LAST BREATH

LAST BREATH

MICHELLE MCGRIFF

URBAN
Renaissance

www.urbanbooks.com

Urban Books
1199 Straight Path
West Babylon, NY 11704

ISBN- 13: 978-1-933967-83-7
ISBN- 10: 1-933967-83-8

First Printing January 2009
Printed in the United States of America

10 9 8 7 6 5 4 3 2 1

Distributed by Kensington Publishing Corp.
Submit Wholesale Orders to:
Kensington Publishing Corp.
C/O Penguin Group (USA) Inc.
Attention: Order Processing
405 Murray Hill Parkway
East Rutherford, NJ 07073-2316
Phone: 1-800-526-0275
Fax: 1-800-227-9604

LAST BREATH

Chapter 1

Sunday night, Christmas Eve 2006

No song of well-wishes and good cheer was heard, only half-uttered affirmations of possible "change a-comin'." Most living on the street could barely remember Christmas Eve indoors, facing tables laden with comfort foods. Their only comfort could be found by huddling around open garbage bins that burned old pieces of furniture from abandoned offices.

It was cold outside, but in the room of one of the discarded buildings that lined the dying streets of the Palemos, things were heating up.

"No! No! Nooooo!" Lionel screamed, fighting like a cat before disappearing through the open window. With one heave-ho, he was on his way like a kite in a stiff breeze, hanging on to nothing but air.

Both Pee Wee and Pepper poked their heads through the broken windowpane of the fifth-story window, mouths agape, eyelids blinking in both surprise and shock. Pepper, with the youthful mind of a nineteen-year-old, attempted to grab hold of the seriousness of the situation.

Pee Wee could only immediately think about Superman or some other cartoon character, only difference being when those superhero guys went through a window, they flew up, not down.

Balamalam!

Lionel missed the dumpster by inches, and with all the trash around—bottles, cans, not to mention cats and rats and all that—his kicking and flailing his arms, hollering and screaming all the way down made for one noisy descent.

"The bigger they are, the harder they fall." Pee Wee's comment regarding Lionel Harrison, the tall, lanky crackhead, came out with a sickening chuckle,

The police sirens could be heard almost immediately.

"Shit! Let's hit it."

Both boys dashed from the empty office space on the fifth floor of the abandoned building, taking off like track stars down the emergency staircase leading out the back door and into the alleyway. The cool, belated winter snap caused their hot-blooded exhalations to billow from them as thick as cigarette smoke.

With bus horns honking and last-minute Christmas shoppers and streetcars slushing through the dark, wet streets, the city sounds were loud and convoluted. Yet Pee Wee and Pepper could hear only the sirens racing closer to that alleyway. They needed to get clean out of the area before the cops came, which didn't take long in their neighborhood, since the cops were always waiting to pick up some punk whether he was guilty or not.

Bandy-legged Pee Wee attempted to keep up with Pepper, but with his loose pants sagging, it was impossible. The boss had told him about wearing all that hip-hop shit. But no, he always wanted to look fly, so now his heavy, loose clothing was slowing his ass down.

Pepper didn't even look back when he hit the fence, clearing it with one try.

Pee Wee wasn't going to be so lucky, and the heavy stomps of the police officers' feet landing as they closed in told him as much.

"Hold it right there!" the cops yelled, service revolvers drawn.

"Shit!" Pee Wee spat, throwing up his hands in pretense of surrender. He had Pepper's pistol in the rim of his shorts and planned to use it. The police officers didn't see it though, until Pee Wee spun around and whipped it out on them.

Pepper could hear the shots even from a block away. He figured Pee Wee had caught 'em. "Dayumm!" Pepper cut around the corner without taking a second off his stride.

Same age as Pee Wee, he played football in high school, until he got kicked out of school his senior year. But it was all good. He was glad he'd had his chance at it, since all that extracurricular activity had actually helped quite a bit in preparing him for the street life and the ability to get away quick.

If only coach could clock my dash now, Pepper thought to himself as he headed back to Damian's place of business, another abandoned building about six blocks away. There were a lot of these empty hulls, memories of what was once a thriving area of legitimate business in the hood. Pepper had heard his parents talk about the devolution often.

"The white man uptown was always talking about redeveloping something. However, none of that talk has made it down here," they would say.

Pepper knew he was going to have to report how bad things had gone down. That cracked-out fool, Lionel, didn't have the "yay" (cocaine) or the money. Why Damian had trusted him with both was a mystery.

Hitting the door, Pepper burst in to find himself instantly standing between Damian and his large busters. He stood less than confident, his mind soaring as the silence grew thick, and his heavy breathing was all that was heard. He waited for Damian to say something. Pepper hated initiating conversation. It was a tactic Damian always used to get people to show their hands. Pepper had seen him do it to other people, only to end up busting their asses for giving out the wrong answers to unasked questions. And now it was his turn to get his ass busted, and for what?

Reliving the moment he and Pee Wee shared with Lionel before the window incident, Pepper was animated and talking fast. "We as'd him twice, 'You got the money, punk?' Just like that, we as'd him."

"So you roughed him up?" Damian asked, without showing expression.

It left Pepper wondering what to say. "We didn't mean to kill him," he attempted to explain, talking fast and sweating. Which was wild, he thought, considering it was hella cold outside. "So now the cops have Pee Wee."

Damian was a cool one, not given to showing his hand. "Well, I'm sure they don't. I'm sure the coroner has Pee Wee. I'm sure Pee Wee is dead."

Pepper chuckled nervously. "Yeah, prolly so, 'cuz you know how he is when he's cornered. He's always gonna fight. And I heard the shots. He had my gun and—"

"You kept running."

"Hell, yeah!" Pepper chuckled again. Damian's solemn expression wasn't helping him at all right now. "You know I did."

"You let Pee Wee hold your gun, knowing how crazy his ass is—was?" Damian, his eyes closed, rubbed his temples. He'd started pacing the last couple of minutes as he listened to Pepper explain the mess he and Pee Wee had made of what should have been a simple transaction. How difficult could it have been? Literally, it was like taking candy from a baby. Truly.

"He wanted to pistol-whip Lionel for not having the money, and well, things got outta hand and shit. Look, Damian, I wasn't Pee Wee's fuckin' keeper and he wasn't my brother," Pepper snapped, causing Damian's eyes to pop open.

The large busters closed in around Pepper.

"What, Damian? What did I say?"

"Well, I *was* his keeper and he *was* my brother," Damian commented coolly, sounding instantly wicked and full of smoldering rage. Pepper had no idea he'd made a fatal mistake, taking Pee Wee's fate so lightly.

It was clear Pepper didn't know Pee Wee was Damian Watson's younger sibling. How could he? Pee Wee didn't look anything like Damian, whose hair was soft and wavy as if he was maybe mixed with some other race, even though his skin was brown. It could maybe have even been red, if someone looked close enough, but nobody ever got that close to Damian. Well, nobody got that close to him more than once.

Always impeccably dressed, Damian, in his white Armani suit, turned and faced the young thug, who stood there with his shirt open, his muscular chest exposed, his pants loose-fitting but tight around his waist, and held in place by a belt. "How many times do I have to tell you fools not to dress that way?" Damian pointed at Pepper's slovenly appearance. "You look a mess."

Pepper gulped audibly, looking down at his clothes.

"You punks are a disgrace."

Pepper's face contorted and, in a moment he would regret, pulled free from the large buster who held his arm and rushed up to Damian. "You worried about how I'm dressed? The cops got my gun, man. Do you know what that means for me?"

The sound of the air could almost be heard behind the speed of Damian's draw. He was as fast as any cowboy in a TV western. Only, he held no Smith and Wesson, no old-fashioned pistol, but a sleek, sharp-looking 9 mm. At least, it looked like one. It was a foreign piece that nobody else around had.

Pepper had to admit, the piece would have looked even sharper if it wasn't pointed in his face, something he realized just before the flash emptied his head of all thought, as well as brain matter.

A silencer was more Damian's style when getting a job done quickly—quietly. He didn't like things that made a lot of noise, and right now Pepper had gotten just a little too loud.

"Clean this shit up." Damian snapped his fingers at his two biggest busters, instructing them to drag Pepper's dead body out of his presence.

Glancing at his chick, Damian smiled. He could see a little fear showing in her eyes, having just witnessed a murder, but the woman was able to hide her feelings well. "Baby, get Simon on the phone. I'm sure the police are going be visiting me soon, and I want to be ready for whatever."

Chapter 2

The year came in quickly, and before you knew it, it was February. With the cold winter, all those around were eagerly waiting for summer, chomping at the bit almost. But Mother Nature was a tease, and the year, despite all its promise of rapid progression, had slowed down suddenly, noticeably. With the advent of spring slated on the calendar for one week from today, the days were still cold and slow to warm up.

The morning ducked under the heavy fog, one that set up a well-constructed net over the bay, spreading out over the city like the wings of a huge eagle. However, no matter how gray the skies were and how much the clouds hovered, life went on unconcerned with its majesty. No one stayed in until after the miasma lifted. It was business as usual for most folks in the city.

And that was okay for Porter, who hated lying around anyway. He liked staying busy to get through his day and avoid thinking about the past, and his loss.

Again last night he'd dreamed about that night. He'd just passed the bar, and the fraternity brothers had decided to celebrate at the frat house. Complete with drinking, girls, and celebrating, it was a cool place to hang out, to party. Then the blue car next to them on the road, the flash, the noise of shattering glass, the screech of the tires, the look on his brother's face before, suddenly, there was only darkness, voices, and the faint howling sound of rescue approaching.

Kiki. It was the last word from his mouth before he died . . . almost.

Porter shook his head free of the memory that began to cloud his day, his good mood. For years his therapist worked with him to get past that morbid description of the car wreck that changed his life, trying to dredge *her* up and purge *her*. Porter's therapist wanted this Kiki to let go of his heart, to free his mind to remember all he needed to remember in order to solve the riddle that night had posed.

Who killed my brother? Who tried to kill me? And why?

Homicide was the final diagnosis. It was unbelievable. Who would want to kill his brother? Well, to be honest, the list could go on and on, and the reasons, even further. He was into shady stuff and kept company with shady people. But youth was on his side, and when you're young and haughty, you don't know good company from bad sometimes. That was Bond Porter. He was making his mark as an up-and-coming private investigator, when his life ended before he'd learned the basics on living and loving, in Porter's opinion.

Love—it was just a fantasy, a beautiful woman—just a dream—or was she?

This girl Kiki—Yes, her name was Kiki, but that was all he remembered about her—did she know who killed his brother? Of course not. She was just a dream girl, right? She wasn't even real, right?

It wasn't as if I've ever seen her again. It wasn't as if

I've worked very hard to find her. Stay focused, Porter. He reprimanded himself the way he always did when thinking of *her*. Porter's mind stayed in a constant state of flux and easy distraction. But he was always focused on the death of his brother, determined to find out who killed him. Maybe that was why he took this job with Simon & Associates. It gave him a legitimate reason to come back to town.

I'm a good lawyer. I can win any case Simon has. But finding Bond's killer just seems so outta reach, and I just wish I knew why.

Sometimes he felt as if Bond spoke to him from the grave, giving him hints, teasing as to who his killer was. But that was just craziness. Sort of like his feelings for Kiki—Just plain, crazy. Yes, sometimes Porter felt as though he was going bonkers. Memory loss can do that, the therapist explained.

Identical twins, Sean and Bond shared more than they should, often getting beat by their father for the same wrongdoing because of their refusal to admit which one was the culprit. But that night Bond had taken a bullet to the head and the chest from a passing car, Sean, who was driving, was thrown from the car when it rolled down an embankment as he lost control from the tires being shot out. Whoever shot at them intended for them both to die that night.

But after an airlift to Los Angeles, California, he survived. Now he had to find out who had punished them both for his brother's wrong. He needed to know who killed his brother, if it was the last thing he did. The night of the murder, Sean was found with two bullets in his body, and in a coma, near the corpse of his brother, who was also been thrown from the car. *Had the killer come down the embankment and shot him point-blank to make sure he was dead too?*

After months of recovery and with a few physical problems, a spotty memory regarding life prior to that incident was all he had left. No one was indicted, and the case was closed, never to be resolved.

Porter eventually left the city and moved to Atlanta, where he had family. After working in the private sector for a while, his uncle offered him a job in his firm. It wasn't the lucrative job offer he'd been promised by one of the elder frat brothers after passing the bar. But as with everything, it was good enough, for what was meant to be would always be there, as he found out when Simon and Associates called a few months back and offered him that lucrative job with their firm. Fifteen years was a long time to wait for it, but it came, and he took it.

"You've held the job for fifteen years?" Porter had asked, holding the chuckle in as best he could. He didn't want to sound pompous, but he had found it rather humorous that suddenly he was in demand. Sure he was a good attorney. *No, a damn good attorney*, he mentally mused, thinking about his no-loss career.

But still, this move back to the Bay Area was his last-ditch hope to cure his unusual case of amnesia. Maybe something here might shock his memory banks and possibly relieve him from the traumatic syndrome he was experiencing, which his therapist reluctantly agreed could occur under the right conditions.

Getting back into life was as hard as living it, Porter quickly found out. But living was what he had to do, no matter what, and fifteen years had been a lifetime of a half-life that he was tired of dealing with.

Porter couldn't remember how much he was involved with his brother's death, but he knew there had to be more there than his mind would accept. His dreams were often frightening. Sometimes, he'd dream that he'd killed his brother, but that could never have happened. Yes, the dreams were horrific, often waking him in a sweat, but he refused the medication to make them go away. Deep inside he knew if he allowed them to wipe away the dreams, he would be giving up on her, his guardian angel—Kiki.

With all her entering into his spiritual world, he'd never taken one step to find out if she was real. But then again, he didn't have half an idea of where to start. During the investigation of the accident there was no indication of female involvement. As far as he knew, Kiki was an angel, taking his hand and pulling him back from the edge of death. And over the years, in his dreams he'd come to depend on her to make the ugliness go away. In his dreams she would come to him and comfort him over the loss of his brother.

He'd long ago accepted that he loved her. Unconditionally. She had become a comfort, one that he had to admit he didn't want to let go of. Nonetheless, he started challenging the haunts, and there had been benchmark memory recall for him. Because of this, his prognosis for full recovery began to look good.

Fifteen years was a long time.

Upon returning to the city to accept the offer a month or so ago, he'd noted the client list. The once perplexing question of why Simon wanted him so badly became a less than challenging conundrum to unravel.

Porter checked the mirror once more for good measure. He was meeting with the DA today, Peter Marcum. Peter was another one from his past. Porter knew with Peter, he'd be in and out in less than an hour. Last he remembered, Peter Marcum was a bit of a knucklehead. Besides, this case was so old, it was growing cobweb behind the ears. Too much longer and the young Pee Wee Watson wouldn't even match his description anymore—he'd be a full-grown man. *Fat chance*, Porter smirked. The chances of this kid becoming a real man were slim to none. It had been a couple of months already since the incident. This case had already gone through one lawyer, so Porter was actually getting a heaping helping of sloppy seconds here.

Chapter 3

Very early Thursday February 15, 2007

It had started with a kiss.

Her mouth opened wide to accept it. She wanted to taste it completely. Deep and passionate it was, and she didn't want to miss any of it. He smiled at her, teasing her eyelids, her forehead, and then her neck with his full lips.

She was "stoned on the musical drug" that blurred the safe lines between love and lust, pulling her forward like an index finger would, curving upward, drawing in the inquisitive closer and closer to satisfaction of a curiosity. Yes, she was being called, and in her heart there was no decision on whether she would go. She had to go. She had to know the answer to her life's question.

Maybe the answer would lie within a dangerous closeness to a deadly heat, a scorching flame. Or within inches of the full, tempting lips of Adonis, who stood before her. Maybe both locations were one and the same. Either way, she was in a hurry to know.

Giggling, from the tickle that his thin, freshly grown facial hair had caused against her soft skin, she ran from him, allowing him to chase her through the field of tall grass. Or were they indoors? Did it matter? It was a dream, after all.

They were naked now. He was firm and tight, and she couldn't resist kissing him over his entire anatomy.

"Shattered dreams, worthless years, here am I encased in a hollow shell," *he sang.*

The mellifluous Stevie Wonder tune carried her on the wings that floated her off the ground and into the air as the young Adonis sang, pulled her into an embrace and rocked her in a slow, swaying motion, holding her tighter and tighter. It was one of her favorite Stevie Wonder songs, and he sang like an angel praying.

How appropriate for a day like today. The day before Christmas it was, and church was where she should have been. Perhaps, some better choices would have been made this night, but tomorrow was another day. She would pray tomorrow.

"So many sounds that meet our ears, many sights our eyes behold."

His gaze burrowed into her head through what was once seeing eyes. He'd blinded her for sure—all clarity was gone.

"I believe when I fall in love with you, it will be forever. Love."

He said it, but was she listening?

"The words I speak will echo in my mind."

He kissed her neck, another sweet spot she had.

The air following and leading the lyrics coming from between his soft, full lips caused a sensuous vibration against her skin. She gasped, holding in her breath.

"Come on, let's fall in love," he responded eagerly and then again regained his calm, his sensual calm.

"Tonight was the night.

Tonight it was right.

You're the woman I've been waiting for"

Climbing on her, pushing her knees apart, he entered her without further ado, without notice of her high-pitched outcry. She knew it would hurt. It was her first time. But he didn't know that and didn't seem to notice or care. He seemed to notice nothing, except the fire between her legs, moving inside her quickly as if her cove were ablaze.

She started to fight him but then, staring into his dark, hypnotic eyes, eventually she realized this was what he wanted in return for his love. And soon what he was doing to her became all right.

Sucking the air through his teeth, seething, he went at her in a mad rush, bringing her voice out in ragged, unfamiliar, throaty groans and moans, as euphoria took over her jerking, trembling body .

Sliding down on her body, drenched in sweat, and fresh funk, his scent intoxicated her. Kissing her between her dampened breasts, her flat stomach, the top of her bikini line, he stopped just above the throbbing mound and kissed her there before glancing up at her. Their eyes again met in a moment of revelation, and again she exposed her innocence.

He smiled slyly before dipping his eyes and parting her lower lips with his tongue. Her first thought was to push his head away, but he took hold of her hands by the wrist, firmly planting them on the bed while he orally pleased her, bringing waves of pleasure to her again within moments.

She was crying now and couldn't stop while he kissed her from head to toe. Never had she felt so many sensations all at once. With his tongue, he lavished her sensitive areas—behind her knees, right below her belly button.

He was enjoying her, entering her slowly with his tongue, weakening her knees and causing her toes to curl, sending waves of orgasm to her core. She would be forever in the moment.

"I believe when I fall in love with you, it will be forever."

Her arms rose above her head, her mouth dropped open as she gasped for air. He had entered her dreams yet another night, invaded her privacy, haunted her peace, rocked her world. In her passion, she sang out, calling to the man of her dreams, who now lay beside her. "Sean, I love you," she said.

It was nearly 2:00 a.m. when Shayla called, "Kiki?" going into her room, causing her to jolt awake, sit up, and glance at the clock.

Chapter 4

Pulling through the gates of the grotesquely ostentatious mansion, Porter felt the creeps coming over him again. Just being here made his skin crawl. It wasn't as if he'd been here before and was having some kind of negative memory flashes so much as the owner of this joint got under his skin, in a bad way. Damian Watson owned this place, no doubt paid for with blood money. Damian was ruthless, from what Porter had reckoned. From the moment they first re-acquainted, Porter was left feeling less than reunited. He felt more like he needed a shower.

At the firm of Simon & Associates, Porter quickly became someone they could trust with their assets, bringing in high-paying African American clients nearly immediately. He was no ambulance chaser, but he had a knack for attracting people who needed legal help. So maybe that's why he got this case, he figured. Perhaps it was considered a reward of some kind.

Nah, just a source of great cosmic disturbance in my soul, he thought to himself.

Porter thought back to the day Damian Watson came into his office.

"Looks like you recovered pretty well. I've never had a chance to tell you how sorry I was about what happened to Bond. But I hear you've done okay. I hear you're the best lawyer around these days," Damian had said, staring out the window after a cool reception from Porter.

Porter remembered Damian's face immediately, and the memory was marred with negativity. Even now, Porter sensed hate in Damian's tone.

"You've become quite aggressive and Bond-like, these days."

"But I'm not my brother. My brother is dead," Porter quickly retorted. "So, no, I'm just being Sean-like, okay."

This conversation took place in his office just days after he moved in. Apparently Damian's brother had been arrested, hospitalized with a minor leg graze, and released on bail at his arraignment right after the incident, and the case had been in continuance since. One of Porter's colleagues, Garret Lansing, had been the attorney to handle the arraignment before Damian requested that Sean take over. Garret was mad as a firecracker about being removed from the case, but held it in well.

Porter was a damn good attorney. He had never lost in court and wasn't about to start losing now behind some bogus shit, whether bad judges, politically motivated deputy DA's, or threatening clients. Yes, Damian was a threat whether anybody wanted to see it or not.

"Yeah, *S* and *A* is a good firm. I'm sure you know that already," Porter said, trying to sound modest but failing.

Damian turned slightly, facing him, then looked back through the window. "Yes, I know this, but I need *you* to be the best, my brotha. I need you to come through for me."

"We've—I've had no complaints from our clients."

"Okay, that's all good too, but listen, I need my fraternity brother to promise me full support on this one. I need more of a commitment than a shrug." Damian moved from the window, his movements were smooth, like those of a dancer or a cat . . . or a second-story man. "I need to know that I've put my money where my baby brother's freedom is. I mean, I'm willing to do my part, and I've been doing that, but I need to know that all my efforts to keep him out of jail won't be in vain. I need my best friend to *remember* how much he owes me."

"I hear what you saying, Damian. I'm not deaf. But, to be real with you, *my brotha*, firstly, I would strongly suggest that, seeing as how that kid Jamon's rap sheet could wallpaper a small apartment, maybe you should consider reform school. Secondly, I need you to *remember* that I *don't* remember owing you a damn thing."

Porter chuckled sarcastically but saw immediately that Damian, although he snickered while shaking his head slightly, didn't find the comment the least bit funny. He decided he needed some tea. The air was getting a bit thick.

"You're right. I guess I keep forgetting you're not your brother. It was he who owed me his life."

"A man's wages are paid in death, so that debt too has been paid. Whatever Bond owed, that's over."

Damian smiled wickedly. "You've always been deep, Sean, not all that loyal to the brotherhood, but surely deep. Nonetheless, regarding the debt comment, it doesn't matter if you're dead or alive. Once you are in the brotherhood, you are forever in debt. Never forget that. I'm sure if Bond was alive he would tell you that."

"But, as I said before, my brother is dead."

"Yes, I know." Damian paced Porter's office a little bit more, glancing at his awards and commendations for his community work and achievements as an attorney in Atlanta. He stared at one picture in particular, the one with

Porter shaking hands with a tall man that towered over him. The photo was eye-catching, considering Porter was nearly 6-4. "Well, seems like you're at the top of your game these last few years. Bond would be proud." Damian then turned and looked at him intently. "Tell me . . . you've been gone forever. You have no family?"

"None I bring to the office," Porter answered, holding his cup in his left hand.

Damian was very observant. "Old southpaw." He nodded approvingly, lifting his tumbler to his thin lips with his left hand, sipping his tea as if was a cocktail.

Porter did the same after nursing the tea for a while.

Damian watched him. "Not many of us left."

"Guess we're a dying breed," Porter added.

"Speaking of dying, I've yet to ask you how you've been . . . without Bond. I guess we all had hoped so much to put the tragedy behind us that we neglected to ask if you had."

"I'm fine," Porter lied, setting the tumbler down on the table.

"Did you ever find the killer?"

Porter was taken aback at the question. Sure he'd said the word *killer* many times, but still. "No. The case is a cold file now."

"Very unfortunate. Well, perhaps you'll find some resolution and peace, now that you've returned to the scene of the crime, so to speak."

"Peace is already mine."

"I see." Damian lifted the tumbler in a toast-like fashion toward Porter, who nodded in acceptance of the congratulatory gesture.

"I hear you weren't even able to practice law until about ten years ago."

"And what does that have to do with anything?"

"Nothing. It just seems as though you've put it together

and shot right to the top, and it seems as though you like it there at the top. You know how to win."

"I'm realistic. It helps."

"Meaning?"

"Meaning, I don't take on a case I can't win." Porter chuckled again, hoping that his words carried the light meaning they were intended to. Maybe it was true, or maybe he was just lucky, but winning cases seemed to be his forte. "I don't like to get involved with anything I can't control. Maybe that's why I never got into drugs."

"Oh my, a personal dig. One for your side." Damian snickered wickedly, downing the tea now as if it was a hard-earned after-five drink. "You do remember some things from that night then, apparently." Damian's tone showed a bit of embarrassment, albeit fake-sounding.

Porter was uncomfortable now, and the memories Damian Watson was dredging up were not ones he wanted to have. He remembered the drugs, and now suddenly, he remembered more than that. "My side?"

"Yeah, Sean, your side. You were always less than a team player, and I guess I could only hope you'd changed."

"I'm a team player." Porter felt cornered now and forced to condescend to the volley of "No, you're not; yes, I am," for the sake of the firm. If Damian Watson walked out, it would cost the firm a fortune in revenue.

Damian smiled, relaxing the tension in the air just a smidgen. "I'm glad to hear it. Then it's a deal. My brother won't go under for killing that Harrison fool." Damian stretched his free hand.

Porter looked at the hand, his stomach tightening instantly. "Murder? They aren't charging him with that murder. Why would you think they would? Did he do it?" Porter felt he knew the answer but didn't let the revelation show on his face.

Damian's smile left his handsome face, and his thin lips

formed a straight line. His eyes tightened just a little. "I guess that's where we begin our jobs, huh? Yours, to prove he didn't, and mine, to make sure you prove he didn't."

"I know you're not threatening me."

"My, my, my . . . are you always so sensitive?"

"Sorry. I guess I am. Yes, Damian, most definitely I will make sure Jamon walks on the drug and weapon charges. I read the file. The DA's charges are weak. Our investigation has gaps, but still, the charges are weak."

"As weak as a little girl"—Damian stopped speaking abruptly. He seemed to want to say more but didn't.

Chapter 5

"So, he's like some loser you know?" Kiki asked.

"Well, no, that's not the case. He's my friend. I'd almost want to call him my best friend, if he didn't get on my last nerves so often." Dana cackled a little after her last comment.

Kiki stood leaning on the counter surrounding her desk. She'd made it to work, but her mood had turned less than pleasant. This was becoming a habit now, and she was going to start looking into the connection. Home, sleep, dreaming: happy. Work, filing, stressing: foul mood. She was certain she wouldn't have too many dots to connect. Being a lawyer was her father's thing for sure, and Kiki wasn't so sure it had fully become hers. But here she was, like it or not.

Dana Tomlinson was a receptionist, but she had no problem being real with the attorneys that worked for the district attorney's office, especially Kiki Turner. Kiki was fairly new here but moving up the ladder smoothly, and without any kinks. It was thought she was born with a silver law spoon up her ass, her grandfather being a former judge, and her father a retired judge who now taught law at the prestigious law school that she just so happened to have graduated from. There were also many rumors flying around about Kiki's personal life, but Dana didn't listen to those, nor did she believe those hateful, jealous innuendos. Dana figured she could get close enough to Kiki to find out enough hateful and jealous goodies on her own, if she wanted to be that way.

But on the fair side of the line, Dana had to admit that Kiki was a hard worker who earned all the breaks she'd been getting lately. Peter had been pretty stingy with the advancing moves, but Dana had heard in the wind that "change gone come" for Ms. Kiki.

Kiki moved Dana's nameplate slightly to the side while sorting her memos, faxes, and messages that Dana had just handed her. The office of the District Attorney was a busy place, and there was never a lack of people calling and trying to get legal representation, only to end up referred to the legal aid department down the street.

With everyone racing in and out, conversations often took place at this counter, and Dana usually got an earful of many confidential matters, as well as gossip from her sibling, who she called regularly during working hours. It wasn't like the firm she used to work at where everything was so hush-hush all the time. Dana had to figure that was the difference between a private firm and the district attorney's office.

Glancing out the large seventh-story bay window, Kiki could see the Bay Area fog rolling out and a hint of a sunny day creeping in behind it. She'd told Dana the other day that she always felt as if she was freezing until at least June or July. It was only February, so surely Kiki felt like a snowman today. December was just a memory now, but she still wore a heavy sweater and tank top underneath for warmth, not to mention that big coat she came in with over her arm, just in case.

Dana caught Kiki's eye after ending her phone call. It was clear Kiki wanted to hear more about this guy she knew. Dana had been talking about him nonstop for over an hour without fully giving Kiki the answer on where this conversation was really going in regards to this guy she knew. By now, Kiki was no doubt wondering why she had brought him up, and to be honest, Dana wasn't sure.

At first Dana was thinking that Kiki could use a hookup, but as uptight as Kiki seemed, maybe it wasn't even worth the effort. She'd probably just have dude investigated. Dana had heard from the other attorneys there that Kiki was celibate. She had also heard that Kiki's mother died when she was seventeen and she took over the task of bringing up her sister, who was now a teenager. It was as if she'd all but inhaled and stopped breathing. Dana didn't believe all that, but maybe it was true. Maybe a lot of rumors she'd heard about Kiki were true, because, for as young as she was, Kiki acted like an old woman most of the time.

"So is he gay?" Kiki asked.

Dana choked on her sip of coffee. Hadn't Kiki been listening? *Apparently not.*

"Because I'm sure you know there are plenty of men out there who keep that little bit of information under cover. And I know you know what I'm saying." Kiki smirked, giving Dana the impression that perhaps she'd been a victim of a down-low or low-down man once or twice before swearing off men altogether.

The thought of Ms. "All-together" Kimani Turner having fallen for anything less than perfection tickled Dana so that a smiled parted her lips. "No," she answered quickly. "That I do know. He's not gay."

"Because what woman turns over a perfectly good

man, unless something is wrong with him? And am I right, you're trying to turn him over, unloading him on me? Am I right? And why? Why would you do that? Why would I want that?"

"I'm not, like, turning him over. It's just, he's my friend, and well, you know, you're my friend and . . ." Dana stammered, slightly embarrassed now for assuming that someone like Kiki Turner was her friend. It was clear that Kiki was from the other side of the tracks, and Kiki's side of the tracks was far from her neck of the woods. She probably didn't even know where the Palemos was. *But then again, what is she really missing in not knowing*?

The Palemos, nestled on the outskirts of Palo Alto, California, was a ghetto across the bridge from where they were in San Francisco. *But it's my home, damnit. Maybe if Kiki came from there she would have a little more passion, compassion, and feeling. Maybe if Kiki'd climb off that white cloud and come down to colored town, she wouldn't be such a damn ice princess! The Palemos'll teach you reality, get you real in a heartbeat.* Dana straightened her shoulders unconsciously.

Everyone who ever lived in the Palemos felt that way about it. Many campaigns were currently going on to revitalize the community and bring it back to life.

Maybe if Kiki and I were better friends, I could convince her to donate a dollar or two to that cause; she's good for it. Besides, she's got nothing better going on in her life, right? Dana looked Kiki over one good time. *If she did, she wouldn't be flipping out over the mere mention of going out with a man.*

Dana had a lot of nerve. Her own life was as boring as all get-out. She'd not had a real date in months, and the last guy was a real loser. *Give me half a man or anything else exciting and I'm like . . . there!* Dana mentally confessed, rethinking unloading her friend on Kiki. *Maybe I should give dude a call myself.*

This woman Kiki didn't need half of anything; she was a complete package—successful, smart, and serious. According to her personnel records, she was around twenty-nine. Dana had only glanced quickly at the file to see Kiki's date of birth and had a hard time adding fast.

Kiki's eyes were light but not colored and, when the sun hit them just right, they took on just a hint of hazel. Her skin was of a light complexion but not high yellow, more like that of a faded Malibu tan. Her hair was thick, but she kept it short and smart-looking—sassy. Kiki, barely making five foot three, was a curvaceous size eight or ten, depending on what she wore. That, Dana noticed, too. Maybe she was even thirty. Who knew? With mature, ageless looks that were above average, her looks were very deceiving.

Dana noticed a lot of things about her demi-boss, but mostly, she noticed that Kiki was bitchy and tense most of the time. It was as if she needed something, like maybe to exhale. So why not take on a cause? *Something*! *Because apparently she doesn't need a man*, Dana thought, unable to keep the smirk from coming to her lips while she listened to Kiki go on a little longer about the pitfalls of blind dates and one-night stands.

Chapter 6

The ethereal serenity was breathtaking, even though Daniel would never admit that it was the landscape he came to enjoy the most when taking a day off work to come here. The crickets called out their mating song, and occasionally a June bug could be heard leaping from a log onto the murky slough, only to be quickly gulped down by a greedy catfish.

"Maybe I need to use those as bait, since y'all seem to like them so much," Daniel fussed audibly, aiming his words toward the muddy water while flicking the ash off the cigarette and tucking it back loosely between his lips. He'd cast out several times, only to come back with nothing more than a drowned worm on the end of his line. It didn't matter. What a perfect day to skip work. At least that's what Daniel thought when he'd called in that morning, pretending to have a scratchy throat. He'd used these theatrics before when desiring to take one day off, but the sore throat gag only worked for one day. If he needed more days, he'd pretend to have eaten something bad.

Ziiiiiiiie was the sound the fishing wire made as it

zipped through the spool before plunking into the water. Again the waterfowl called out against the otherwise serene setting.

I'm gonna move down some, Daniel decided, reeling in impatiently. He'd given this spot about ten minutes and was sure he'd do better moving down the bank a bit.

"Damnit!" he barked, realizing his line was caught and no longer coming in easily. "What the hell!" he fussed, noticing the large clump of floating brush.

Cussing and fussing, he stomped down the jagged, rocky hillside of that secluded spot to clear his line. This spot was a secret good-luck spot. Nobody knew about this fishing cove not far from the bay, or at least he thought nobody did.

Reaching in the brush, his hand touched the fabric of the boy's shirt. Ripping at it to free the line, he saw what appeared to be flesh. Unsure of what he was seeing, he leaned in closer, only to find himself staring in the eyes of death. "Ohhhh God!" he screamed.

Never once had Daniel needed to present a doctor's notice or anything upon his return to work, but after today, he was going to need something, as he'd already thrown up twice and was still a little weak in the knees by the time the police got there. There was no way he was going to work tomorrow.

The body of that young black boy surfaced with just a few hard tugs of his fishing pole. It was pretty clear that the body was that of a black kid, and it was his matted kinky black hair and loose youthful-looking colorful clothing that he had . . . jeans, tennis shoes . . . well at least one, that told Daniel it was even more than likely a boy.

The female homicide detective pointed over Daniel's shoulder, toward the water behind him. "And that's where you found him?"

"Ye-yes," Daniel answered, realizing his teeth was chattering.

Daniel was scared. He wasn't gonna even lie about it. He'd never seen a dead body up close before, nor one with a bullet hole between cloudy, opened eyes. There was also a bullet in the chest, and at the ends of both puffy, grayish-blue arms, his hands were cut off.

"We got enough pictures, guys?" the male detective asked then, yelling out to the photographers, who carefully waded through the shallow waters, getting snapshot after snapshot.

With all the yellow tape going up, Daniel felt almost as if he was hemmed in. He wanted to leave. He wanted his wife to come pick him up, or maybe even his mother.

It wasn't at all like TV. The photographers seemed to have endless film as they quietly worked for what felt like hours, no jokes, no crude comments. They didn't seem to find the situation funny at all. Daniel knew he hadn't found it anything but horrible.

"So you come here often? Are you very familiar with this place?"

Daniel wondered why the female detective had asked those questions. He was hoping it didn't mean he would have to look at the body again. He never wanted to see anything so horrible again. He prayed they didn't think he could have possibly had anything to do with such a heinous crime. It was obvious the boy had been shot. *Nobody ever shoots himself two times.* Daniel could sense the authorities were preparing to move the body. He could hear much more talking than before, and besides that, he had seen the coroners carrying the gurney down the hillside and got just a glimpse of the black plastic bag.

"Do you know who he was?" Daniel asked, trying not to look over his shoulder at the gruesome scene playing out behind him

"Please . . . his own mama wouldn't know who he was at this point," the female detective muttered, mindlessly flipping the pages of her notepad.

If Daniel had a second to catch up to this moment, he would have considered the young woman's comment far from lady-like.

She reached in the pocket of her manly-looking blazer and handed him a card. "Here. Call me if you think of something else, okay," she requested gruffly, before moving past him as if his usefulness was finished.

He glanced at the card. Tommy Turner was her name.

Chapter 7

The conference table was fairly quiet, short of Dan's unwrapping of his monster muffin from the noisy tinfoil wrapper. His wife was a baker or something. Whatever the case, she sent him a meal in the shape of a pastry muffin-like thing every morning.

To the stares of disbelief that a muffin could be so big, his common inquiry was, "Want some?"

"No," came back from everyone, as was common.

Porter cleared his throat as Simon came in. "Good morning to you too, Mr. Porter," Simon said jokingly.

Porter smiled and nodded. "I'm no troglodyte. I can speak cordially. Good morning, Simon."

Everyone chuckled. Porter was always amazed at the booty-kissing that went on here. Surely everyone owned stock in ChapStick. Glancing around, he caught the eye of Garret Lansing. Sour grapes still had a hold on him.

Garret just twisted his lips and pretended to be concerned with the lead in his mechanical pencil.

If Porter even cared, he'd say Garret didn't like him. But noticing his lecherous come-ons with the female colleagues there and his blatant resistance to following Simon's simple instructions, Porter would gather that not too many people were particularly fond of him, short of Dan, who would always ask him, "Want some?"

"Okay, so down to business. Carter, want you to check on some things in connection with the Madison case. Come by my office. Porter, you have a meeting with the DA today, correct?"

"Yes, I do, in about two hours. Enough time to go pick up my client, yada, yada," Porter answered.

"I wonder how Damian Watson would feel, knowing his brother was referred to as a *yada*," Garret mumbled under his breath, still working diligently on his pencil.

"I think *yada* is politically correct," Dan said, nodding and chewing on his muffin.

Garret rolled his eyes, as others again chuckled. Even Simon found that one funny and quickly handed out assignments for the day, with Garret getting the bottom of the barrel.

Copyright dispute. Yaaaawn, boring, Porter thought. *Poor Garret, but oh well, I'm off to Oz and can't be too worried.*

"Great day to be alive, eh, Porter," Garret said, passing him in the hall a few moments later.

The comment struck him as strange suddenly, but he had to admit, "Yeah, Lansing, it is."

The People v. *Jamon "Pee Wee" Watson*: Illegal weapon; resisting arrest; carrying a concealed weapon (CCW); felonious assault; fleeing and eluding police; and for good measure, aggravated attempted murder on a police officer.

Kiki began to read between the lines quickly, trying her best to deduce what should have been clear. If only she could see what was really going on here. "No witnesses on the murder thing." Kiki flipped pages, pages with one omission after the next. "Who the hell is his attorney?" Kiki said aloud, shaking her head at how bad it was all starting to look. *Black kid running in the ghetto streets. Suddenly he's a murderer; suddenly he's free.* "And where are the witnesses? This case stinks." Kiki then read the side notes.

It was revealed in discovery that while in the hospital, during questioning, Jamon "Pee Wee" Watson, confessed to the murder of Lionel Harrison, but added that he was not alone in the act. Then right after his attorney visited him in the hospital, he quickly denied it altogether. The man who Pee Wee had named as an accomplice prior to his attorney's counsel to shut his mouth—Pepper Johnson—had not surfaced since that day.

"Okay, so that explains not indicting him, but I would have indicted him anyway," Kiki mumbled under her breath. She nodded, agreeing with her own thoughts. "Black kids running in the ghetto, dead crackhead . . . of course they did it, right?" She heard her own words and realized how prejudiced and stereotypical they sounded. This case was weak. "Yeah, I see why we didn't indict." She continued to read the superficial evidence found on the victim.

"And who knows, you might get your chance to change that, Ms. Turner."

Kiki looked up to see Peter standing in her doorway. "What?"

"Jamon 'Pee Wee' Watson." Peter smiled wickedly, almost slithering into her office.

"Should I know that name outside of this file?" Kiki asked, feeling a little out of the loop. He reminded her of a giddy girl with a big juicy secret.

Learning that crimes came with names was something new that Kiki was going to have to get used to. For the last six months, since joining the prosecutor's office, she was trying to adjust to the differences in the case files.

She'd been working out of family court since graduating from law school. Those cases had numbers, as most of the clients she represented were minors. Flipping rapidly through the pages of the file in front of her, she looked hard to see if anything jumped off any of them.

Peter slid his narrow hips onto the edge of her desk. "You don't know the name *Watson*?"

"Well, sure, but that's not what you asked. You asked if—"

"Okay, okay," Peter interrupted, "let me stop with the games. You're no fun anyway. Jamon Watson's brother is a diabolical maniac whose actions have 'unmanageable mobster' written all over them. He was born in Miami, grew up on the streets there. He moved here to the West Coast, got in law school somehow, and quickly built a reputation, using both sides of the law to his advantage. Sure, he's a lawyer, but as far as I'm concerned, he's nothing but a two-bit hood, an accomplice to all the crimes that weigh so heavily over our fair city like a dark cloud, raining down drugs on top of our innocent children, taking advantage of the weak."

Kiki had never noticed before how Peter's way of speaking when explaining something took on all the markings of a political campaign speech. *Must be practicing*, she reasoned internally. *Now what does Jamon Watson's brother have to do with anything?* "Wait, you're telling me Jamon and Damian Watson are brothers. This, this"—She held up a page from the file.

Peter smiled and nodded vigorously. "We've never been able to connect him with anything illegal directly, but now we have his brother . . . or we will have him." Peter brought his hands together as if meshing the two cases and floating them along a wave, while finishing his animated speech. "I feel the end of an evil reign coming."

Glancing back down at the file, Kiki realized that this

case was nothing more than a big fluffy feather in the cap of the district attorney's office. To snag the brother of the infamous Damian Watson would be kudos, for sure. If nothing else, it would make for some ugly headlines, and that would be what Peter needed to push his political career to the next level.

"This case is already three months old. It's a drug case. I mean, the guy pleaded not guilty. The case has been in continuance forever. It's circumstantial at best. Well, is there something about this case that I'm missing, or what?"

Kiki continued to flip through the pages, trying to catch as much as she could. She wished that she'd had more time to read it thoroughly, in private. This impromptu review of the case wasn't sitting well with her. "There are no witnesses, no accomplice, and worse, to be truthful, Peter, I don't see how we have Pee Wee for the murder of Lionel Harrison either. That could be why we never indicted. I mean, I see a little something here, but I'd have to ask more questions before putting us out there like that."

"And the problem with that is?" Peter asked.

Kiki shrugged.

"So what do you think about this case?"

Kiki shrugged again.

"Good answer, because I think this case would be a perfect opportunity for you to step up to the plate, start earning your salary around here."

"Pardon me?"

"Your daddy, the former Superior Court Judge Frank Turner, who just so happens to be an alumnus of my alma mater and one of the founding members of my fraternity, didn't send you to law school to become an administrative assistant, did he?"

Kiki looked around as if he was speaking to someone else. She couldn't believe they were having this conversation. She hated his crudeness, but besides all that, she was trying to think fast so as to understand fully what he was saying.

So my father is involved with all this. It figures.

Was he requesting that she try this case before a judge and jury? After just this short time with the file, was Peter actually asking her to be second chair on a major criminal case like this one? Was this what he considered a briefing?

"You are kidding me, right? You expect me to try this case? This is major crazy, Peter!"

Peter fanned his hand as if swatting at a slow-moving fly. "Major? This isn't major or crazy. I could show you major and major crazy. And win? *Pisshawl*, we will win this with one hand tied behind our backs. You must not have seen this kid's rap sheet."

"No, no, that's not it. This is major . . . major enough." Kiki smiled widely, touching her forehead with one hand, her other hand spread out protectively over the open file. *A potential murder case, oh yeah.* Kiki was thinking ahead. From family court to criminal court, yeah, this was major for her.

But one thing still bothered her when she looked up into Peter's dancing blue eyes. There had to be a reason for this sudden confidence in her abilities. She'd only prepared one motion from scratch since starting this job. Sure, she was turning into a great clerk, always having the files in tip-top shape when Peter got to court, but still, she was an attorney who hadn't seen the courtroom.

"What's the catch?" she asked before internalizing the question.

Peter laughed sardonically and patted her shoulder.

"You women, always thinking there's a catch when a man has a great offer for you."

"Peter, now you know that wasn't nice to say." Kiki was hoping that he wasn't about to totter on the politically incorrect fence he often teetered on.

"I know, I know." Peter pretended to button his lips.

He and Kiki had been down this road before. Peter was a lot like her father, however, and she had to remember not to jump down his throat the way she always did with her father when he went there with the rude talk.

Trying to keep the smirk from her lips while continuing to fondle the file, she ignored her initial thoughts and began to imagine trying the case—the glamour, the prestige. Perhaps, it was the feeling of power that suddenly consumed her, but she immediately knew where she would start. Mr. Watson's attorney.

Kiki finally saw the name of the representing firm, Simon & Associates, the firm Garret was with. Garret had a crush on her. He'd had one most of her teenage and adult life, now that she thought about it. He was a bit older, and she was far from interested. But it didn't matter to him, as he just always seemed so very fond of her. He'd had a hell of a time passing the bar, claiming prejudice. Somebody was out to get him, or whatever. He just loved to tell his law journey. Kiki's father, Frank, hated the guy and said terrible things about him constantly. She remembered her father calling him a slacker, brownnoser, stuff like that.

Garret had wanted to intern with her father after his one and only intern left abruptly, but Kiki's father wasn't having it, saying that Garret couldn't tie the shoelaces of the former intern. Kiki knew how narrow her father's mind could be on things, so she actually felt rather bad for Garret. Kiki never saw her father in any coveted light. He was just an old coot, as far as she was concerned, but apparently being an intern of the great Judge Turner was a feather in any young lawyer's cap. Even Peter sang her father's praises, as if he did a little "Judge Turner worship" on his pillow at night. Maybe hiring her was part of a love gesture, and maybe Garret figured being a suitor of Judge Turner's daughter would work just as well.

But then again, she had some ulterior motives for all those rain checks she'd been banking away. Maybe with this case involving the firm he was with, she'd simply call Garret, take him up on one of those dinner offers, see what he knew.

"These guys are tough," she admitted. "And I'm-a need some serious ammo." She was thinking about Garret but didn't say it.

"Yeah, but you can handle them—him. You think about it. You have"—Peter looked at his watch— "until, well, until right now to give me an answer." He pointed at her with a trigger finger, adding to his dramatic play.

Kiki chuckled nervously, licked her lips, and then nodded before she could think it through and refuse. This was her big break, her chance to prove what she was made of. How could she pass this up?

"Yes, of course. I'd love to take it. I'll start investigations right away."

"Investigations? It's a simple open-and-shut thing."

"It's never simple, Peter, and never open-and-shut. You've said that a million times yourself." She chuckled.

"I guess I did." Peter smiled crookedly. "But this one is open-and-shut." He clapped his hands. "Let's go."

"What?"

"They're here. Let's go."

Chapter 8

This case, although nearly three months old, was yet to go to trial. At the initial arraignment, Jamon "Pee Wee" Watson had pleaded not guilty. From the notes, it was clear that Peter Marcum, the DA, was more than ready to work with the police in pressing every thinkable charge, and maybe even a couple of unthinkable ones—anything to get this young man back in jail.

Reading the file, Porter could almost see the ellipses at the end of each lesser charge leading to the larger charge of murder—the murder of Lionel Harrison, the man found in the alley at the time of Pee Wee's arrest.

Owning a lengthy rap sheet filled with one misdemeanor after another, Jamon "Pee Wee" Watson's pending charges would clearly darken the ink a bit on the term *habitual criminal.*

The arresting officer stated that Jamon "Pee Wee" Watson allegedly committed murder, shoving Lionel Harrison out of a window after roughing him up during an alleged drug deal gone bad on Christmas Eve. Jamon "Pee Wee" Watson was then apprehended on the scene during his alleged attempt to escape capture. Yet the charge of murder had not been made, nor had that issue been pleaded in court. Only the illegal weapon and drug charge had been addressed before a judge and was now in continuance, where it looked as if it was destined to die. Porter knew his job was to make sure it did.

Peter Marcum would be a piece of cake. He was another one Porter remembered immediately. Porter didn't remember him as a DA, but as a bumbling, wannabe-cool, run-with-the-up-and-coming-Negroes, white boy. That was Peter.

"Well, I guess he got his wish. He's a 'cool fool' now, with all kinds of *Negroes* working for him," Porter said under his breath as he pulled into the underground parking. One name on the roster rang a bell—Kimani Turner. Porter remembered a pretty big-time judge with that last name. It would be like Peter to make a power move like that. But the likelihood of the two Turners being related was far-fetched, to say the least. Porter had learned a while ago that trying to link the obvious wasn't always the way to get the chain complete.

He glanced over at his client. The smug thug sat bopping his head to the rap music that poured out of the radio. Speaking of chains, this kid here was surely the weakest link in his family line.

"Now don't get out until I get the wheelchair and come around. I'd hate for you to fall or whatever," Porter stated, sounding more sarcastic than caring.

The boy smacked his thin lips, the only part of his face that resembled his brother's, Damian Watson, in the slightest.

Awkwardly, Porter hoisted the boy into the chair and pushed him into the building and into the elevator, where they crept up to the seventh floor.

Chapter 9

Kiki gulped down the bite she'd taken of her bagel. "Right now? Peter, this is crazy." She quickly gathered the file. She had barely skimmed the file and realized she would have to wing it during this first meeting with one of the Simon & Associates' attorneys, who all had reputations for being unstoppable when it came to defending their clients. With high-profile clients, they were extremely sophisticated attorneys, sly even, and if she wanted to sound full of hate," she would even call them slightly shady—"By hook or crook," her father would have said—judging by Garret, who'd finally made it to their lawyer A-list.

They were the firm you really didn't enjoy coming up against; at least that was the rumor. She hadn't gone up against anyone in court, except on paper, so she had no measure, but the grapevine had been good enough in this instance.

She gasped at the thought of actually fighting it out with another attorney, a "big dog," as Garret put it when he'd called her to tell her about losing his chance at a big case. He'd claimed that a big dog had just swooped and took his airspace. He was fit to be tied. Garret had said hateful things that she'd decided not to hold against him. She understood his frustration, being treated like nothing more than a clerk herself all these months.

Kiki instantly wanted to call her best friend and only confidant, Tamika Turner, aka Tommy. Kiki and Tommy had been best friends since their days in continuation school. Kiki was there because of the missed year, and Tommy there because . . . well, before she was Tommy. Tommy's mother had died and she was in sore need of a mother's care. Boyish, crude, and always getting into some kind of trouble—that was Tommy—and that's how she ended up in continuation school. Kiki loved her like a sister.

Kiki had her father's love, but for Tommy there was only the court-ordered care of an older brother and a check from some secret benefactor she'd never met to keep her secure as she grew from girl to woman. Their meeting was created by chance, but their friendship was created by fate, and as they both would often say, the same last name was pure coincidence.

The two of them shared everything with each other's life and knew each other's failings, flaws, and secrets, even the big ones, Tommy, acting boyish to hide her girlish fears, and Kiki acting adult to hide her need for Daddy. Despite her advantages, Kiki felt no better off than Tommy.

Lately their time together was strained and becoming infrequent as Kiki was progressing in her career and Tommy was promoted to homicide detective, both of their climbs to the top involving long hours and a less than glamorous life.

How often, when Kiki was a kid, she used to feel neglected by her father's long hours away. He was never home while his career progressed, and more so, after her mother died.

Kiki all but raised herself, and surely she had raised Shayla.

Her baby . . . sister. So many secrets . . .

There was never a thank-you for the life that Kiki had sacrificed, for a childhood she'd never had. It was as if a big "So what?" was all her life had amounted to. As far as a relationship with a man, it wasn't even a thought. She was what was known as a "sworn-again" virgin. Kiki's therapist had even called her a candidate for a "love care-package," for she was just that deficient. But then what Kiki's therapist didn't know could fill an ocean.

What Kiki loved most about Tommy was that Tommy never tried to "figure her out" or judge her. Tommy shot from the hip and spoke her mind, and best of all, she knew how to keep a secret and be a friend. There were things Tommy knew that Shayla would never know, if Kiki had her way about it.

The thoughts of Shayla made Kiki want to go pick her up from school and head home right now, turn on a good movie, curl up with her on the sofa and eat pizza the way they did the night before. Smiling at the thought, Kiki realized how much she loved Shayla.

"And the answer is no." Peter turned to her and pointed his finger toward the hallway.

Get your mind back here. Kiki nodded heartily at Peter's instruction, although she'd missed several comments leading into it. She wanted to ask, "No, what?"

Heading out of her office, trailing closely behind Peter, Kiki held the Pendaflex file tightly under her arm. Her heart was pumping harder than she ever remembered. She reassessed her black outfit. Perfect. No signs of her nervousness would show. Her teeth freshly brushed and flossed after a quick pit stop, considering Peter had caught her mid-bite, she couldn't have been more aesthetically ready than if she had planned this turn of events. She'd met with defendant's representatives before, usually in the capacity of a paralegal or clerk, and never on a case that she would be so closely involved with. Usually it was simply for a final *nolle prosequi* draft, a phone call, or some other form that caused the case to avoid the courtroom. She'd never dealt with Simon and Associates in person. Garret didn't count; he'd made sure his visits were purely social.

Kiki could feel in her bones that this case had more going on than what the surface presented, and today's impromptu meeting was going to be the turning point in her career. She just felt it. Whatever was going on though had put a boyish twinkle in Peter's eyes and had him all fired up to get this case back on the docket. Just the mere mention of the infamous Damian Watson and his relation to the accused told her as much.

The name Damian stuck in Kiki's brain like a nagging something that she just knew would come up when she least expected it. She wished she could go back to her office and re-read the brief. She'd skimmed the file all the way through and was actually on her second, more detailed reading when Peter interrupted her.

Moving past Dana's desk, Kiki caught Dana's smile—a shared pride between equals. They were both young black women trying to make their mark on the business world, the same mark, just different tools, Kiki having gone to law school, and Dana just finishing four years of college with a BS in office automation.

Dana even winked quickly, which Kiki didn't quite get

until she entered the conference room. That's when it hit. It was like a blast from the past. Kiki was sucked instantly into a portal and then spat back out. The wave of déjà vu was nauseating when the man, tall, dark, and handsome, turned to face her.

Chapter 10

Snatched back in time and then thrown relentlessly into the present, Porter's brain all but snapped at the sight of the beautiful woman who entered the conference room. Yes, she was older. *But of course she would be, Sean, ya idiot! It was fifteen years ago.*

I know that, but the dreams . . . in the dreams she's just a girl. She's . . . she's an angel.

But she's not an angel, she's a real person, a woman, his inner haunt responded, seemingly shocked at the sight of her as well.

He wanted to grab her, kiss her, and love her, as he had done last night in his dream, but no, he was awake now and dared not touch her. Not even to greet her with a handshake. He looked at his hand, which was shaking slightly, so he hid it by sorting papers. His mind soared to unreachable heights before crashing again, causing him to rub his forehead, bite his lip, sweat.

Play it cool, Porter. He had to hold tightly to the few cards he had left in his deck. If he didn't, he would snap, explode, just cut a fool all over this room and make a total ass of himself. *Everybody has a twin in this world, right?* Hell, he did. At least he used to. *So why not the angel*? The thought calmed him immensely.

Yes, she has a twin. Whew! Twin angels. Nice thought, Porter.

"Peter," thanks for meeting with us," he said, hoping his voice didn't show any signs of his inner disturbance.

Chapter 11

Shaking it off, Kiki immediately assessed "the enemy." Yes, he was the enemy, since he was defending the guilty. He had on a black pinstriped suit with a smart-looking gold mandarin print tie. His shoes were expensive, his hair was closely cropped, and his face impeccably lined with a thin beard that perfectly framed his jaw.

When he looked at her, she saw his flaws in his eyes, noticing the break in his front when he licked and then bit nervously on his full lips, squinting his left eye as soon as he saw her entering the room. From somewhere deep in her unconscious, she knew this man had invaded her life. It wasn't as if he was a stranger. She'd known him all her life. But did he know her? She could only pray he remembered; she could only pray he'd forgotten.

Shaking the thoughts from her head, Kiki was drawn back to the now. Before anyone spoke, she noticed the young man in the wheelchair. Her thoughts scrambled a little, but staying focused on the case, she thought now about the file. *Wheelchair*? Had she missed this part? Where had it said that Jamon "Pee Wee" Watson was permanently handicapped? Was the state really trying to put this crippled young man behind bars?

Wait, this "crippled" young man was a drug dealer, caught red-handed at the scene of a crime. He'd pulled a gun on the arresting officers and fired it. Evidence was pointing to a connection between him and the dead man in that alley. Hell, this boy is nothing more than a street punk, chair or no chair. And his brother was the infamous attorney Damian Watson, who everyone tipped around as if he was some demigod.

The connection is . . . ? Kiki always prided herself on her ability to synthesize a situation quickly, an art she'd learned from Tommy, but this one wasn't melding. No doubt, it was the young man's representation that had scrambled her thought pattern. *Her dream man. Oh my God, the dreams! Clothes shedding in the heat of the small room, skin rubbing, hands groping, panting . . . seething . . . passion . . . love.*

Kiki's dry mouth opened and closed again quickly before her breath could release a gasp. She squeezed her eyes closed tight and shook her head to jar the thoughts. Here he was. None other than—

"Porter . . . Sean Porter," Peter greeted the man, reaching out for a hearty handshake.

Chapter 12

Kiki didn't move. *Oh my God, the dreams! His mouth on hers, his eyes melting into hers, the desire, the passion.*

Sean, the man who on many nights, more nights than she wanted to confess to, had brought her to orgasmic ecstasy, now had a last name—Porter. She swooned just a bit but quickly quieted her spirit before anyone caught the quaking. Kiki then reprimanded herself immediately for getting mentally off track again and also for not having all the facts of the case in order, but she was given only moments to look it over.

"This, this is Ms. Turner. Kimani, this is—"

"Hello, Mr. Porter," she said, trying to keep the sharp periphery on her words. A tough exterior was imperative right about now. She was a lawyer first. Besides, maybe this wasn't the man. Maybe she'd seen him in *Essence* or *Black Enterprise* and just imagined.

"Hello, Kiki," Porter replied, smiling almost warmly.

It truly was him! His voice was unmistakable. Here he

was, outside of the otherworld, walking, breathing, real. "How have you been?"

"You know each other?" Peter asked, not showing on his face if he thought this was a good thing or not.

"No," Sean answered quickly.

"Yes," Kiki said, as they both spoke at once. "Oh, I, uh, I thought we did," Kiki added, her face on fire.

"I'd remember," his response came, sounding nearly flirtatious, rumbling through her, taking her breath away.

"You called me Ki—" She paused, fighting to keep from gasping in air and hyperventilating as she did when extremely upset. She was filled with emotions she'd not had time to decipher. His voice was so wonderfully comforting, but the memory surrounding it was so ugly yet. He was so beautiful. She'd missed him. She'd hated him. She'd loved him. And for what? She hadn't even been on his mind. He didn't even remember her. The confusion of the conflicting emotions was starting to make her ill.

"I'm sorry. I took the liberty. That was my bad, as they say. I just love nicknames," he said. "I would imagine that to be yours." He was cooler than cool. He was ice-cold, playing with her head now.

This is war! She heard her father's voice.

"So as far as having met you before, I'm afraid I'm at a disadvantage, Ms. Turner, because, for the life of me, I don't remember meeting you, short of my inquiry into Mr. Watson's representation. Your name was on the list as one of the firm's attorneys. But if we've met, you surely have a better memory than I."

Recovering as best she could, Kiki said, "Apparently. But then perhaps I'm mistaken about having met you." She spoke in a flat tone while sitting the file on the table, signaling a start of business.

Without missing a beat, Porter then introduced Jamon

"Pee Wee" Watson to Kiki and Peter. Pee Wee just nodded in Kiki's direction, totally ignoring Peter.

Kiki noticed the boy's attraction for her in his eyes instantly.

"I want to get to the point quickly here, Peter. Mr. Watson isn't going to help you build a case against his brother in exchange for a reduced sentence, especially with the nature of the charges against him. I'm sure that's why we're here, correct? We're here to waste Mr. Watson's time because the fact is, he's not who you have on your radar. It's an old war, Peter, one you should have surrendered a long time ago." Porter sat down as he spoke.

It was clear Porter and Peter knew each other—well. And it was even clearer that Porter wasn't in the least bit interested in Kiki or shaken by her presence in the room. She only wished she could say the same.

"Now, Porter, you know I don't work like that," Peter began. "Your boy here is a criminal."

"Who you calling a *boy*?" Pee Wee blurted, taking his attention from Kiki for just a moment.

Porter held out a hand to calm him. The tension in the air was instant.

Peter quickly attempted to correct the terminology. "I didn't mean—"

"Now, Jamon, I'm sure Peter was simply referring to your age. Peter doesn't have any problems with race, not with who he's got working for him as a clerk."

"She's not my clerk, she's my first chair on this case," Peter said quickly, hoping to keep Kiki from going totally off at the comment that topped even his level of rudeness. "She's Judge Turner's daughter," he said, as if that last part helped explain things further.

Chapter 13

Judge's daughter? Shame on you, Peter. Porter smiled knowingly, nodding slyly, as he bit his bottom lip. "Ah, I think I understand now, Peter. Thank you for clearing that up." He knew she was an attorney, but he was messing with her head. Hell, she'd messed with his long enough.

Kiki . . . how ironic, he thought. But, then again, with the wave of ethnic names in the '70s, Kimani wasn't so uncommon. But it was when he called her Kiki . . . the look on her face; it all but flipped his stomach. But that was just because she was beautiful, Porter reasoned. She must surely have a million men thinking they knew her, and half of them were probably young attorneys looking for a leg up, or old farts like him looking for a chance to feel young again.

If she was the woman from the dream, he would know it, right? He would have felt it in his bones. He would have reacted in his flesh. Okay, so he was hard as a rock and prayed it didn't show, but still . . .

As he looked up, both Peter and Kiki were staring at him. The sudden attention was unsettling. *Did it show?*

Why was she on this case? Of all the prosecuting attorneys in the city, why her? Could it be that she was the token black woman for the state. He hadn't seen any other female names that sounded African American on the list. Things were becoming clear as glass to him now. It was clear that Peter was planning to throw the book at Jamon "Pee Wee" Watson as soon as he got the opportunity and use the double minority black female attorney face to do it.

It was wickedly simplistic in Porter's mind. Thus, he was certain now there had to be more to it. Maybe Peter just wanted to humiliate Damian Watson, and as much as Damian disrespected women, losing the case to a woman would be a whammy. *Of course, that wasn't going to happen.*

While Porter worked to prove Pee Wee's innocence, Kiki would be on the other side, proving to the state that this "Pee Wee" Watson, like all misled inner city boys like him—uneducated, unemployable, unremarkable in the eyes of society—deserved nothing more than to spend the rest of his life in prison. Was that what this was about?

Hope not, Porter thought. He was planning to show that not all black people felt the same way about black on black crime. Sure, someone still needed to be punished for killing Lionel Harrison, but Pee Wee was innocent, and he sure didn't need to pay for being Damian Watson's brother. No man should have to pay for his brother's sins.

"So, Ms. . . . Kiki," Porter spoke, drawing Kiki into a staring match with him by speaking her name as if he truly did know her. He was certain no one called her *Kiki* when speaking in a professional setting.

Chapter 14

"Ms. Turner," Kiki answered smartly. If she allowed her mind to wander there, she could have sworn she saw twinkles come to Sean's eyes, but surely she imagined it. "Ms. Kimani Turner is my name, Mr. Porter," she corrected. "And here I was thinking you knew me. I guess that's what I get for giving people too much credit."

The boy smiled as if filing away the information regarding the sassy Ms. Kiki for a later time, or maybe he was noting the heat between this foxy mama and his attorney. Or maybe Sean had told him something regarding his plans to whip her butt in court without much trouble. The wild thoughts curled Kiki's lip in disgust; she didn't feel like being the fuel to some "guy" thing. "I think your client should wait outside," Kiki suggested.

"Why?" Porter asked.

"I just . . ." she began. It was too late. Porter had seen her flinch. She could tell.

He smiled slyly. "Jamon, would you mind waiting a moment outside while we regroup for a couple of seconds?"

Pee Wee bit his lip and smiled wickedly, as if showing his clear understanding of what was occurring. "You gon' stay out here wit' me?"

"In my worst of dreams," Kiki muttered, wheeling the young man quickly into the hallway. She nodded at Dana to tend to the young man while she quickly returned to the heated conference.

Simon & Associates was a prestigious firm, handling many wealthy clients, and so this pitiful-looking boy, paralyzed in this wheelchair, while still trying to pour on some weak-ass mack, just didn't fit the clientele they normally represented.

Kiki was no genius true, but she knew this young man, Jamon Watson, couldn't possibly be paying the tab for his legal representation, and wondered if S &A had accepted blood money, and if they had done it knowingly. Had Sean taken on this scum of a client with his eyes wide open? Looking at Porter, noticing his pompous body language and pretentious manner, Kiki wondered hard about him. It couldn't be her dream man. The Sean she knew was loving and caring. He was sensitive and fun. But, then again, a lot could change in fifteen years. Heaven knows, she'd changed nearly one hundred percent. *But what we had was special, wasn't it? What we shared that night meant everything to both of us, didn't it? Apparently not*, she figured.

When she walked back into the conference room, Peter and Porter were going at it.

"Jamon will testify that he was there with Pepper Johnson when Mr. Harrison went out that window, since he was forced to admit to being there by some overzealous officers who threatened him at gunpoint. By the way, speaking of guns, you know the gun found on Mr. Watson was not his, and we feel that his choice to be in the alley at that time had nothing to do with Mr. Harrison's flight out of that window. Your efforts to connect the two has no glue. Drugs, maybe. Sure, Mr. Watson will perhaps admit to a small drug purchase; however, what you are suggesting regarding Mr. Watson's involvement is some kind of major drug deal that eventually led to Mr. Harrison's taking a swan dive into an empty dumpster—"

"And missing it, by the way," Peter added, holding onto a serious face.

Porter pointed his finger emphatically. "Exactly! Well"—He then shook his head as if totally done talking about this entire matter—"I guess you know I expect this whole thing to be thrown out of court."

"What about the evidence found on the body, Porter? If it's true and this young man has no reason to be in a courtroom on murder charges, then ask your client to assist us in apprehending the man who deserves to be there," Peter yelped.

"And who is that, Pepper Johnson?" Porter asked, sounding sarcastic.

Peter shook his head. "Right." He glowered, with a sarcastic snarl in his tone. "Pepper Johnson."

Porter glanced at Kiki. She couldn't read his face.

"I'm sure that's who you meant," he then said.

No, she was nowhere on Sean's mind, at that moment she realized that.

"We are doing everything in our power to assist the police in finding Mr. Pepper Johnson, as I assume you are. We want to get to the bottom of this Harrison situation. And our hope is that your client here is agreeable to pleading to the lesser charges in exchange for information regarding Mr. Pepper Johnson."

Kiki remembered this part of the file. Even in the short time she had to skim it, this part stood out—the phantom witness, Mr. Pepper Johnson. From what she was hearing and piecing together, she knew exactly where this was going and it was making her sick. Peter no more wanted Pepper Johnson than the man in the moon. Who knew if there even really was a Pepper Johnson? Peter wanted someone else behind bars.

Someone else . . . who? She wasn't sure yet, but she was going to find out after she tried this case and put Pee Wee Watson behind bars for murder. Sure, the case was weak, but her frustration was fueling her now. Suddenly she felt as if she could push the envelope as far as it could go, but first, she was going to find out what was really going on here today.

In listening just this few moments, she realized these two men found law a game, and she wasn't about to play with them. What was the objective? What was the prize? Dream lover or not, and he was acting as if NOT, Sean Porter wasn't looking out for the best interest of the state or her heart, so to hell with him, and Peter too, for that matter. Peter was playing ring around the rosies here, and this all smacked of politics.

"You both are making me kinda ill," Kiki interrupted then. "We both know that Mr. Johnson is a ghost, and the true criminal here is Mr. Jamon Watson. Gentlemen, let's stop playing games. Jamon Watson killed Mr. Harrison. Pepper Johnson—if there is a Pepper Johnson—is just an accomplice. Evidence points—"

"I don't think so," Porter interrupted, smiling slyly, shaking his head, and looking a little surprised at Kiki's outburst, but ready to take her on without missing a beat. "Besides, Ms. Turner, we aren't looking to indict for murder here. We are not even talking about murder." He then glared at Peter. "Is there is something you haven't told me, Peter."

"Nothing," Peter said, backing down slightly, trying to

discreetly give Kiki the cut-it-out sign, slicing under his chin ever so covertly.

Kiki looked the other way, in defiance of his sign language. "Drop what? A murder charge, Peter?"

"Drop it," Peter growled now.

"Peter, come on!" Kiki yelled.

"There is no murder charge!" Peter yelled back.

"There will be. What about the gun found? You know it had a body on it, and . . ." Kiki said, trying to calm down a bit. She knew she was taking a chance with this one, but she'd seen Peter do it a million times. Well, maybe not a million times, and hardly did the ploy ever work, but she was going for it. *Good lawyer, bad lawyer—it works for the cops.*

"Oh Peter, come on! When did this happen?" Porter yelped, turning his attention back to Peter, who just shrugged.

Porter's body language showed Kiki that she was about to be tuned out while he spoke to Peter man-to-man. "Two young black men running through the streets of the Palemos, a known ghetto, where crime happens every few minutes—no, seconds—and a dead crackhead shows up an alley where the forensic team alleges he was pushed from the window by who knows who! And suddenly we have a murder charge with my client's name on it. Surely you can do better than that. What is this, Ms. Turner—your first case since law school?"

Kiki moved into Porter's view, and so he gave her a full glare.

"Oh now you didn't just go there."

"I see no murder here and you know that gun is not dirty, Kiki," he continued, rolling her name over his bright white teeth as he gritted them. "Why are we getting so creative here? What do you really want? What? We need to get down to business or end this mess right here. I've got real work to do!" Porter's voice rose to an unnecessarily high pitch.

"Why you getting all loud?" Kiki asked, slamming her hands on her hips.

"Now you actin' like you know me!" Porter all but hollered.

A deafening silence exploded in the room.

Chapter 15

Porter, get a grip! Porter barked internally. This encounter was getting out of hand, and he couldn't take it anymore. In his dreams he was always in control. He had his way with her. Always. But that's the way she liked it. Not today though, there was no having his way with this real woman, who was fierce and giving him a run for his money.

Kiki's eyes widened with his growing volume and attitude. It was clear to him that frustrations and heated rage were racing into her chest.

It had been years since he'd spoken with anyone in this manner, and with this much emotion, but it was like riding a bike, and he was ready to pedal this one all the way around the block. He felt the need to tear into her—Why? He knew why. Kiki, the girl of his dreams, had made his life bearable, but this Kiki, the woman who stood before him now was ruining his day. And his open-and-shut case!

Kiki wanted to jump on him, maybe even scratch his eyes out, but grabbing at all of her professionalism, she attempted to stay on point, that being the young thug in that wheelchair waiting out in the lobby. *Probably flirting his butt off with Dana right about now.* "Ugh!" she groaned.

"Don't throw a tantrum," he remarked, continuing to goad her. His words came surprisingly cool and distant.

"What the hell did you just say to me?" Kiki exploded, all professionalism gone. He'd done it. He'd taken her there.

"I said, 'Don't have a tantrum,' girl. You're an adult, act like it," he barked.

"I know I'm fully grown. What about you, boy?"

"Oh, you must wanna stand up here and take me on like a man? 'Cuz I got cho, boy."

"You don't want me to take you on man to man because you would be outnumbered!"

"Whoa, guys," Peter interjected, holding up his hands in a football *T* for time-out, hoping for a truce.

"I hope you are getting someone else to handle this case, Peter. It's clear, *Miss* Turner . . ." Porter paused dramatically, trying to dig further. He'd seen no ring. She was clearly just another career woman—selfish and self-centered, and lonely. "It's clear she isn't ready to face me"—He paused again, his dark eyes like molten onyx stone—"in court."

"*Ms.* Turner is *readier* than you think," Kiki stated flatly. "She's been ready to face you for years." Kiki sneered.

Porter's heart jumped in his chest. The involuntary action within his body nearly nauseated him. Again she was implying familiarity with him, acting as though the history he had only imagined was real. She was wreaking havoc on his brain and probably didn't even know it. No, by the look in her eyes, her beautiful, haunting eyes, she knew exactly what she was doing.

"She *don't* act ready," he growled, hoping to fight her off, push her back out of his dotted memories. She wasn't ready. There was no way she was ready for what he was not. "She acts intimidated, and I can't have the jury feeling sorry for her," Porter snapped. "I can't have the jury seeing this case as something it's not—the big bad man against the cute little lady." He'd lost it now.

Chapter 16

There was another adjusting silence.

"I'm not intimidated," Kiki repeated, ignoring his clearly crude, and if one stretched their imagination, half-assed, flirtatious comment. It was true, she was a bit stunned by how fast this was moving and how passionate Porter was about defending this client, but intimidated? "I'm not intimidated in the least."

She was more than ready to go up against "Pee Wee" Watson or Damian Watson or any other Watson they wanted to bring up in there. She may not have been raised in the ghetto, but she knew a street thug when she saw one, and they had never impressed or overawed her. And as far as her being moved by the comments regarding the big bad man, Sean Porter, she wasn't even going to go there. Peter was right, the case was far from major, but what Peter didn't know was that going up against Sean was.

Suddenly with instant flashes of memory filling her brain, Kiki became nearly overwhelmed. Her life had been thrown into fast reverse in a matter of moments, taking her back to that small room. Perhaps it was all the emotion that brought on the premature hot flash, but there they were in that small room together. Heated pants filling the air as they ripped at each other's clothing. It was as if she was starving, craving him to an unnatural degree. She'd given him her pride along with her virginity. Shamefully brazen and drunk, she gave it up with nothing coming in return for her actions but more shame and a lifetime of broken promises.

Sean Porter, he sang to her that night, spoke poetry to her, kissed her, and touched her. It was Sunday, Christmas Eve, and she had just turned fifteen. She had decided to go to the party with some of the girls from her school. Insecurity over her weight and need to belong to something other than her boring life had thrown her and these pretty girls together this night. She hadn't met Tommy yet; that came about two years later. That year, the one that quickly rushed to her mind, she'd only met lies and deceit, and wrongfully considered them her friends.

He said everyone called him SP, but she could call him Sean. He was one of the college boys there at this party. He was much older than her, but he didn't know that. Her friends didn't seem bothered by it, but then again, since they had confessed that it wasn't their first time lying about their ages and getting into the party, it wasn't as if anyone was in a position to make a judgment call.

Once in the door, her friends were hard to find, and so the fake ID they had given her was helpful in getting around. She wasn't even considering the fact that just being there at a frat party was an illicit act on her part. Kiki should have been at church praying, where her father thought she was, instead of there with this dark angel. The beautiful dark angel who talked about music, foods, travel and clothes. Who sang to her, who kissed her, who touched her.

He was so grown up, not like her; she'd lied about her own age. She liked him immediately, but more importantly, he liked her. Finally, after wooing, promising, beguiling, and convincing her that being with him was the right place to be, she gave herself to him under the most humiliating circumstances—on a mattress that lay on the floor, no blanket, and no pillow. There were only the sounds of his hunger for comfort. It wasn't the way she planned for her first time to go, but it went that way.

After finishing with her, he heard a noise, or so he said, told her he'd be right back, slipped on his clothes and left.

How could she have ever thought she loved a liar like that? How could someone as rude as this man here going toe to toe with her be the man of her dreams?

Just then Porter glanced up at her from where he stood across the conference table. His dark orbs dug deep into her soul, her subconscious.

Sean Porter. Kiki's head hurt with the refreshing of the memories while watching SP, Sean Porter, shuffle his notes. Kiki had to figure he must have been developing his career that night in the small room. He was probably molding his art of sophistry, conjuring, lying, cheating, and playing underhanded dirty pool even back then. It was a perfect career for such a beautiful one, and what a stunning one he was that night. More so now, if she wanted to admit it. Which she didn't.

She had trusted him that night, felt safe with him. Safer than she should have, because rape was the final diagnosis given to her parents by the ER doctor. Her parents had found her in the bathroom vomiting her guts out from the overdose of alcohol and disgrace. They rushed her to ER to have her body examined, poked, and prodded for signs of invasion, penetration, and bruising, of which they found plenty. Unable to face the shame of not so much as having a full name to claim as a partner for her trip into womanhood, Kiki told a lie. She let everyone at the hospital think she had indeed been taken against her will, raped by a nameless stranger.

Kiki's mother's humiliation and a year in Europe to stay with her mother's sister was all there was to fix the situation.

Upon coming home, her life changed, her parents changed, and a new baby in the house, a baby sister, made life very different. There was no more talking, no more attempts at closeness with her parents, and after her mother was diagnosed with terminal cancer, there was no comfort. Only the screams of a baby sister that Kiki had a seemingly unnatural attachment to, according to her mother's friends.

"Kimani needs to be with people her own age, make friends," they said.

So after her mother died, Shayla was taken from her care by an aunt who kept her for five years, until Kiki reached her early twenties. All Kiki had in the meantime, until Shayla's return to her life, was the man of her dreams. She'd grown to depend on him to comfort her during the loss of Shayla.

But how could she love a rapist? That's what her father called him.

He didn't rape me. She looked at him, stared at him, falling in love with him all over again. "Oh my God," she mumbled while watching him, his smooth, dark skin unmarred, his beauty undiminished by the foul mood he showed her. She had fallen in love with him that night and still she loved him. "Oh my God," she mumbled again. *Maybe it's not him. It can't be. He doesn't remember me. I love him, and he doesn't remember me.* Her eyes burned. *The Sean I know would have remembered me!* She was mortified, angry—no, hateful.

Stop it, Kiki. This is serious. You don't love him, you don't hate him. You don't even know him. You didn't even know his full name until today, and now . . . now you're just guessing that it's even the same man.

But he was the same man, standing there talking to her as if nothing had happened between them.

Something happened, all right. Shayla is proof of that. God, I've admitted it to myself, God, and all the angels. I've broken my promise to the spirit of my mother and admitted the truth about Shayla.

I'm so sorry, mama. I'm so sorry, mama.

Suddenly Kiki all but wanted to cry out, howl, and drop to her knee, to bay like a wolf calling to a full moon. She'd thought about what she'd promised her mother she never would say aloud. She'd admitted even to God what she sworn to her mother she would never confess to.

Just then she noticed Porter staring at her, through her, across the conference table, their minds seemingly connecting. She saw it in his eyes. The truth. She saw it, and it made her lip curl in a wicked half-grin.

"Can we get focused here? Can we get back to business," he said to her.

"We have no more business," she growled, her voice coming guttural and unnatural-sounding.

Chapter 17

Desperation and fear are the best weapons of your opponent, and once you know that, you need not be afraid. Just conquer them with their own fears. Kiki cleared her thought, and apparently her mind. "So how long will Mr. Pee, uh, Wee," she paused sarcastically, smacking her full lips between the compound name, "be in that chair?" she asked, showing both Peter and him that she was looking at this case from all the angles. Or maybe she was probably just trying to get back on track with this case.

Porter knew he had thrown her for a loop for a minute for sure, but she was back now and ready to fight him some more. "We believe he will be permanently paralyzed," he answered too quickly. He knew his lie read like ticker tape across his face.

"Really?" Kiki looked up from the brief she had earlier pulled from the Pendaflex and laid on the table.

"Why do you ask?" Peter asked.

Kiki then smiled at Peter, a show of confidence, Porter

could tell. She was on to something. The wheelchair wasn't working. What he'd come to the table with as a ploy wasn't cutting it.

"I'm just wondering if he will be on his feet when he gets to court. I mean, we'd hate to have emotions flying and the jury feeling sorry for him, big bad deputy DA versus the poor crippled thug." Looking at Porter with her eyes narrowed and intense, Kiki depicted anything other than weakness because it was now clear Ms. Turner was not weak. Angry as hell, but weak? Never!

"Mr. Porter, this office will be proceeding on all charges that our investigation into this case presents. That includes all the charges we've previous stated in the petition. But, hear me now, someone is going to prison for murder." Kiki's voice was cool and controlled now. "There has been a serious crime committed, Mr. Sean Porter." She said his name again formally, as if tasting it, rolling it around in her mouth. "There has been a murder, committed during a drug deal and your client"—Kiki pointed toward the door where Jamon waited outside—"committed it, was an accessory to it, or witnessed it. Either way, he was at the scene with a dirty gun, which he attempted using to shoot and possibly kill law enforcement. And I'm sure blood analysis will show he made contact with Mr. Harrison. Annnnd"—Kiki glanced again at the file to gather a quick reference—"at the time he was admitted to the hospital, he was under the influence of a hallucinogen, the same as found in Mr. Harrison. Now why, why was your client there in that alley at that time? Running an errand? I think not."

Porter could see out of the corner of his eye that Peter was impressed.

"Humph. I don't recall a mention of Mr. Hamilton's autopsy indicating drugs," he huffed, under his breath.

"Well, it did," Kiki bluffed further. "So I'll find all the

medical reports stating his permanent disability in here?" She pointed at the Pendaflex. "As well as his blood workup from ER and DNA test, etcetera, etcetera."

Porter smiled then, showing that he too was impressed with Ms. Cute Junior Attorney. "What you need will be in that Pendaflex when you need it."

"So does this mean we're gonna dance?" Peter asked excitedly.

"Looks like it, but not before I know if you plan to indict my client on any other charges, because I'm not going to let this young man here go to jail for something he didn't do. And I'm not going to allow you to build this case into a political platform. I'm not going to allow my client to pay for your bad temper." He meant that one for Kiki.

"He's getting charged for the activities that led to Harrison flying out of a window. And he'll be charged for the illegal weapon he tried to killed the arresting officer with," Peter said, taking over where Kiki reluctantly left off.

"None of this fleeing and eluding police, or aggravated attempted murder on a police officer," Porter insisted, huffing again, nodding at Kiki. "It's just window dressing and a waste of good ink." He noticed her lips curve into a smirk. Porter was extremely irritated and wanted away from this case, from this room. Away from Kiki and her bad temper.

Chapter 18

Yeah, you think you've seen a bad temper, Mr. Sean Porter? You ain't seen nothin' yet.

Simon & Associates was not going to be happy with Porter's report when he got back to the firm. They were going to court to defend a thug. This couldn't be good for their reputation. Simon & Associates was used to winning cases, and they didn't stand a chance on keeping Mr. Jamon "Pee Wee" Watson out of jail, even on the lesser charges.

Surely, when Porter walked in here today he was planning to settle this out of the view of a judge and jury. She was sure he had planned on charges getting dropped, with the promise to exchange Pepper Johnson. But Pepper had not shown. And Kiki didn't expect him to. Pee Wee was as guilty as they came. And about his attorney Mr. Porter, he too was fraying around the edges. Kiki planned to pull the unraveling strings as hard as she could. She wanted to see what was underneath that Armani suit, because there was no way the Sean she loved was there.

"Based on new evidence in the case, we are requesting

a revocation of bail," Peter stated, grinning like a Cheshire cat. "Please be advised that upon the judge's acceptance of our plea, Watson be picked up, unless you want to advise him to turn himself into the police after the revocation is issued."

Kiki was a little surprised that after her diatribe, Peter still hadn't included a murder charge, but she let it go. She had time to build that case, and build she would.

"Peter, I see where this is going. Don't think for a moment I'm beguiled," Porter said.

"A *surrender* might help with the bail issue," Peter told him.

The door opened, and they poured out of the conference room. Kiki looked at Jamon "Pee Wee" Watson sitting there in that chair as if he was a true victim. He probably did deserve to do the time that Porter was trying to keep him from.

The young man licked his lips, eyeing her up and down again, seemingly unconcerned with the charges that had just been laid out.

Kiki began to wonder. *Maybe Simon & Associates had a few games up their sleeve.* Surely they had to know he was guilty too. But clearly Simon & Associates had collected a hefty retainer from Mr. Damian Watson to make sure Pee Wee did no time, but that wasn't going to happen, not as long as Kiki was on the case. She was out for blood. She wanted to see Sean Porter bleed like a stuck pig, and Pee Wee get what was justly coming to him, of course. *Stay focused, Kiki.*

Porter gripped the back of the chair and pushed Jamon toward the elevator without saying anything else or even looking back. The door opened, and he entered without even turning around to face outward before the door closed.

"So do I understand this right? You really do want

Jamon for murder, right?" Kiki asked as soon as the lights showed the elevator lowering to the ground floor.

Peter directed her back into the conference room and closed the door. No doubt, he'd noticed Dana's interest in the law.

"As I've wanted nothing else. What part did you miss?"

"Well, for one, Jamon's murder charges. I guess you were holding that off for another reason. Maybe you wanted to indict later or—"

"That young man in that chair is scared. He knows we want to try him for murder, and he's scared. He's scared of prison, this mysterious Pepper Johnson, but mostly of taking this rap alone. No matter how tough he looks, Jamon is small potatoes. But if Sean Porter doesn't want to play nice, we'll turn him into the main course." Peter again sounded campaign-like in his speech. "Didn't you see the fear in that kid's eyes when we came out and Porter grabbed that chair?"

"Actually, no."

"That's because you were too busy *PMS*ing on Mr. Porter. What was that about? One minute you don't have faith we can win this case, then ten minutes in a room with Porter and you're ready to throw the book at that kid without even knowing why."

"That's not true," Kiki lied. She began straightening the room, pushing in chairs, pulling the conference phone into the center of the large conference table.

"So where do you know SP from?" Peter finally asked.

Kiki wanted to avoid his question at first, holding onto her tightest poker face while tidying up the room. She couldn't believe what he had just called Sean Porter. "SP?" she asked innocently.

"Sean Porter." Peter smiled wickedly, holding the door open for her to pass after she'd finished tidying the room. "You sure have a short attention span."

"I never heard him called that today."

"Oh, I guess not. We used to call him that in college."

"You went to college with him?"

Peter shook his head again. "Real short attention span. Anyway, you realize he's gonna be hell in the courtroom. I hope you're as ready as you say. I have some calls to make, you know, work," he said, walking away.

Glancing out the window down below, Kiki caught a glimpse of Porter as he and his client pulled out of the roundabout in front of the building. Again she thought about Shayla. "Please. I'm past ready to take you on, Sean Porter . . . SP," she mumbled under her breath. "More than ready."

Passing Dana's desk, Kiki recognized the look of sudden preoccupation, noticing that Dana appeared overly busy and totally into her computer monitor. She'd probably been online shopping before they came from the conference room. She could only wonder what was on Dana's mind and what she'd heard. Holding her heavy head high, Kiki headed back to her office.

Chapter 19

"Looks like that bitch tore you a new one," Pee Wee snickered wickedly under his breath, bringing Porter's mind reluctantly back to the situation he was in.

Porter glared at Pee Wee out of the corner of his eye, keeping his hands tightly on the steering wheel. "First, she is not a bitch, and I don't ever want to hear you addressing any officer of the court that way." Porter didn't point his finger at Pee Wee, but he wanted to. Pee Wee had stomped on several of his last nerves already today and was heading for an ass-beatin' if he kept it up. At this point Porter couldn't give a good gotdamn about Damian Watson, what he was, or who he was. He was gonna whip baby brother's behind with the buckle of his belt before too much longer.

Kiki . . . ugh! Porter groaned internally before slamming his palm on the steering wheel. Why, of all people, the one woman whose very essence, let alone presence, sent his blood to the boiling point? His mind fought the instant memory that flooded his thoughts. The memory of the night his brother died. The night he and Kiki met. The two memories collided in a paradoxical conundrum of sound, thoughts, smells, and pain.

Kiki. That name was all he knew regarding the identity of the woman in his dreams. The woman who held answers to his riddled memories. But today he'd seen her face. "Ugh," he groaned again, this time audibly.

"Cool out, man. Why she got you twisted so tight?" Pee Wee asked, seemingly unconcerned or unaware about the depth of what went down during their visit to the district attorney's office today.

Porter's brain was filled with more thoughts than he wanted to separate right now, whereas Pee Wee, on the other hand, didn't seem to have one working notion in his head.

Glaring at him, Porter spoke coolly, "Secondly, do you, or do you not realize that you are going to jail? You were inches from being indicted for murder."

"Murder? Look, fool, my brother said—"

"I'm no fool, and your brother is the reason this is all happening to you. When are you going to see that?"

"Hey, I thought you were our attorney. I thought you were on our side."

"I'm *your* attorney. I'm on *your* side, man. Your brother is just paying the bill. You're the one going to pay for this crime. Tell me again that you didn't kill Harrison. Tell me where Pepper is. Tell me something. Shit!"

"I told you I don't know. You keep as'n' me that. And I told you I'm not the one that sent dude flyin' like some broke-ass superman." Pee Wee turned and looked out the window. "Besides, what does Pepper have to do with anything anyway?"

Porter smacked his full lips and ignored the question. Pepper Johnson was the sacrificial lamb needed for this burning bush. Without him Pee Wee was going to go down for this crime, and that could prove bad for everyone. Damian was crazy and maybe just crazy enough to follow through on the clandestine threats he'd been making for the last few months, threats that no one else at Simon & Associates seemed to realize he was making. But Porter was from the streets; he knew what a man like Damian was capable of when he didn't get his way.

Sean's brother, Bond, worked for Damian back when they were all new and fresh to their careers, and even then Damian showed his potential to be a borderline mobster. It wasn't surprising to come back and find that Damian had his hand less than clean. Bond and Damian were associates. Bond had just started working for Damian's firm as his personal investigator, but it wasn't working out. That's what Bond had said anyway. Bond was aggressive and maybe willing to take things to the edge—but never further and further was where Damian was pushing him. That night, Bond was planning to end their relationship. Porter remembered that now. He'd had another offer that clearly was more interesting.

There was darkness surrounding Damian Watson, and his presence weighted heavily on Sean's mind. But without Bond to assist in getting past the large blanks that punctured big holes in his memory banks, Porter had been depending on Damian's recent reminiscing about his and Bond's relationship to fill some gaps. Lately Damian had been talking a lot about Bond; it was almost as if he missed him. Maybe they had been better friends than Bond let on. Who could know?

"The DA can't put nothing on me," Pee Wee said, bringing Porter's mind back to the now, and Peter Marcum, another frat brother of theirs.

What was he up to? Porter wondered. That was what Porter wanted to know more than anything at this exact moment. With the negative vibe Porter picked up from Peter today, he would hate to think that Peter was another link to finding peace of mind and pieces of memory.

Just then the sounds outside of the Chrysler 300 caught his attention. The jet-black Hummer swerved in his direction, surely to hit him broadside—on his side!

"Ohh shit! What the"—Porter twisted the wheel with all his strength, the mighty vehicle reluctantly curving in a tight circle, as if it was a sports car instead of the monster it was. The Hummer's horn blared as the brakes screamed and the vehicle came to a halt.

Heart racing, Porter quickly lowered the glass to see if he could identify the driver and passenger if any, but the Hummer's windows had a dark tint. Suddenly, the Hummer backed up quickly and then turned around, running the red light as the driver sped off.

This was a deliberate close call. No accident. If he wanted to go so far, he would have called it some kind of attempt, but what kind? To kill him? To mess up his car? What? Had he gotten too close to something? Had he crossed a line somewhere and pissed somebody off?

The memory of that night flashed again in his mind, and he glanced over at Pee Wee. He panicked for half a second, wondering if maybe Pee Wee had been shot. Had he been shot through the window as Bond was? Porter remembered the blood on the seat, the window, and on him, as the car raced passed before another shot sent the car off the road and into the ravine.

Pulling over, Porter leaned over to get a closer look at Pee Wee, whose eyes were closed. He nudged him. "You dead?"

Pee Wee cracked open one eye and looked around. "What the fuck was that?"

"Nah, you ain't dead."

"Man, you better get your head right. You almost killed me."

Porter tuned him out immediately. Of course there wasn't a cop around, and no one on the street seemed concerned enough to have gotten a license plate number. No one was running over to see if they were all right. So Porter cautiously pulled back out to the street and continued on, looking in his rearview mirror for a few blocks, just in case the Hummer returned to start some trouble.

This case was darkening, and it was less than appealing. Something beyond the obvious was going on, and frankly, Porter wanted nothing more to do with it. After that meeting and hearing all the information Peter had hidden between his lines and lies, and now this close call, triggering Porter's paranoia button, he wanted out.

But backing out now was impossible. Simon & Associates had already taken a hefty retainer, and Damian's unethical means of making things happen had already been set in motion. After today he was sure of it. But why kill him? How could taking him out help win this case?

Porter's mind soared now. *This whole case is a bunch of bogus shit that, frankly, I don't have time for, let alone dealing with Ms. Kiki and her iss*—Porter couldn't even finish the thought, coming back to the now, sitting behind the wheel. Calmer. Whatever Ms. Turner's issues, they were apparently no greater than his right now.

God, she's real. And she remembers me.

All this time Porter truly thought she was just a dream. Where did she fit into his life? He knew she fit in somewhere major because he dreamed of her constantly, dreams that, over the years had become a love affair of the greatest kind. But that's what dreams did, right? Distort and misconstrue the truth, right? We were never lovers, right?

But she knows me, and hell, I know her, so I have to

figure she was tied to that night and me. Stop playing, Sean. You did nothing but talk about her that night. The way she smelled. The way she tasted—". . . fresh as a Georgia peach," you said. And I told you I didn't want to hear that shit. I told you it was wayyyy more than I wanted to know about your business. I said that, but it wasn't true. I was listening hard because I knew she was dangerous.

"Is she the reason they tried to kill us?" Porter mumbled.

"Nah, nigga, ain't no *us* in this. Must be you they wanted. Ain't nobody even know me. I'm innocent," Pee Wee said, thinking he understood what Porter was talking to himself about.

Porter glared at him. "Shut the hell up."

What did Bond mean? What was he trying to tell me about that night with Kimani Turner?

Just the thought that so much was blocked, that so much of his past was blurred, Porter groaned again out loud. Had it blocked it? No. Well, only the parts that hurt too much. Only the pleasant thoughts about his brother and him growing up together, fighting, forgiving, sharing, caring, loving and hating each other had come through without any gaps or missing spots. Porter enjoyed that part. He also enjoyed the memories of Kiki. Made up as they went along, they were still the best of memories of all. Those memories heated his loins in a good way.

But right now, Porter had no time for those kinds of thoughts. He had a maniac on his hands, and Kiki was working for the district attorney's office, the clear object of this madman's obsession. Kiki was planning to prosecute and probably convict the crazy man's younger brother. And in her innocent determination, she was about to be pegged as Damian Watson's personal enemy.

She needs to get off this case. Porter realized immediately. She was his dream girl, and he had to protect her, right? Damian already had him on the edge of ethics with Pee Wee and these whack-ass defense tactics, and he hated the position.

Porter had thought he was going to be working with Peter Marcum on this case. He thought he was going to be able to work a deal, "keep it in the family," so to speak. As much as Porter hated this Frat friggin' loyalty scam, he knew when to use it to his benefit. But now things had been flipped upside down.

Working with Peter Marcum, he could have come to an equitable agreement quickly and ended this, right or wrong. They could have worked this out so that each party was happy, but now someone new was on the case, someone distracting and troubling to his spirit. Porter had a feeling defending Pee Wee was going to take him where he never wanted to go in his legal career, but he never figured it was going to take him here.

Pulling through the gate and into the roundabout, Porter, stopping at the door, glanced over at Jamon again. "Look, we need Pepper Johnson. You need to talk to your brother about making him appear, and I mean mad fast, okay. But for now, your bail is being revoked, and you're going back to jail. I know the judge is going to agree to it, so just go along. At least they aren't charging you with Harrison's murder." *Yet*, he thought but did not say. "But they are raising the bar from the simple possession to possession for sale, and a gun charge, so get ready. I'll be at the arraignment and get you right back out again, but for now, you need to just do what you're told."

Pee Wee slammed the car door before turning and strolling toward the door.

Suddenly the car door opened behind his head, catching Porter off guard. "Hey! What the!"

"Gettin' the chair, man, chill," one of Damian's goons explained.

"Yeah, yeah, I almost forgot." *It's not like he needs it*, Porter thought to himself.

After the goons pulled the almost forgotten wheelchair from the backseat and playfully wheeled it into the slow-opening garage, Porter blew out hot air, resting his head for a moment on the steering wheel. "What a ride home this was. I almost get killed, and these fools are playing around like this all is a game." Porter ran his large hand over his closely cropped head.

Again he thought about Kiki and her powers of observation. There was no way he was going to be able to convince her that Pee Wee was chair-bound, not without doing something illegal. Like breaking the boy's legs. No, he'd already eased as far down the yellow brick road toward the Land of unethical Oz as he wanted to go. Forging medical records would be a full gallop, one that would end with him being disbarred.

"Besides, Sean Porter is not a criminal," Porter fussed aloud. He looked up toward the huge house, where inside, Damian Watson, no doubt, sat, cooking up something corrupt. He groaned again. "This whole thing is sooo not going to work," he mumbled under his breath. "I should have let the Hummer hit us. At least he might have actually gotten hurt."

Tonight Porter would break his first of many promises to himself. He was going out to have a drink. But first he'd have to go back to the office and write his report, sit through a boring meeting or two, and last but not least, he'd deal with Damian a little longer, answering his call and questions about why his precious little brother was going back to jail tomorrow.

Yes, by five o'clock he'd be more than ready for some booze.

Chapter 20

"I thought you said she wouldn't be a problem."

"She's not. Why would you think otherwise?"

"She's being less than cooperative."

"She's always been less than cooperative, but that's to our benefit this time. And that's all that matters, doesn't it? You won't have to worry about Kimani Turner."

"Now, why don't I believe that?"

"Trust me. Didn't I tell you I had this all under control?"

"I hope so, because I wouldn't want to have to take matters in my own hands."

"I told you, you don't have to do that. This just isn't that serious. Just calm down."

"Calm down? Did you tell me to calm down? Don't you ever question my emotional state. You better check yourself."

"My God. You . . . this is—"

"This is serious—that's what this is, my man, very, very serious." Damian finished the sentence, hanging up the phone, showing his full control over the situation. No nappy-head ho was gonna stop this show. No woman had that much power. Pee Wee wasn't going to jail, period.

Thinking of Pee Wee, Damian grew angry all over again. *Loyalty had a price, but no timeline.* He picked up the phone to call Sean Porter.

Chapter 21

Friday, February 16, 2007. Late afternoon.

If Kiki could have had a worse day, she didn't want to think about it, because today had to have been the worst ever.

"Sean Porter . . . ugh," she groaned, raising her head off her arms. She'd been laying there on her desk for nearly an hour. Her appetite was long gone, and all she could do was spend the ticking moments thinking about her missed lunch, life—the past, the present, and the future, if you wanted to call what she was anticipating in the next few years a future.

She'd made a total fool of herself in that conference room today, and Peter saw it. Or maybe he didn't. Maybe what she showed him was her ability to fight dirty, which was what she was going to have to do to win this case against Sean Porter.

"Big dog, my ass," she growled. She thought about Garret. "I know what I have to do now . . . sort of."

She picked up the phone and dialed *a regret*. That's

what she needed to call Garret's phone number—*1 - 800 - dial-a-mistake.* After a moment of small talk, she asked, "Did you know Sean Porter was representing Jamon "Pee Wee" Watson?"

"Sure, I knew. What did you think I was talking about when I called him a—"

"Big dog, yeah, yeah."

It was clear that Garret had no way of knowing the connection between she and the guy, so she kept talking, hoping something would drop out of Garret's head into his mouth and she would be able to formulate a plan from all this craziness.

"So Sean Porter is the man that's been giving you the blues all this time?"

"Yeah. You know him?"

Kiki paused for a moment to fold her lie like a paper airplane, toss it out, and see if it would fly. "No."

"Well, good for that, because he's trouble. Always has been. He's a cocky prick. Thinks he's some demigod. He's playing ball with our richest, most dangerous client and without a mitt. If Porter screws this up, we're sunk. I'm telling you, Kiki, this case is choice and—"

"Why do you keep calling this a choice case? It isn't choice. The case is weak, and you guys have no way of winning."

"How do you know? Don't tell me you're trying it."

"Maybe."

"Then you must not know."

"Know what, Garret? Why don't you quit playing ball with me and spit it out?"

"Let's meet for dinner and talk."

"No, let's talk on the phone."

"We can't. It's not cool. And what I have to tell you is so very cool. It's about your boss, my boss, the big dog,

Damian Watson and this case, and why I know we're gonna win."

Garret could be so girlish when he wanted to be. Why didn't he just say what was on his mind? He never acted his age. He was forty-something, if a day.

"You're not going to win."

"Sure, we are," he said. "Wanna know why?"

"Okay, Garret, I'm biting. Why?"

"Really, you're biting?"

"Yes, Garret, I'll meet you at Tobachi's. It's not far from here. It's—"

"I know where it is. See you in a half an hour?"

"Sure."

Kiki was sure Garret didn't know about her and Sean. She didn't even really know. Sean Porter's attitude toward her had made her wonder if she really knew him or not. Had that night really happened or not? Was she that drunk? Maybe she truly had made a mistake, and it wasn't Sean Porter at all.

"Doesn't even matter," she lied, throwing up her hands and gathering herself together. She wanted to know what Garret knew about everything else having to do with this case. Maybe he could help her make the biggest move of her career. Or the biggest mistake. Whichever it was, it was going to happen in a half an hour. At this point either one would okay. At least it would be movement, for right now she felt totally constipated.

Ripping the case file from the Pendaflex, slamming it into her briefcase and gathering her purse, Kiki started for her door, only to nearly bump into Peter on his way in.

"Where ya going?"

"Meeting a friend."

"Who?"

"Peter, that's none of your business."

"You're meeting with Garret Lansing?"

"You were listening to my phone call?"

"You weren't quiet. Listen here, missy, meeting anyone from that firm is a mistake, and especially someone who is not representing the client you are prosecuting. Listening to hearsay is only hurtful to this case. As of today, you and Simon & Associates are on opposite sides of the room, okay. No footsy, no fu—fraternizing," Peter said, catching his words on the tip of his pointed finger.

Kiki glared at his finger that pointed too close to her face. "I'm meeting my friend Tommy Turner."

"Good. Go shopping or whatever you girls do, but this case needs no more footwork, okay. I hope you were kidding earlier when you said you wanted to investigate it. It's over. You just need to take it to court."

Kiki wasn't sure what she was hearing, but it didn't feel right in her ears. "Just take it to court? How am I supposed to prosecute without—?"

"Read the file, honey. The case has already been investigated. Can't you understand that?" Peter's voice rose and then quickly toned down. "Now we just need to show some muscles, which we did today."

Kiki wanted to know why he was so upset. If she'd screwed up today, he needed to just tell her and get it over with. "Peter, are you mad at me? What's going on?" Kiki gulped audibly, knowing, sensing, and feeling Peter was leaving something she needed to know.

"Nothing that we can't overcome, Kimani," he said.

"Fine. I won't meet Garret. I guess I didn't realize how sensitive things were."

"You got us there, honey, so realize it," Peter said.

Still Kiki couldn't read his tone. Was he happy or not?

Chapter 22

"What's her name? You don't even know her name," Bond taunted in his usual manner when half-jealous.

Sean was angry beyond belief and wasn't even pretending that he wasn't, despite how good he felt inside. When he got back to the room, she was gone. The girl of his dreams was gone. It was surprising that she had been sober enough to move, let alone get dressed and get herself out of the room, out of the house. And he had looked in every room in that house. All he found was new lovers creating relationships, old lovers developing theirs, intellectuals discussing policy, and drunks finding their relief on the edge of porcelain. He couldn't call her name because for a moment he had forgotten, but while riding in the passenger seat of his own car, it came to him.

"Kiki!" he growled while Bond laughed at him.

They both would be hungover tomorrow, but what else was expected after a celebration party? He'd already planned to take the next day off. Having boxed it up with that clown hadn't helped much either. Who was that guy anyway? Didn't matter.

At the time Sean was interning for stiff-staunch, no-joke, no-laughs Judge Turner. The judge was all about business all the time. Even his office held no personal effects that spoke to a family or loved ones. But tonight, the judge had toned a bit. After getting the news of him passing the bar, even the judge seemed to understand his need to have this time to celebrate. And he had celebrated big time. The frat brothers had thrown a major stomp for him, and it was fantastic. The party was complete with girls, food, dancing, and cameras snapping memorable pictures. So much love all around, or so he thought.

"The fight," Porter said, remembering for the first time the argument he and his brother had that night. It was over the incriminating picture. "Why hadn't I remembered that before?"

"I don't know. Only you do."

"I know why."

"You see, Mr. Porter, basically we're down to some selection issues here. From here out, it's up to you what you will remember. I'm here to help you, but you're going to have to start pushing the pain a little harder," Anjuelle, his therapist insisted, closing another unsuccessful session.

"I've pushed about as hard as I can," he confessed. "Maybe the fight wasn't important."

Anjuelle didn't look convinced, but Sean didn't care. His head ached, and he was done for the day.

That was over a year ago, and still the dreams continued. Dreams of Kiki, Kimani Turner, and his dreams of the night his brother died. He hadn't done much work with his therapist on the dream girl, so as to minimize her importance in his life. Besides, he wanted to avoid using the words *angel* and *salvation* while speaking to a therapist.

That was the last thing he wanted her to hear. He was a professional, for crying out loud, educated, and, well, hell, he was a man! There was no way he was going to admit to anyone he believed in angels. But it was time to talk about her.

Thinking about that day, Porter verbally urged Anjuelle to pick up. “Pick up, come on,” he groaned. Glancing at his watch, he realized it was still fairly early Georgia time, but she apparently had left for the day. When the machine came on, he hung up. “I’ll just catch her Monday. By then, I’ll have another way of wording things,” he said to himself, pulling into the parking lot of Harvey’s.

Chapter 23

Stepping into the condo, Shayla greeted her with a big hello. "How was your day?" she asked.

Kiki could barely look at her. How ashamed she felt. How could she even talk to her after betraying her the way she did? Kiki gazed at her beautiful ebony baby, watching her full lips move before staring into her dark eyes. Familiar eyes. Eyes she'd only seen in a dream until today. "I'm sorry."

"Sorry?"

"I mean, I'm sorry, what did you ask me?"

Kiki decided tonight wasn't the night to tear Shayla's life apart. Tonight she would not end the secret relationship they'd shared all of Shayla's life. How could she do that? What would she give her in return? Could she tell her she was her mother and Sean Porter was her father? Hell, no!

Kiki tugged at her short hair. The hair she regretted cutting so short. She rubbed at her burning eyes, eyes that fought back tears.

"Man, your day musta been heck on wheels." Shayla

moved in closer, so close that Kiki could smell her breath flavored with the strong cinnamon flavor of her favorite candy—Altoids. "Are you crying?"

Kiki moved back from her.

"I know my breath ain't bad. I just had a grip of Altoids." Shayla chuckled, tugging at the top that rose slightly, exposing just a little belly.

Kiki hated that Shayla was so thick. She was prematurely developed and curvy. Shayla had a look all her own, tall, exotic and beautiful with rich skin tones and dark brown eyes, full lips, which she kept glossed and shiny, a head full of thick, long hair and full hips. It was hard for her to look her age. *Kinda like it was for me*, Kiki thought now, looking at her daughter, admitting to herself for the first time, with a struggle, that Shayla was her child.

Just then the phone rang. It was her father. "So you've got your big case?" he asked, a smile in his words.

"So you know?"

"Of course, I know."

"So you know everything?"

"Like what?" Frank asked, sounding more than suspicious.

"Sean Porter. Daddy, you know I'm going to court against Sean Porter."

"You betcha, and I couldn't be more excited, my two mentees going against each other. I'm—how does Shayla say it?—geeked fa sho."

Kiki exploded, more confused than ever now. "Daddy! Sean Porter? Mentee?" *He knew Sean Porter? How could he know?*

"Yes, he was my intern before. Well, he was the best one I ever had, well before he was involved in a terrible tragedy that took him out of the game for a while. I'm sure you remember me speaking about him. He had tremendous potential. That fool Garret couldn't even tie his shoelaces," Frank added. "But ha ha! Sean is back and ready to play ball. Man, I wish I was still a judge. I would personally request to try this case. I mean, well, I guess I couldn't, with you trying it, but you know what I mean. I'd love to sit before Porter, listen to his defense. Ohhh, he was so tricky." Frank smiled boyishly at the memory. "I haven't wished for the bench in years."

Kiki had never heard so much affection in his voice. "You seem to like him."

"He was a champ. I mean, sure, I liked him. I hated losing touch. I wished I had made it to his party because it was that night he had that tragic accident. He's back, but Peter says he's changed, not the same man, so to speak. Shame. I guess that's why he's not been by to see me."

"You keep saying that. What happened?"

"Oh, it's too awful to even repeat. Suffice it to say, it's a miracle he survived. I'm just realizing he's back in town. Peter kept it from me. I wonder why. Just told me other day."

"Yeah. He's only back a few weeks," Kiki answered in a monotone, and less than enthused. She hated her father right now. Why, she wasn't sure. She just needed to hate someone, and he was bugging the hell out of her right now. So why not him? How dare he care so much about the man he accused of raping her? The man he swore he would kill with his bare hands? If only he knew it was his protégé who had ripped his daughter's innocence away, tore their family apart.

"Well, dad, Shayla wants to talk to you." Kiki held the phone out to Shayla, who shook her head vehemently, mouthing the word *no.*

"Hello, Papaaaaa," Shayla sang, putting on her fake voice. She looked over at Kiki, who had moved to the kitchen. "I don't know. Just a funk, I guess. Sure, I'd love to come over. Come get me."

About that time, the doorbell rang and was followed by a familiar knock. It was Tommy. Kiki let her in.

"What's your problem?" she asked, recognizing Kiki's funk before it even came completely on.

"Nothing, really. Wanna take in a movie?"

"Yeah, a movie would be swell." Tommy rolled her eyes a little bit. Sure, Kiki was square, but it was better than being the whore her mother had called her once.

Chapter 24

That Friday night at Harvey's Dana waited for her sister to show up. She hated going out with her. She always had to wait until her sister's boyfriend decided to give permission. *It's as if that girl can't take a breath without dude's permission.*

Dana was glad she didn't have those kinds of troubles. She didn't even have a man, and she liked it like that. Well, not really, but it always sounded good to say.

"And that heiffa has two men," she grumbled, thinking of her sister again. "Feast or famine, I guess." Dana sighed, looking around at the slim pickings pouring into the club. If they weren't looking like death on holiday, they were sitting up under white women. W*hich wouldn't be a problem if I was white*, she thought to herself, watching an inter-racial hookup in action.

Harvey's was a hotspot for trendy and progressive professional folks, college boys, grown-ups, and those trying to be adult. People who felt they were too old for the clubs, but too young to give up on the nightlife. Serving well-made happy-hour-priced drinks along with snappy, hot, spicy, and delicious finger foods, Harvey's was the place to be.

The waitress stopped at Dana's table again. Nothing more than a ghetto princess, she moved the loose braids out of her face with her long, fancily painted acrylic nails. "What'll you have, sweetie? You still waitin'? He ain't coming?"

Dana thought about the day when she would have chosen that length, color, and similar design, but no longer. She was a legal secretary now going places now. "No, I'm not stood up."

"Mm-hmm, right," the girl said, humoring Dana.

"No, seriously. For your information . . ."

Just then he walked in, Sean Porter, looking even better than he did that morning when he came in with that thug in the wheelchair pretending to be crippled. Yeah, Dana was hip to that game. She wondered for a second what a man like him was doing representing a criminal like that. After double-checking the calendar, she saw that he was a lawyer from Simon & Associates, her old stomping ground. She had been a legal secretary there for about a year before coming over to the DA's office. They usually handled high-profile cases, and she had kind of wondered all day about that boy in the chair, and who he might have been. He didn't look like any rap singer she'd seen before. He wasn't big enough to be an athlete. The case couldn't have been an insurance fraud case; their branch of the DA's office wasn't the place for that kinda mess. Plus, that kind of lame case wouldn't have paid any of Simon & Associates' bills, nor help Peter Marcum get where he was heading in his political career.

Around lunchtime, Dana called her sister to see if perhaps she had missed something in the news, but Roxi wasn't home, or just wasn't answering her phone. Dana should have taken that as a sign that she just might not show up tonight. *Note to Dana: Ask Kimani about the case on Monday.*

Dana would have asked her before leaving for the day, but after meeting with "Chocolate Dream" and Peter, Ms. Kiki had a serious attitude all the rest of the day.

But back to Sean Porter and his beautiful smile. He was about 6-2, 6-3, handsome, and dark like rich Ghirardelli Espresso Escape chocolate, the kind that's supposed to be good for you if you have it on a regular basis.

"Dayum!" was all she and the server who was still standing there could say on that one.

"And don't think I wouldn't want to have him any time," Dana purred. *Yeah, if Kiki didn't notice this man today, she truly had some serious issues.*

Looking in her direction and then, as if recognizing her, Porter headed toward Dana's table, smiling as he approached her. "Hello there, Dana," he said.

Dana all but slapped the girl's hand in an I-told-you-so reaction. "You remember my name?"

"I always take special note of a pretty woman's nameplate. Besides, I understand you used to work at *S* and *A*." Looking around slightly, he caught her back up in his winsome gaze. "Are you here alone?"

"Uh, yes," Dana answered, hoping not to get a response from the server, who still stood by the table waiting to take an order.

"Thought maybe you might be here with your boss."

"Boss? Oh, hell no!" Dana thought immediately of Kiki and her square self. "You mean Peter?"

"Yeah, right, Peter." Porter noticed the server now. "Scotch," he told her.

"And?"

"Straight," he answered nonchalantly. "And another of whatever the lady was drinking," he said, taking the liberty.

"Strong drink?" Dana flirted after the server walked away. Glancing around, she could only hope now that her sister didn't show up.

"It's not strong enough sometimes."

The comment came slightly under his breath, but she heard it.

"Stressful day?"

"Yeah, as a matter of fact, it was. Your boss, Ms. Turner, doesn't make things easy on a brotha, but it's all good though."

Dana wondered if he was going to say anything about Kiki. Most men noticed her, not hating, just commenting. "Yes, Kiki is a tough cookie, but she's really great to work for."

Dana noticed the server returned twice as fast as when she had ordered the first time. She cut her eyes at the little gold digger. *Prospecting in the wrong river will get your head held under.*

Porter had sat but stood quickly to retrieve their drinks. He paid the server and didn't give her another glance as he handed Dana her drink. "Pink Passion. I'd know this drink anywhere. It's a sexy brew," he said, sounding flirtatious. "Not much alcohol, though. It's totally a lady's drink."

Dana was nearly beside herself with excitement. He was talking to her like a man talked to a woman. "And I'm totally a lady." She giggled. It had been a while since she'd had a real man's attention, and she could tell Sean Porter was a real man. A real hunk of a man.

Glancing at his large hands and then down at his feet, she knew he was "everything she could want in that department too." His suit was expensive, tasteful, and put together well, but aside from the diamond pinkie ring he wore, there were no other outward signs of female attachment.

"You here alone?" she asked.

"Yeah, I used to come here a lot when I was in college, but since getting back to town about six months ago, I've not been in, and, man, it's changed." Porter rubbed his forehead and looked around again, as if hoping for something or someone familiar to jump out at him. "Anyway, I've not been in. I thought I was going to have some memories here but"—He downed his drink and glanced over his shoulder for the server.

And as if his eyes were magnets, she showed up immediately. She was rubbing Dana's nerves raw. Porter repeated his drink order, requesting now that she run a tab for the two of them.

Dana hadn't even started her Pink Passion, but now took a modest sip. It would be her third while waiting for her sister, but he didn't need to know that.

"So you're not married, Mr. Porter?" Dana asked, pouring on as much sex appeal as she could muster.

Porter smiled broadly. "Never went there."

"Wow! Must be a good thing."

"I think so."

"You got kids?" she asked.

Porter hesitated. He hated that question. "No children. I'm not father material." He smiled. "Is that okay with you?" he asked jokingly.

"Well, hell yeah." Dana chortled, watching him down his next drink as if it was a short cool glass of water and not the harsh liquor it was.

Chapter 25

Kiki could be such a wet blanket when she wanted to be. All evening all she wanted to talk about was the case and the possibility of going up against the fantastically handsome guy who she gave up the cherry too, maybe. And got pregnant by, maybe.

She still doesn't know for sure. Shame on her. But something obviously happened. Either way, she can't figure out if she hates or loves him. Sheesh!

Every time Tommy heard the story, it still seemed so wild that she actually knew someone in Kiki's position. She was a victim, to be true, but she'd lied about her age, gone where she had no business being, and consensually got what she got from Mr. Sean Porter before he got up and got ghost. Then she was forced by her dominating father to raise her daughter as her sister.

And now she had to face "the phantom baby daddy" in court on the opposite side of an ugly case, with him acting as if he remembered even less than she did about their encounter.

Tommy pondered internally, half-listening to Kiki's moaning. *Whew! Kiki, you've been through it, but still you act like you're the only one with troubles. It was over fifteen years ago. You lied about your age. Now you have to live with that. You're fine, Shayla's fine. Now you got us up here on our way to the theatre to watch some cornball movie when what you need to be doing to get through all this is drinking and dancing. I can teach you how to get over shit.*

Tommy couldn't believe that they were freewheeling all night, and all Kiki wanted to do was sit in the theatre eating greasy, fattening popcorn, overhearing people making out behind them.

Ugh, Tommy thought, accepting for a second how long it had been since she'd made out in a theatre or anywhere for that matter. Yeah, she needed to take a lesson from her own book on getting over a man, even if she didn't have one to get over. *Forget this madness*, Tommy thought, turning in the opposite direction of the Regal Cinemas.

"Where are we going?" Kiki asked.

"I need a drink."

"Tommy, you do not need a drink. Now let's go to the show." Kiki glanced at her watch. "We are gonna be late."

"No, we're not late. Harvey's is probably just starting to kick."

Kiki threw herself back in the seat and groaned loudly.

Porter and Dana were on the dance floor. Dana was surprised that he had such smooth moves. He was way past college boy, but ohhh, was he on fire!

Spinning her under his arm, he broke into a cha-cha move, swiveling his hips.

"Dayum!" she exclaimed. Hot Harvey's was even hotter the later it got.

Porter moved as if he did nothing but listen to the radio and practice his dance steps all day. He knew all the current moves and seemed to know all the songs, but then again, many of them sounded alike, so you really one only had to know a couple. A few times she moved in for the rubdown. Yeah, Porter was all the man she could want. She could tell.

Raising his arms, he seemed to be encouraging her familiarity with his frame, and by the size of the bump she was raising on him, she was more than happy to follow his encouragement.

Tommy hit the door moving, bopping her head and wiggling her hips. Kiki, on the other hand, tucked in close behind her, like a schoolgirl.

Harvey's, Kiki thought. *Why here?* It wasn't the dancing she was shying away from, although it had been a while. She'd not come since before Shayla, when she snuck in here with her friends. This place and the memories, the memories that were thicker than the hot air that threatened to take her breath away, were getting to her. Harvey's was another part of the ugly past she wanted to forget.

Tommy grabbed her arm, pulling her to the dance floor, spinning her wildly then letting her go. "Come on, girl. You act like he's gonna show up here or something. Get over Sean Porter."

Unprepared for Tommy's strength, Kiki nearly fell, bumping into the couple dancing next to them.

"Hey, watch it!" the tall man yelped, turning quickly, catching her before she stumbled and fell.

They stared deep into each other's eyes for at least thirty seconds until finally Porter's lips parted slightly.

"Is it you?" Kiki asked.

Squinting ever so slightly, Porter shook his head. "No."

Suddenly, Kiki's head snapped as if slapped awake from a dream. "You lying bastard, why are you doing this?"

Dana and Tommy's eyes met, and they both knew instantly that this was a moment that couldn't have been worse, if planned.

Chapter 26

Roxi lay in bed. Stiff with fear, she stared at the ceiling. Why she was suddenly so afraid, she wasn't sure. It wasn't as if she hadn't witnessed the murder of the young boy they called Pepper just a few months earlier. As much as she wanted to close her eyes and maybe even faint, she'd done neither and saw Damian, the man who slept so peacefully, almost innocently, beside her, shoot him twice, once in the head and once in the chest, the bullets whispering death instantly. Why was she acting as if hearing this morning on the early news that he was dead was such a shocking and disturbing surprise? She'd not lost a night of sleep since that day, but then again, she wasn't high right now. She wondered if she'd ever sleep again.

Reality was settling in now. Her sober mind was able to comprehend all that had occurred that day in December when she watched Pepper get shot. Roxi blinked slowly, remembering how he looked when the bullet hit him, how he crumpled to the floor like a rag doll.

All this time Pepper had been missing, all these months,

his mother had no idea where he was. She'd probably thought he was laid up safe and sound with some girl. But, no, he was hidden beneath a muddy slough. But an eager angler had hooked him, and managed to surface his body.

Roxi was sure it was Pepper that had been found. Despite the report on the news of the body being unidentified, Roxi knew it was him. They described his clothes. She remembered what he had on that day, and thinking how he must have bought his clothes at Wal-Mart, as they were ill-fitted *knock-offs* of the name brands he should have been able to afford, considering that Damian paid those thugs—Pepper, Pee Wee and the others—a lot of money.

Stirring, Damian's hand landed on her thigh. Even under the blanket his hands were cold, just like his heart.

Roxi again looked over at the man whose bed she'd shared since the night she met him. He was so handsome, mysterious, cool. Everything Damian did was powerful, and nobody ever questioned him, not even the police. He was a powerful attorney and cold-blooded killer, but apparently nobody knew that part or had the nerve to accuse him.

Since the day he'd killed Pepper, Damian had continued to do nothing but break the law to cover it up. Even after finding out his brother Pee Wee was alive, he unethically used his business connections to obtain legal counsel for him. Roxi had all but heard him admit to buying a judge and bringing in some big-shot, hot-shot, never-lose attorney from Georgia.

Damian had even started his own investigation into all the potential allegations that Pee Wee could be charged with, making sure he had enough weight against the DA's office so that he could fight that if need be. It was like a chess game. He carefully calculated the cost on who he'd have the power to extort, coerce, threaten, and maybe even kill to keep Pee Wee from going to jail.

While talking to his cohort on the phone, Damian laughed as if this was all fun and games. But this wasn't fun. This was becoming very dangerous, and Roxi was scared and wanted out.

Hammett had told her, "Just leave."

Of course, it seemed easy for him to say something like that because he was big and fearless. He didn't know who Damian was. Nor did he know anything about her or the life she lived. All he knew was she was some foxy mama he'd met at a club, and she had a man at home that she no longer wanted to be with. So in Hammett's eyes, it was as easy as packing her stuff and leaving.

Roxi smiled as she thought about meeting Hammett for the first time at a club last month when she went out with her sister Dana. Damian let her go out with her sister pretty often, and surprisingly enough, he didn't follow her to make sure she was where she said she was. He trusted Dana, perhaps because she worked for the DA's office.

Staying close to the enemy, Roxi had to figure, considering the situation Pee Wee was in now.

Hammett was fine and had money aplenty. He had an honest job; at least he told Roxi he did. And he wasn't a bully, shaking up people and dealing drugs to weak people who had vices they couldn't control. Roxi once had a drug problem, but now she had it under control, no thanks to Damian. He'd not even noticed that she was only smoking tobacco now.

The night she met Hammett, she could see first off that he was a good dancer, and on the slow song, when his hands wandered, she would let them travel freely up and down her backside. The next weekend when she went out, she lied to Damian about going to the club with her sister, and instead, she met Hammett at his apartment. He had a nice place. Nothing like the place Damian had though, but then again, there was no way Hammett had the money Damian had. Hammett had honest money, clean money.

"Just leave him," Hammett explained simply, while washing her back as she sat in the tub indulging in his pampering.

Hammett washed her, lotioned her up, and loved her down on this memorable night, one she couldn't wait to have again. But, first, she needed to get away from Damian. Her sister was right. She needed to turn him in to the police.

Dana just figured he was a lowlife or a simple street drug dealer, and it would be easy to just get away from him and call the police. But she just didn't know. Damian wasn't just a run-of-the-mill drug dealer. No, people who *worked* for him were drug dealers. He was like a drug lord, and he was a killer. Dana didn't know that, so she didn't realize the true situation that Roxi needed to get out of.

Sliding from under Damian's hand, Roxi palmed her cell phone from the bedside table. Looking back toward the bed, she assured herself that he was asleep and slowly crept toward the bathroom. Shutting the door carefully and turning the lock, she flipped open the small cell phone. She noticed a missed call from Hammett. Her heart raced with excitement to return the call.

"*You have reached Dana, and I'm either not home or hungover—just playin',*" her sister's playful voice was heard saying, on her VM recording.

"Damn, Dana, just pick up the phone," Roxi whispered into the small receiver. "I need you to do something for me."

"At the sound of the beep, leave your message."

BEEP

Roxi whispered, “Dana, that body found in South Bay Slough this morning, I know who that was, and I-I-I can’t say any more on the phone, but I need to see you, right now.”

Looking up suddenly, Roxi saw Damian’s reflection in the mirror. Her heart leapt from her chest as quickly as her cell phone left her hand. “Damian, how did you get in here?”

Damian snatched her phone from her hand.

Fear caught Roxi in a grip, and she realized she had to get out of there. Without hesitating a second longer, she broke for the door, only to have Damian catch her by her tightly connected hair weave. “Damian! Damian!” she pleaded, her voice reaching a soprano as she turned to face him.

Holding her by the hair, he asked, “Who were you calling, baby?”

“Damian, I wasn’t calling nobody,” she lied, whimpering and stroking his face, his mouth, hoping to maybe reach him, touch his heart.

Damian stood cool, watching her squirm, his face emotionless. He pulled her in a tight embrace then let her hair go. “Then why you runnin’? Who were you calling, baby?” he asked again, his voice just above a whisper.

“Ain’t nobody gonna come, Damian. Ain’t nobod—”

“Shhhh.” He kissed her lips quickly and smiled. “Come to bed. I was missing you.” He roughly led her back to the large California King they’d shared for the last six months.

“I know, I know.” Roxi simpered, her voice coming without any thought.

Roxi was scared beyond reason and wasn’t thinking clearly at all. Her instinct said to run. Even if he shot her, the police would come. Someone would hear, and the police would come. Maybe she wouldn’t be dead by the time someone came. Damian always kept his gun in the dresser beside the bed.

"What were you thinking, baby?" he asked.

Roxi shook her head.

With one hand he pushed her back on the bed and held her down, forcing a small red pill between her lips. "Don't you think I know what I'm doing? I know how to cover my tracks. I'm a professional . . . unstoppable." He went on confessing to his sins, knowing she would only remember snippets of what he was saying once she woke up.

Roxi knew within a few minutes she would be feeling lighter, higher. Damian had good drugs, the like of which she never had while hustling on the street.

"That was a mistake, Roxi," Damian told her. "Telling your sister or anybody about me is a mistake. Always know that." He tugged roughly on his appendage, urging his body to hardness, and climbed on her.

"I know, and I'm sorry." Roxi grunted upon his entry and lay penned beneath his weight, while the drug took her strength and will.

Damian ferociously sexed her as if she had no feelings, as if she was a blow-up doll.

"Damian, baby, you're hurting me. Please, stop a minute. Let me make it good," she said, her voice growing softer as she gave in to the abuse, unable to fight him.

Damian ignored her pain-filled simpers, closing his eyes, his hand around her neck.

For a second, Roxi found a window of strength and clawed at his wrists with both hands, but it was only momentary for, within seconds, she was weak, and attempting to fight was no use. He was bigger, stronger, and she was lost to the drug. As his sexual pace quickened, his grip tightened around her neck until her head swooned.

"Damian, I'm sorry, baby," she whispered, giving in to the high, loosening her weak clutch on his wrist.

"I know you are," Damian finally whispered into her ear, speaking only into her dreams as she lay unconscious. Damian wasn't one for fighting with women, wooing or seduction. He always liked his sex quick and easy.

Chapter 27

Saturday morning, February 17th, 2007.

The morning after came quickly, but not as quickly as Kiki's hangover. "Damn you, Sean Porter," she groaned, rolling off her sofa and onto her plush white carpet, knocking over the empty bottle of White Zinfandel and scattering the loose pages of the Watson brief.

Kiki always kept her place extraordinarily clean, but with white carpet, and soft white faux leather sofa with matching recliner, it was a must. Everyone who knew about her décor thought she was crazy to have white furniture with a teenager in the house. But after Shayla came to live with her, she just seemed to know how to behave and live with her "big sister's" quirks.

"Big sister," Kiki groaned aloud. "Porter, ugh, why is every thought I've ever had coming back at me like this? Why didn't I prepare better for this day?" Kiki whined, her head pounding.

The walls of Kiki's apartment were covered with black-and-white stills of her family, her grandparents, her mother and father, Shayla. She had many stills of her mother, and several of her, Tommy, and a few of her girlfriends during the road trips they used to take during college days. She went to college right after graduating from the continuation school. There was no holding her back, not if daddy had anything to say about it. She went to college and then to law school. Tommy went to junior college and then the police academy.

Kiki had to wonder if Tommy would ever speak to her again, let alone take another road trip or photo with her. "I acted so badly last night," she groaned, crawling toward the bathroom.

"What are you doing here?" she had asked him last night, after gathering her wits and accepting that this wasn't a dream. She was truly in Sean Porter's arms again, sober this time.

"What are you doing here, Kiki?" Dana asked. *Is there attitude in her voice? Is she here with Sean? Is this why Dana was trying to introduce her to that loser friend of hers? So that she could make a move on Sean Porter?* Dana had to have known that Porter worked at Simon & Associates.

"Bitch!" Kiki growled into the mirror now, staring at her bloodshot eyes and puffy face. "No, wait. Dana isn't a bitch. No, she's not a bitch; she just didn't know. How could she know?"

Kiki shook her head, trying to remember the rest of the disastrous evening. But at least now the ground rules were set, and everybody knew where they stood. Well, at least Sean Porter did. He would never have to wonder how Kiki felt about him again. Nobody in earshot of the Golden Gate Bridge had to wonder how she felt about him.

"Ohhh, why didn't Tommy just arrest me?" Kiki splashed water on her face before opening her facial cleanser. She avoided the mirror the rest of the time she was in the bathroom. She looked frightful. Even after washing her face, she could still feel the tightness in her eyes.

"Now I want a damn drink!" she'd screamed at the top of her lungs last night after calling Porter and his mama out of their names. At least she felt like she was screaming.

The music was so flippin' loud, who could know. I mean, if I didn't know better, I would think Porter was yelling back at me.

Kiki tried to remember the whole scene before Sean grabbed Dana by the arm and stormed out.

All he had to say was, "No, I've never with slept you. I have no idea what you're talking about. I got your name from a roster. You just think I was the guy of your dreams because I'm fine and you're lonely and my name is Sean. Frat party fifteen years ago? Me fucking you while you were drunk? Rape? I did nothing of the kind. I don't know what the hell you're talking about, you crazy woman. You are a psycho idiot!

But no, he said, something even worse when she asked him where in the hell he thought he was going with Dana.

"I'm going to call the pound, but in the meantime I'm saving an innocent woman from the bite of a rabid bitch on the loose."

Just the thought of Sean, the man of her dreams, saying such hateful words, burned Kiki's eyes again.

The automatic coffee pot sounded off, filling the kitchen with the aromatic scent of an expensive Ethiopian blend just as the doorbell rang. Veering from her caffeine-driven direction, she headed to the front door and peeked through the peephole. It was her father and Shayla. Smoothing back her hair, she opened the door and caught Shayla eyeing her up and down before passing on her way in.

"What's wrong with you?" her father asked, noticing her tired-looking face.

"Nothing," she lied. "I'm sick."

"What is it—Nothing, or are you sick?"

Glaring at him while following Shayla to the kitchen, Kiki wondered what would happen if she cussed her father the way she'd cussed out Porter last night. "Neither," she answered.

"Oh, do I sense a bad vibe in here? You and Tommy fighting?"

"Oh, Daddy, knock it off. You know she and Tommy are *BFF*s. You can't break them up the way you broke up—"

"*BFFs*? What is that? Can you speak English?" Frank asked.

"Best friends for life." Kiki looked back at Shayla. "Broke up who? Who?"

"Best friends forever," Shayla corrected. "Nobody."

"Some no-good hood rat boy. Tell her, Shayla," Frank said, exposing Shayla's business.

"Boys are not hood rats. Hood rats are girls. And Isaiah was my friend."

"Who is Isaiah? Are you seeing someone, Shayla?" Kiki asked.

Shayla's eyes widened in her attempt to recapture her innocence.

"Exactly! My questions exactly!"

"God, Kiki, you act like you're my mother! God!" Shayla yelled.

Kiki's lips buckled. This was the first time Shayla had ever said anything like this to her. It was the perfect time to say the truth. But she couldn't.

"And I just want to know what's going on here? You losing control? Before we know it, Shayla will start lying and making the same mistakes you did at her age. History will start repeating itself." Frank's tone was accusative as he went on with the farce, ignoring Shayla words as if they were nowhere near the truth.

Had he come to believe the lie after all these years? Kiki's eyes tightened. This was almost too much to take in right now. Couldn't he see she was hungover? Couldn't he see she was having some serious issues right now? Her life had caught up with her. Her lies had overtaken her. Her secrets were smothering her. She couldn't breathe.

"What? What mistakes, Kiki?" Shayla asked.

"Nothing, Shayla. We'll talk later."

Suddenly Frank's attention was commandeered. "About what? You don't need to tell her anything about"—He outstretched his hands, palms up, as if the rest of the sentence was going to drop in them—"about anything, Kiki. You don't need to talk about anything at all," he said, sounding guilty, and sorry for even bringing it up.

"What suddenly happened here? Is this about me or you?" Shayla asked Kiki, sounding confused and innocent, as always.

Frank shook his head and headed to the kitchen.

"Nothing. Nobody. I don't want to talk about it," Kiki said now, blurring the lines further.

"I hate feeling confused!" Shayla yelped, storming off to her room.

"What was that all about? Years go by, and here I am thinking we've moved on, progressed, but no, apparently we are right here again," Kiki growled as soon as Shayla was out of earshot. "Accusing me—"

"You're the one who immediately fell back into some juvenile . . . *tsk.*" Frank smacked his lips. "Drinking and acting a fool in public. Look here, Kimani," Frank began, moving in front of the counter so as to look her square on, "it's the lies that get people in trouble. Why would you act like that with Sean Porter?" He whispered, "Why would you show your"—He glanced around for Shayla—"your ass in front of a man like that?"

"Why would you ask me that? And stop whispering. Shayla is not a child! She's heard the words *ass*, *shit*, *damn* and *fuck* before!"

"Kiki, stop it. Peter called me and—"

"Okay, okay!" Kiki yelled, catching Shayla's attention on her way back into the kitchen, as if remembering that she was hungry. "Enough of getting in my business! Enough. I made a mistake once. Once, for God sake! I've lived with the guilt for fifteen years, and it's over, okay!"

This time Shayla was listening to the conversation closely.

"So knock it off, Daddy, you and Peter, and anyone else you have spying on me. And if you've got some sick crush on Sean Porter, it's not welcome here. I don't want to hear about it."

"I'm not spying on you," Frank explained, sounding very blasé and matter-of-fact about the whole matter. "I was spying on Shayla. I just happened to trip over you."

"Ugh." Kiki held up her hand to shut her father's words up. She took a deep breath then and closed her eyes tightly. Opening them, she ignored Shayla's concerned face. "Now, do you want some coffee, or do you have something else to do, somewhere else to be?"

"Excuse the hell out of me." Frank shook her paper open and looked it over.

As Kiki pulled down a coffee mug, the phone rang.

"Don't say *hell*, Papa," Shayla said softly, correcting his use of bad language.

Peter's voice came on the answering machine. "Kiki, if you're there, you need to pick up the phone. I got a call this morning, and we've located the ghost."

Kiki quickly grabbed the phone. She noticed her father's attention piquing. "What?"

"Pepper Johnson . . . found him. He's dead, of course."

"Then there ya go. Let's indict."

"Hold on now. We're going to follow through on the first matter. There are steps to take when catching a fish."

"I don't think we should wait, Peter. The fish is tugging at the line already. We got him. I say it's time to reel. It's the last thing Porter would expect, and so we've got him. The defense has no witnesses now; they have no case. What are we waiting for, Peter? It's time to strike."

"Kinda like you did during your meeting with Porter last night."

"I didn't have a meeting last night. Trust me, you would have been the first to invite, if I did." Kiki smarted off, and then quickly regained her professionalism. "I'm sure if we comb that case we can find a witness that puts Pee Wee in that building at the time Harrison left it, via that window."

"Kiki, this case is hotter than we first thought it would be."

"I figured that, Peter. Even my father is over here frothing at the chops. We need to indict Mr. Watson for murder." Kiki slowly began to move toward the living room for more privacy.

"Jamon will do plenty of time on the drug rap. Without Pepper we're sunk on a murder charge. Let's be okay with the drug charge, okay."

Kiki was determined to indict Jamon "Pee Wee" Watson for murder. She was determined to win too. "But I'm not okay with that. That poor man, Lionel Harrison, has been dead since before Christmas. Somebody somewhere in the Palemos waited that night with bowls of potato salad and stringed popcorn, ready to celebrate Christmas with that man. They waited for him to come home."

"Nobody was waiting for him . . . geeeesh us H. What in the world are you talking about? You're starting to sound like me."

"Thank you." Kiki winked as if Peter could see her. "But seriously, Peter, since the day I got handed this case and was briefed, which didn't go well by the way, I've been reading this file in place of my Bible." Kiki was exaggerating. She'd given the case another once-over before passing out last night, but that was about all. "And let me tell you, there isn't much about this case that I don't know. And winning, well, it'll be less than tricky. Here is how I see it—Jamon "Pee Wee" Watson was in an abandoned building on December 24th of last year—"

"Exactly and . . ."

Kiki's hand rose to shush him even though he couldn't see her through the phone. She quickly moved into her bedroom with her cordless and shut the door. "For whatever reasons, Peter, and at this moment, it's not important why or who. What's important is that Jamon "Pee Wee" Watson was there in that building, and the business was illegal drugs. Nothing has even been said about the drugs. What about the drugs?"

"Ah, ah, ahhhh, at this moment—Okay, forget about the drugs, but we all know this was about drugs."

Kiki made quotation marks around the word *drugs*. "So, with that little mention, there was an altercation. There is evidence that they had an altercation, Peter. It's right there in the file. DNA. My God, am I the only one to see that? Lionel fought and scratched Jamon and then was hit with a pistol several times." Kiki paused, waiting for Peter to jump in again, but he didn't. "By Jamon, who then pushed him out of that fifth-story window, where Lionel then died upon hitting the ground. Accident or not, Lionel is dead now, and the only witness was Pepper Johnson, and he's dead. So, in my opinion, Jamon's attorney should be trying to build a manslaughter case instead of spending his time trying to prove innocence on some drug charge or riding on continuances. What is Porter trying to do here? What are you trying to do here? Why the smokescreen? What's really going on?"

"I want Jamon in jail just as much as you do."

"Good. Then what's the problem if we indict? All this dancing about a gun and running from the cops, what about the bigger issue here? Lionel Harrison?"

"Why are you going after Porter like this?"

"What? This isn't about Sean Porter."

"I heard about last night. Don't think I didn't."

Peter paused a long time, as if Kiki could say anything that would explain her bad behavior the night before.

The only thing Kiki wanted to say was, "Who in the hell told you about that?" Had Sean tattled on her? He didn't seem like a punk, but fifteen years is a long time. Moving back from her bedroom to the kitchen, Kiki glanced at her father.

Frank sipped his coffee that he had poured himself while trying to pretend he wasn't interested in her call.

"Look, that was personal and had nothing to do with this case. Don't start doubting me. Don't do it, Peter."

"Well, don't give me reason, and I won't. *Drunken Public Spectacle* is not the DA's middle name. Do you understand?"

"I wasn't drunk, and how dare you tell my father that I was."

"Well, that's not what I heard, and I didn't tell your father anything."

"Well, whoever is stalking me and tattling to you and my father is a liar, Peter, so let's drop it and get out of my personal life and back to my job! I'll get the paperwork done for what we discussed."

"You know I have to agree with your decision here, but I don't have to like it. I felt the need to say that, since you are so determined, and you think the defense don't have a case. Now, you do what you feel you have to do. I mean, I did turn this over to you to handle."

"You know I always do, and yes, you did."

"I just can't believe you think you stand a chance against Porter, unless of course you two have reached some kind of understanding since your last meeting."

"Whatever, Peter."

"Have you seen your dad?"

"No," Kiki lied. "I'll talk to you later."

After hanging up, Kiki noticed Shayla eating toast and her father drinking the last of the coffee, both of them pretending that Kiki wasn't acting out of the ordinary. The scene would have been comical, if it wasn't so pathetic. "I've got to go to work. Shay. Can you hang out with Dad for a while? I know I promised the mall but . . ."

"Certainly." Frank grinned. "She and I have some unfinished business."

"Ugh, God," Shayla groaned.

Chapter 28

"Oh my God, last night was not a dream, and she's no angel," Porter admitted finally, staring at the ceiling. He'd not slept well the night before, thinking of how terrible the night had been.

Kiki's words kept him awake all night. She all but called him a rapist. He couldn't have been so doggish a man as she described. She was hurt and angry, but the bottom line was that she'd had him on her mind all these years and he couldn't remember her beyond his dreams. What a supernatural phenomenon.

"How could she remember what didn't happen? Or at least didn't happen with me? Or did it? She had to be around fifteen years old. And, me, I had to be at least twenty-five. I can't believe I would have done what she said. But she knew my name. There is no mistake she knew me. She even sang my favorite song. I believe when I fall in love . . . ohhhhh." Porter groaned.

Apparently what they had was "Hotter Than July" and that "Golden Lady" had made him an "All Day Sucker." Of course he would always "Blame It on the Sun," and just chalk up what he went through as "Ordinary Pain," although the girl must have truly knocked him off his feet, "Because, in the words of the great one, *I was made to love her*," Porter sang, before bursting into laughter at his Stevie wanderings.

Rolling out of the bed, Porter rubbed his head hard, trying to juggle his thoughts. Last night was bad, and today was going to be worse. Kiki had made a big dent in her professional and personal bumper, he could tell. She'd gone off in front of Dana, a colleague and a friend, Tommy Turner, who also happened to be a member of law enforcement. Recovering from showing her ass like that was going to take more than a minute to fix, unlike his life, which he knew to be still very messed up.

Even after all this time, apparently he didn't have to fix shit until he was good and ready. But he was ready. Ready to fix the guilt. So much guilt. It consumed him. Why? What had he done to deserve such a vexing problem? He was driving, and his brother was killed. *Okay already!* "Ugggh," Porter groaned thinking of that night again, looking over at Bond grinning at him. It was as if looking in a mirror. Staring at his reflection, Porter could almost feel his brother's presence. They were so different, yet so alike.

Last night lying in the bed, the night came back to him so vividly. Porter could almost taste Kiki's lips, smell her skin. It was as if he could reach out and touch, but then there was nothing. Nothing, but the darkness. Kiki, at Harvey's was insisting that what he had dreamed had indeed occurred between them. And now he had to admit to himself that, no doubt, it had. The memory of Kiki Turner was too alive for it not to have been true.

Porter's fight with the growing memories was like grappling with a bear. He was going to lose, and the memories were going to come. They were going to come and probably kill him just like they killed his brother. So often, Porter felt unworthy to still be living.

Maybe the memories will kill me. What a relief that would be. Keep your mind on the case, Porter. It's the only way you're going to make it.

Damian was talking all crazy. The voice messages Porter had heard on the phone last night when he got home from Harvey's were just short of threats. Porter, at the last minute, had decided to skip the meeting with Damian, and well, his answering machine paid the price for that decision. Apparently, Jamon had told Damian what Porter had suggested as a best choice—surrender.

It was just a drug charge, for crying out loud. Let the brat do a couple of years. It might do him good. Porter sighed while thinking about the situation. Besides, he was more than likely the one who threw Lionel out that window just the way Jamon had claimed, and he was willing to drop it at that and wanted Peter to do the same. Surely, putting Damian's brother in jail for anything would be enough grandstanding for this quarter, and he would be a shoo-in for election.

Peter Marcum was out to get Damian. But then again, who wasn't? That was the first thing Porter had learned when he returned. Damian had enemies, but he'd earned them. Years of making friends on the wrong side of the law hadn't helped the situation either. That was Bond's trouble. He had started keeping bad associates, Damian Watson for one. They had become cohorts of sorts, *pawdnas*. "How did I know that?" Porter asked himself.

"Keep your friends close and enemies even closer," Bond would say.

"But, Bond, what if you can't tell the difference between the two?" Porter mumbled the question while brushing his teeth.

"Because I've told you that white boy is not your friend," Bond answered.

Sean glared at his reflection. "What white boy?"

Bond didn't answer. He was done talking.

"Maybe I'll give Kiki, Jamon and his funky little possession charge, felonious assault, blah, blah, blah. Get out of this and move on to something else." Porter shook his head then continued his one-way conversation with his reflection. "No way."

Porter was determined to win this case. It was a matter of loyalty, right? He owed his frat brother, Damian, that much, right? Whether he liked him or not, he owed the brotherhood that much, right? Sean Porter was a loyal man, right?

"Just try the case, Sean. Act like it's just a normal case. Stop getting all crazy. Get it behind you so you can get to the more important stuff, like who killed your brother." Porter huffed and then puffed up a little bit.

"Yeah, that's right. Just put ya foot square in her back and stomp her down in court, right in front of the judge. Take no prisoners. Teach her who is boss, since she's thinking you're some frigging dream man." Porter fussed into the mirror, thinking of Kiki again and her confession to dreaming about him over the last fifteen years. He didn't dare confess to the same regarding her. There was no way.

Porter continued talking to himself in the mirror. "Yeah, think of it this way—since you're a dream, Sean, you can give her the nightmare she'll never forget." He had Bond's help now, pumping himself up for the upcoming court battle.

It was a weird practice Porter had, probably unhealthy, but he would always talk to the mirror as if talking with his identical twin, Bond. He shook the water from his toothbrush roughly, sucking water from his clean teeth as he again glared at the mirror. "Who gives a good gotdamn about her and her memories?"

Suddenly Porter realized how much he was sounding like Bond, and feeling and thinking like him too. This practice was surely unhealthy, for Porter believed he even looked like him right now, as the wicked curve came to his lip, and squint to his eye. It gave him a chill. He shivered slightly.

"Wow! That was weird."

He looked around, feeling invaded. Suddenly the vision of Kiki's face flashed before him, her blazing light eyes. Eyes he could have sworn he saw well up with tears last night.

"I should have just told her the truth. I should have just said, 'I don't remember having sex with you." Porter shook his head. "Right, Sean. That would have really helped the situation. Great explanation. Any jury in the world would buy that one."

Catching his reflection, again Porter felt the invasion.

"What if you die tonight? You lied to that woman. You gonna burn in hell for that. You know her. You did nothing but talk about her right before that blue car drove past and gunshot-busted the front window. You said you loved her. I heard it right before I died."

"Bond stop," Sean ordered.

"Now do you remember? It was crazy how you fell in love with her that night. I told you that you were crazy."

"I said shut up."

"You're always wondering what we were talking about before we died. We were talking about Kiki. You said her name right before I took a bullet in my head and you closed your eyes. It was with your dying breath you called her name."

Just then the phone rang. It was Peter. "Houston, we have a problem."

"We, or just you do, and you really want me to believe that I have one too?"

"Stop the drama. Pepper Johnson showed up dead. You have no witnesses now, thanks to Damian, I'm sure."

"Again we're blaming Damian for our troubles?"

"Bullets in Pepper are foreign, a Luger. Sound familiar. Anyway, Johnson is another case altogether. But as far as Harrison, Tommy Turner is on the case, so being Ms. Turner's best bud and all, she was quick to dial her number. Ms. Kiki is now in the process of getting the judge to okay a warrant for Jamon's arrest. Not a little drug charge or any of those other ones you could flick off. It's called *murder*, my friend, in the first degree. She's a smart little cookie, that girl," Peter reported.

"Like you didn't give her the okay to do that. You act like she's the deputy DA. This is what you wanted, Peter. Why? I haven't quite figured it out, but I know you planned this. What in the hell are you trying to do here? You may have fooled her, but don't try to make me think a murder charge isn't exactly what you wanted."

"I could take her off the case, or you could get off the case, I mean, with your history of improprieties and all."

"Look, you could stop this game you're playing. That would be best for all of us. I told Jamon to give himself up to a drug charge, not a murder charge." Porter ignored Peter's threat. "And why didn't you call me earlier, before issuing that warrant? It's already noon. I'm certain she's already gotten the damn warrant. They've probably picked him up. I promised that kid I would be there to take him in. Shit, Peter. You talk about impropriety. Well, I'm-a be talking *mistrial* here."

"Hey, not my fault. She moved like lightning on this, man."

"Riiight. You are fuckin' with me now, and I don't like it." Porter pointed his finger at the phone.

"Me? Fuck with you? Don't you mean—"

"Look, somebody tried to have me and Pee Wee killed yesterday. Was it you?" Porter asked. Why not ask? Sometimes the truth comes out when one least expects it.

"Why would I want to kill you?"

"Just wondering. I mean, somebody did once."

"Sean, brotherrrrr, come on. I know you are not in your wildest dreams thinking I had any connection with that attempt on you and Bond's life."

"It wasn't an attempt on Bond, remember? It was a success."

"Cheeese us, H! That night is as foggy to me as apparently it is for you. We were all fucked-up that night. Sure, Bond and I had a little run-in, but that was it. And it was over."

"Run-in about what?"

"If you don't remember, it wasn't important. Drop it."

"No, you brought the shit up, and you keep bringing it up. You and Ms. Turner, you both just seem to be living in that night. So what's the fuss? What the hell really happened?"

"We need to meet. Maybe lunch . . . my place," Peter said before the line went dead.

Porter had hung up. "I'm not looking to date you, you mutha. I have a client to see." He tossed the cell phone and quickly began searching for clothes.

Chapter 29

Damian was livid, that was clear. He nearly lost it, but kept things as cool as he could when the tall, pretty female cop and her partner showed up at his house to arrest Jamon. And what was worse, Jamon wasn't in his chair. He was in the music room hanging out with the guys, listening to that rap music and playing pool. Porter had called him warning him about the arrest, but it was just a bit too late.

Murder! Damian's head was spinning. Kimani Turner was starting to cause him more than just a little anxiety. She was a ploy, a puppet, but whether she was aware of what she was doing to him or not, she was dangerous. Just her audacity to bring murder charges against Jamon after meeting with Sean and promising not to do it.

Lying women gave Damian a tick in his upper lip. And this Kimani Turner, especially, caused a knot in his belly. From the moment he heard she had joined the DA's office he had watched her. *The Judge thought he was slick, putting his kid through law school. I guess he was hoping for a clone.* But from what Damian had been hearing,

Kiki had been reduced to nothing more than a clerk, until now. *What was Peter thinking, putting her on this case?* Damian had some questions that just weren't getting answered to his satisfaction.

"Where is Sean Porter?" Jamon howled. "Why isn't he stopping this?"

Yeah, where was Porter, and how could he allow this to happen? Never had Porter bent to the district attorney this way. In the three months they had been working together since his return to the city, he had been nothing but aggressive in keeping this case out of court, but suddenly, since this little meeting with Peter and this Kimani Turner, to whom Jamon reported, flipped his game, Porter was acting very passive.

Where women were concerned, Bond was much more unmoved. He could care less what a woman thought or felt. He would have been all over this Kiki Turner. He could dig up dirt on anybody. She'd be toast by now. By the time they finished playing musical attorneys on this case, it would be history, not even important anymore. Off the books. Forgotten. But, no, this was headed for front page fucking news.

"Where is Sean?" Jamon cried out again during the reading of his Miranda rights.

"Shut up, Jamon," Damian snapped. "Just don't say anything." He was trying to think. With all Jamon's howls, how could he?

"That's right, big brother. You school him in how to get arrested the right way," the female cop who came to pick Jamon up remarked. "Just shut up and enjoy the ride. It will be the most comfortable one you're gonna get from now on."

"He said this wasn't going to happen!" Jamon cried, jerking against the handcuffs. "He said I was only getting arrested for the drugs. I didn't kill Pepper."

"He'll be there when you get to the jail," Damian told him.

"You sure you don't want to just come on down too, save some time, make it easy on all of us?" Tommy said under her breath knowing Damian was the only one to hear her. "I'm sure your days are just about numbered."

Their eyes met.

Damian was hell to deal with. He knew it. The cops hated him. This one was no exception. They would put the bad guys in the clank, and in the wink of an eye, he would have them back on the street, indebted to him and willing to do his bidding. He'd been around a long time just hiding out above board with the upstanding folks while wreaking havoc with the cops. He had cohorts all along the lines of the law though. Even now, he was thinking about who to call, since Porter was a no-show. This was the second time a Porter had let him down.

"We'll have you out by morning lil' brother," Damian called as they escorted Jamon to the squad car. It was a spectacular and showy arrest—six squad cars and at least eight uniformed officers. The police and the district attorney trying to make a statement on every page of this case, Damian figured, as he looked around at his nosey neighbors getting an eye full through the open gate.

Roxi stood quietly at the top of the stairs. She could see the tightening of Damian's jawline when he walked back in the house, even from where she stood on the stairs. She knew what that meant. He was going to kick her ass if she said anything he didn't like. He'd been knocking her around for the last couple of days, ever since he'd nearly killed her the other day when he caught her on the phone trying to call her sister.

I've got to get outta here, she thought to herself.

About that time, as if feeling her stare, Damian turned

to face her. His expression was tense, molding his face to fit his anger. Everyone scattered as if sensing his growing rage, but she was paralyzed with fear as his eyes were locked on hers.

Run! she told herself. *Dammit, run, stupid!*

He climbed the stairs slowly without taking his eyes off her. When he reached her, allowing his large hand to slide down the sides of her neck he said, "You wish that had been me, huh?"

She shook in fear at his touch. She shook her head slowly.

"Don't lie. I hate being around so many liars. Do you want to leave me?"

Again, she shook her head, feeling his hand tightening just a little.

His breathing was ragged, as if just the sight of her fear aroused him. "Come to bed then," he whispered.

"Damian, your brother just went to jail. How could you want to—"

Damian slapped her quickly, knocking her down onto the top step. Roxi screamed.

"Shut up!" he yelled, when she screamed. "You know I hate all that damn noise!"

This morning Roxi didn't care; she continued to scream as if losing her mind. Damian dragged her to her feet with her kicking at him. Something inside her decided she would rather take a beating over a rape.

Chapter 30

The delivery boy handed Porter a manila envelope. Porter recognized the packaging. It was confidential mail. "What the hell is this?" he asked the boy, digging around his inner jacket pocket for his money clip.

The boy shrugged and accepted his generous tip.

Opening the seal, his heart thumped hard in his chest. The photos were graphic, inexplicable, and highly incriminating. "Dayum!" he yelped, slamming them down to his side, as if everyone in the neighborhood had seen them.

"Catch somebody cheating?" The boy slipped on his bike helmet. It was clear he was used to delivering packages to attorneys and P.I.'s. He obviously recognized the "gotcha" look.

Porter's face was still twisted when he glared at the boy. "What?"

"The pictures. You look like you caught somebody red-handed or whatever," he said, his face quickly flashing a blush.

"Yeah, yeah," Porter barked, rudely slamming the door.

"Aw damn!" Porter sighed, glancing through the pictures of a young girl being sexed in every imaginable position. The young girl was none other than Kiki—Kimani Turner, deputy DA—and the young man, none other than Sean Porter. "How in the hell could I not remember this? Whhhoa shit!" His brow glistened from the instant reaction to seeing her full breasts and both of their ecstasy-filled expressions.

"Watch your step," the note read. "I won't miss next time." Reading further, he saw the signature, *Brotherhood forever.*

Porter was furious. Slamming the pornographic photos to the floor, he immediately thought about his cleaning woman. "That's all I need . . . for Monica to misunderstand this." He picked them up and thought about a hiding place.

Porter dashed upstairs and tucked the photos deep into his closet. "This doesn't work." He wanted to destroy them, but he needed them. He knew he did. This was blackmail, extortion, some kind of crazy shit, and he needed these photos to lead him to the culprit. Surely, this picture had many copies. "Blackmailers keep Kinko's in business!" he blurted again, thinking about the pictures. He looked at them again. His body reacted but still not his mind.

Still the memory of that moment wouldn't come, no matter how hard Porter tried to pull it in. And right now, as sick as it was, he was trying with all his might. He needed to talk to Kiki. He had to get to the bottom of this.

Forget Jamon. Let him figure out his own mess.

Chapter 31

Damian looked out the window of his second-story bedroom. Glancing over his shoulder, he could see that Roxi was still sleeping. She was a pretty woman when her face didn't bear the after-effects of his anger. Damian remembered his mother's face, how pretty it was when it wasn't all bruised up from his father's "love."

It was hard not to get aggressive when having sex. It was as if the violence fed the mood. This aggression made it awfully damn hard for a young law student to stay out of the limelight. Thank goodness for a friend like Bond. He was great at getting people out of a jam. He was a great friend and brother. He had one flaw, and only one, his brother Sean. Bond would die for Sean, and unfortunately, he did.

It had been difficult to find a replacement for Bond, but Damian did, not a neat and tidy one, but better than nothing.

"A murder charge? I'm furious how you think I'm feeling?" Damian spoke calmly, bringing his attention back to this phone call. "And here is what I want you to do about it," he said into the receiver, holding it close to his mouth so as not to raise his voice.

"I'm listening."

"You have until Monday, maybe, to stop the forward motion on this case. If Sean is worth his salt"—Damian paused dramatically—"he'll get Pee Wee out by Tuesday, and then we'll get outta here."

"And if he doesn't?"

"He will, despite how he fell apart on me today."

"I'm beginning to think he's got his own agenda. Ever since he met with Ms. Thick Booty, he's been—how can I put it?—secretive. He and Simon are meeting behind closed doors as we speak. This Kimani Turner woman is pretty fine. Have you ever seen her?"

"Not up close, but from the picture, I can see her as a potential problem for a weak man. I never considered Porter to be that, so his giving in to Ms. Thick Booty, as you call her, for whatever reason, is not an acceptable option."

"Okay. So don't believe me. Whatever. What do you want me to do?"

"Jamon needs to be out of jail soon. His time in there makes me nervous. He gets edgy, and he talks too much. I'd hate to have him spreading rumors."

"Rumors?"

"Yeah, rumors. He's very sensitive."

"Unlike you."

"Exactly. So I have a backup plan."

"You gonna let me in?"

"No, but trust me, if I have to use it, you're just the man to help me. And if I do go there, it's going to shake up the DA's office for a few minutes, catch them mid-breath, and stop them in their tracks. That will give me enough time to finish up my business and get outta this one-horse town."

"I've never heard Frisco referred to as *one-horse.*"

"Then you've not been around."

"Been around longer than you think."

Just then Damian's intercom sounded off.

"You have a package, Mr. Watson."

"I've got to go." Damian hung up, glanced at Roxanne once more, and headed downstairs.

Chapter 32

"Play dirty?" Peter asked innocently. He looked around the café. They had chosen a seat outside.

After Porter got the envelope and ran around his house for over an hour, he decided he really couldn't do Jamon any good, and so he decided to tend to his own business, that of finding his blackmailer.

"Dirty. You are filthy dirty," Porter stated matter-of-factly.

"I was taught to always clean up after myself, Porter. Playing dirty would never have crossed my mind."

Something beyond loyalty was indeed going on, and Porter felt that he was in the middle of some wacky family feud, both sides bringing out the big guns. They were an odd group of frat brothers. Truly loyalty wasn't their stronger suit. There was a time when they had each other's back, but not anymore. Porter had gathered upon his return that Damian had caused many riffs between them over the years. He'd been a major problem, yet Simon, in some sort of loyal convolution, had taken a retainer from his frat brother-turned-professional colleague.

"So what's your angle in all this, Marcum? I'm sure you have one."

"I thought you might wonder what my angle was. I mean, considering the sexual misconduct you've had with Ms. Turner when she was a minor, and the totally inappropriate behavior she exhibited last night, all but accusing you of rape, and at a public bar. And despite all that, I've not taken her off this case." Peter smacked his lips in disgust. "Maybe I'll remove Ms. Kimani and take this case myself. Just you and me, *mano a mano*."

"Please . . . you don't want to fight me in court. Why not just request a mistrial, get it over with? There isn't a case, not a platform, Marcum. Just a black kid running in an alley and a dead crackhead. We both know you are only doing this to piss Damian off. You're only doing this to humiliate him. Now why you want to humiliate Ms. Turner, I don't know. But me, you can't touch me."

"Mistrial? Wouldn't think of it. We're going to the wall with this one, my man."

Porter's head spun. "You sound like a maniac?"

"Me crazy? No, I think you were, for having sex with a minor the night you passed the bar. I mean, did you really want to be a lawyer or what? Can you imagine if Judge Turner ever found out what you had done to his little girl? Wheeewwww," Peter whistled before taking a sip of his tea. "Your career would've been over before it started. But, no, Turner never found out. I had your back, brother, and now you owe me."

"Peter, tell me you didn't piece that crazy puzzle together on your own." Porter was flabbergasted. "Talk about impropriety? Oh my God. Peter, you seem like someone who would be a little tidier about blackmailing." Porter then threw the envelope on the table. "Oh, and by the way, Harvey's is not a bar. Well, not like a bar, bar. It's got a bar, but . . . anyway, it doesn't matter, because whoever it was spying on me and Kiki didn't give you the right informa—"

"Oh, it's Kiki now, is it? Pretty cozy. After all these years the reunion musta been sweet." Peter then slowly opened the envelope. His eyes bugged out of his head. He looked around before quickly slipping them back in the envelope. "What the hell are those?"

"Like you don't know."

"Mannnnn, I don't know, but you better burn them." Peter chuckled nervously.

Porter stared at him, looking for the break, looking for the lie. He couldn't see it. "So you're telling me that you didn't take those pictures?"

"Man, I wouldn't have been able to take those pictures." He peeked in the envelope once more. "Oh my God!"

Porter snatched it back. "Then why are you trying to humiliate Kiki this way by putting our business in the street?"

"I wasn't aware you guys had business." Peter chuckled.

"You're telling me you didn't try to have me run over by a Hummer yesterday?"

"Hummer? My God, you've gotten paranoid in your old age."

"Never mind," Porter growled, his lip buckling in his frustration. "It would be nice if I had a clue who wanted to blackmail me over this one night. Hell, it would be nice to have remembered this night, period!"

"My, my, my, you really don't remember that night? I'm sure that really pissed her off." Peter said, full of mischief. "I thought you were bullshitting in the meeting, but wow! You really don't remember. How very convenient for you because, believe me or not, it was a crazy night for all of us. And then to find out Bond was murdered. Cheese us, H! Yeah, it was a rough night." Peter held up his tea. "I've not taken a drink since."

Porter felt his forehead begin to glisten. Peter Marcum was involved in that night. The players were mounting, and yet he was no further from the finish line than he was when it all began. He couldn't imagine he'd ever be caught up in mess like this. It was a dangerous game and one that was sure to end badly. What had Bond done to make everyone hate him this way?

"Who killed my brother?" Porter decided to ask.

"I have no idea."

"Okay, so let me get this straight. It wasn't you?"

"Me kill Bond? Are you insane? Why would I kill Bond? He was my friend. Hell, he was everybody's friend."

"Well, somebody didn't like him much, and I'm going to find out who it was."

"Is that why you came back?"

"Maybe."

Peter pointed at the envelope. "Or was that why?"

Scooping the envelope up and shoving it in his jacket, Porter stood. "Our meeting is over. I'm staying on the case. You try to blackmail me, and you'll regret it."

"Ohhh, wow! Sounds like a threat."

"Or a promise. Take it like you want it, because it's good for me either way."

Chapter 33

Later Saturday afternoon

"Your arraignment is Tuesday. You won't get out until Tuesday," Porter told Jamon, speaking to him over the phone through the glass.

"Tuesday! What the fuck, Mr. Porter! You said I wouldn't have to stay in that long. You said that you would get me right back out!"

"They are charging you with murder. I wasn't expecting this. It just might not be that easy to get you out without getting some serious money together." Porter hated telling him that. It made him seem unprepared, but he was caught off guard by Peter's underhanded deal. There was no chance in hell of getting Pee Wee out on bail now.

Using Kiki for his dirty work this way, Peter's plan was going to work out perfectly. There was no way she was going to hold up a public humiliation, the likes of which Peter had planned. Peter was after Damian, and going through Porter and using Kiki. What a piece of work Peter was.

"Brotherhood. Whatever, Peter. Let's call it like it is." Porter knew the only way to save Kiki was to get off the case. But there was no way he could do that. His pride just wouldn't allow it, so it was a draw. And the pictures were in the deal. This was getting messy.

Porter planned to deal with those as soon as he finished calming Jamon down. It would probably be crystal clear what was going on if he could only find a moment to stop, drop, and think. He was still tossed about who was zooming who in this whole thing. Maybe nobody was. Maybe it was all just a case of unfortunate circumstance.

No way, he reasoned. *Those pictures didn't take themselves, and they didn't mail themselves*. Somebody had a plan, and they'd waited a long time to put it into play.

Porter thought he was on his way to the jail, after doing the math in his head. She had to be no older than fifteen or sixteen in that picture. *And me, God, I was twenty-five. Yeah, it was rape.* He shook his head clear of the thought. And a thought was all it was, because there was no memory of taking that young girl's innocence.

Porter spoke in a low tone to Jamon. "Stay calm. Tuesday morning I'll be in court trying to get this continued, but between now and then, I have to work on getting you out on bail. The judge will have to see that the evidence is circumstantial, and with my key witness dead now—"

"Damian's got the money. Get Damian to bail me out now!"

"Jamon stop," Porter growled. "The judge may not—"

"Look here, Mr. Porter, I hear it was Damian's gun that shot Pepper." Jamon's voice had a little panic attached to it. "What is they gon' do 'bout him being the one paying my way like this? I'm very confused, and I don't like them as'n' me all those questions and telling me stuff."

Quickly Porter scanned the room before demanding Jamon's silence again. "Who told you that? Don't say that again, Jamon. Now just shut your mouth and do your weekend. Don't say your brother's name again while you're here. Don't talk to anybody about your brother."

"But the DA was here talking to me, telling me they could cut me a deal and—"

"Kimani Turner was here?"

"Nah, she wadn't here. It was that white dude, the one callin' me *boy* an' shit. He had his ass up here right before you came, and of course that white-bitch cop and her partner was trying to get me to talk all the way here. You need to talk to dem 'bout dat. They violated my rights, right? They was as'n' me all kinds of questions about Dame."

"What did I tell you about calling women *bitches*? Stop that. But, anyway, what did you say to them?"

Jamon twisted his face. "I told them to get fucked."

"Good. I mean, no." Porter shook his head. "Look, Jamon, I'll come see you Monday after I speak to the judge. You just be quiet. Just stay to yourself. Read a magazine or whatever. Just keep your mouth closed."

"Do you think Damian iced Pepper? Why would he do that? Pepper was my homie. He didn't do nothing wrong, and he sure as hell didn't ice Lionel on purpose." Sober for nearly a whole day, Pee Wee's thoughts were jumbled. That was clear. He stammered, "I-I know Dame was mad he left me in that alley, but damn, now that Pepper is dead, they gonna pin everything on me, unless I can clear it all up. I have to tell them what I know. Why did he kill Pepper?" Jamon sighed, pulling his finger through his loose curls. "Killing Pepper sure as hell fucked shit up for me!"

Peter had added bricks to his gloves on this one. He'd planned on a one-two punch just in case things were too loose on the drug case. Listening to Jamon and watching him squirm, Porter thought that Peter must've figured that Jamon would roll over on his brother within twenty-four hours.

The up-and-coming black female attorney just knew she was about to make her mark in her little law memoir by putting the young black thug away for peddling drugs in the street and throwing crackheads out of windows. She had to have thought that before Peter put it in her head that this should turn into a murder charge. He played her like a fiddle. It was a cinch that Kiki would have won the drug case against Jamon with one hand tied behind her back. She would feel accomplished and sleep well at night.

But Peter wanted blood. He wanted Damian. *Poof!* A murder charge, Kiki gets removed, and Peter goes up against the great Sean Porter. Then suddenly Porter is out of the game . . . impropriety.

"Damn, Peter, you're good."

Peter had it all but signed, sealed, and delivered. Porter could tell by the little baiting game Peter had played that morning with the threats about Kiki being pulled off the case if he didn't resign, or whatever, that Peter knew about him and Kiki all along. But how?

Maybe she told him, but then that would be crazy. But, then again, Kiki was awfully bitter about a one-night stand that he didn't even remember. But bitter and foolish were two different things, and she didn't seem like a fool. Surely, she knew getting pulled off her first case for an impropriety would end her credibility for sure. She'd be out. Truly she'd not worked this hard to get where she was just to throw it all to the wind. Because, despite what happened that night, Porter didn't remember it, and she had no proof it occurred, so her efforts to discredit him would be crazy. Unless she knew about the pictures, and then, yes, her knowing about the pictures, or possibly even sending him the pictures, yes, that would qualify her for crazy.

"Shut up, Jamon. Look, I'm leaving." Porter hung up the phone and stood quickly. His heartburn was instant, and he needed a swig or two of Mylanta Ultimate Strength, and then, as much as he wanted to put it off, he needed to visit Kiki Turner.

Porter wondered now how could he explain all this to Kiki without her again going off on him. Last night she called him an opportunist and warned Dana to watch her back "since riding someone's ass is what he does best."

Ouch! His heart tightened. Yes, Kiki inflicted a "Master Blaster" last night, but enough tripping down Stevie Wonder lane. "Dammit, I don't want to do this," Porter blurted, slamming his hand on his steering wheel after leaving the jail visiting with Jamon. Again he was dancing the ethics cha-cha, one step forward, two steps back, cha-cha-cha. *I want out of this whole thing. All I had to do was tell her the truth. I don't remember!* The pictures came to mind. *Like she would believe it now anyway! Why didn't she just tell Peter no, when she saw it was me? I can't believe she would put herself out there like that to win a case. Doesn't she realize what this could do to her career? To my career? I don't believe she would have done this.*

Porter pulled out his cell phone. He flipped it open, debating if the number he'd gotten from the directory was current. It was listed under Frank Turner, Kiki's father, but perhaps Frank would give him Kiki's home number. All he wanted and needed was for the former judge to be reasonable where his daughter was concerned. But he never liked the judge, right? Or maybe he did. He couldn't even remember now. Nonetheless, if he got crazy and started asking too many questions, Porter had all his ducks in a row and an answer for that too.

Stop being so damn paranoid, Porter, and make the damn call.

Chapter 34

Dana felt like crap. She was torn about who she was madder at, Porter or Kiki. She felt stepped on and a little crushed by what happened at the club Friday night. Kiki going off like that and saying all those hateful things to her as if she was just somebody she didn't know was the worst.

Why didn't Kiki just tell somebody that she knew Sean Porter like that? Like I could have guessed that she would have had it in her to even go there with a man of his caliber.

Dana fantasized again about Sean Porter. He'd kissed her good night after giving her a lift home. She'd caught a cab to Harvey's that night and had planned to ride home with her sister, who usually got picked up by some big dudes in a Hummer. *Big-ass armored car, like she was money.*

But Roxi was a no-show.

As a matter of fact Dana needed to give her another call. Dana had missed her voice mail message; her raggedy-ass cell phone had it all garbled up, so she deleted the message without trying to understand it. Maybe Mr. Mystery Rich Lawyer dude had her tied up in the closet or some crazy mess like that, and that's why she was a no-show.

Dana chuckled at her thoughts concerning her sister's life. Nothing so exciting ever went on in her own boring life. It was every day like the last for her. Well, until Friday night. Friday night stood out, and she was going to do some researching on that mess before Monday morning.

"What is up with Ms. Kimani and her secrets?" Dana asked Mr. Porter, with his pretty lips. Kiki all but scratched his eyes out, and hers too, for that matter.

Porter drove just what she expected for a man like him, something big, shiny, and expensive. The car was nearly as big and bodacious as what her sister rode in, but it was definitely classier. "My God, I can't believe Kimani acted like that," Dana had said to Porter, as soon as they reached his car.

Sean was shook by what had happened back at the club. She could tell by his reluctance to talk to about it. When he got to her apartment, he alluded to wanting to see her again. She was good at reading between the lines.

"I regret that our evening was interrupted by Ms. Turner's terrible misunderstanding. But us . . . perhaps another time," he said, avoiding any comment regarding what Kiki had said and done at Harvey's. He even gave her a kiss. He must have really wanted to see her again because Kiki was nowhere between his lips and hers.

The phone rang, interrupting Dana's reverie. It was a former colleague, Garret Lansing. Maybe at one time he could have almost been called a boyfriend, but anyway, for now, he was just calling to gossip. Maybe with Garret, she would get a chance to practice her story regarding the night before, the good parts, at least.

"And I want to see him again too. I gave him my card, and he smiled really big." Dana related, trying out the story for the first time on Garret for audience appeal, to see if she might need to embellish here or there.

"Wow! This guy seems to be on everybody's radar," Garret said, trying to hide his jealousy.

It didn't work. Since the day Sean Porter landed, Garret was nearly driving himself crazy, drinking tubs and tubs of the green-eyed devil's blood.

"Jealous, baby?" Dana teased.

"Don't call me ya fucking baby. I ain't sucking on ya titty anymore."

"You are so hateful."

"No, I'm not. I just hate lying women. You were all over him last night."

"I didn't lie. You were there? I didn't see you there. Where were you hiding? And why did you let me tell you the story? Anyway, you're still talking to me, so you don't hate me that bad."

"Why not let me come over there and show you much I hate your ass."

Dana giggled. Old, gossipy, greedy, and backstabbing, Garret was so not her type. He was worse than a teenage girl, when it came to being spiteful. It was during their brief "whatever it was" that she noticed how whiny he was. He wanted Kiki but didn't have the guts to even go after her. He had so many issues that his being white was low on the do-I-even-care-about-that meter. She had a feeling he was doing coke. He was straight-up crazy sometimes.

But Dana wasn't scared of no crackhead, and she was enjoying nothing more than feeding his thoughts that Kiki, the object of his desire, had a thing for the debonair Mr. Porter. She could tell he hated Porter because he was a man with true grit. Wish he would "jump bad" with her.

She'd open his eyes about a few things. Because, little did Garret know, Ms. Kiki didn't have a thing for anybody, and after the way she'd showed her behind last night, if she ever had a thing for Sean Porter, she didn't anymore.

She all but called him a rapist. What was up with that? Dana sighed as she thought further about Sean Porter, while Garret went on in his attempts to get in her bed.

It was funny that as long has it had been for Dana, sex with Garret did not make her want to end her dry spell. But now that Porter knew where she lived, it was gonna be smooth on real soon. He would never have to worry about raping me. He can have me.

Dana needed to end this conversation with Garret and share the Porter news with her sister. Roxi was always telling her about some rich or famous man finding her in a crowd and taking her out to dinner, or moving her in with him. Like the mystery man she was with now. She'd been with Rich Mystery Guy since right before Christmas. He was apparently pretty nice to her because sometimes Dana couldn't reach her sister for days. Like now.

"Maybe Roxi left an explanation on my raggedy-ass cell phone. Who could know?" Dana mumbled, noticing the broken phone lying on her table. "It's not like I can get the messages off."

"Guy must think he's superman," Garret said, bringing Dana's attention back.

"No, that's who you are. Look, boo," Dana said, hiding the sarcasm badly, "I have to make a call, buh-bye."

Roxi's phone rang and rang until the voice mail picked up.

"Call me, sistergirl. I have something to tell you. I met a man. And he is fine." Dana giggled into the recording. "He's a lawyer, and I think he might be the one. He's tall and gorgeous. A bit older than what I'm used to, but hey,

I'm due for a change. I know what you're thinking, but, look, if you can find a good man, one that's willing to care for you and take care of all your needs, why can't I? We kissed last night. Oh my God, the sweetest kiss I've ever tasted. Garret is all hatin' now. But you know his ass is *S.O.L.*, if he thinks I'm gonna fly his way ever again. Anyway, by the way, where was your ass last night? I really needed you there. I almost got in a fight. I'll have to tell you about that one. Freaked me out. Remember I told you about my boss, right. Well, she's prosecuting this case, right . . . some bad-ass thug. Well, guess what? My dude is defending the thug, and they almost went to blows. That chick don't play when it comes to the law, I guess. Anyway, it was wild. Apparently, he made a pass or something and she misunderstood and overreacted. But, anyway, I don't have all the details. I'll have to tell you more later. Oh, I almost forgot, his name is Sha—"

Roxi's phone beeped, indicating the end of the message tape.

Dana looked at the phone as if it was a rude person. "Whateverrrrr," she sneered, hanging up the phone.

Just then her phone rang. The caller ID said Sean Porter. She squealed with delight before answering it.

Chapter 35

Kiki paced nervously, kneading the dough in the bowl. She'd done it. She'd had Jamon arrested on murder charges over six hours ago and nothing had happened. The world hadn't come to an end, but she had a feeling it was going to any minute, for sure. Any minute Jamon was going to come to her door and shoot her. Or Peter was going to call and fire her. Or Porter was going to come and blurt out that she had made everything up and he had never slept with her. Or, worse, that he was indeed Shayla's father.

"Why in the hell would he do that?" she mumbled under her breath, again thinking of Shayla and the secret she'd been keeping from her. How do you tell your sister that you are really her mother?

"I can't do it. I won't do it. I don't have to do it actually. It's not like Sean Porter has even admitted to having had sex with me, so I mean, why should I tell Shayla anything? As a matter of fact, I think I'm going to just forget this whole Porter thing too."

Kiki enjoyed cooking, and Shayla enjoyed cooking too. Kiki was sure Shayla would become a chef once she got older, and was already looking into culinary schools. "Lord knows, I don't want you be a lawyer," Kiki had told her.

Cooking brought Kiki joy. More joy then being a lawyer, she had to admit. She thought about becoming a chef when she was younger, but of course, Daddy wasn't gonna have that. She was born to be a lawyer, according to him. He didn't know anything about her. Maybe she didn't know anything about herself. Sean Porter had put that question in her head. He had made her realize that her life had been nothing but fake, a pretense of reality. What did she expect to happen? What did she expect from him? Of all times for him to come back into her life, why now?

Why later? Why at all? Her life had been just fine the way it was. Yes, she was very happy, as long as she didn't think about it. *Okay, yes, I just won't think about it ever again. Try the case and move forward with my life.*

Just then Kiki's phone rang. She dusted most of the crumbly dough crumbs from her hands on the apron she wore and sang, "Helloooo," into the phone. Yes, cooking definitely lightened her mood.

"Kiki, we need to talk."

Kiki would know Porter's voice anywhere. Her breath stayed in her chest, and her forehead immediately glistened. "How in the hell did you get my private number? What made you think you could call me?" she growled into the phone, not giving him a moment's break.

"Will you be quiet for a minute? My God, woman!"

Kiki's chest heaved. How mortified she felt. All over again she felt it. From head to toe, it covered her like a heavy, wet blanket intricately decorated with indignity and guilt, then overlaid with even more ignominy. "What do you want from me, Mr. Porter?"

"I could ask you the same question, Ms. Turner, but before I jump down your throat, I'd like some facts. I'm one of those like-the-facts-first kinda people. We really need to talk. I want to meet with you."

"Monday at the office is good, or maybe even Tuesday before we head to court. Ten a.m., I believe, is our time on the docket."

"I don't think so. I think we should talk today—like now. I can come by and—"

"Don't you even think about coming to my home! Are you outta your black mind?"

"My black mind?" Porter chuckled.

Kiki was terrified. He could hear it in her voice. It trembled, much the way it did last night at Harvey's. She'd put on such a show of bravery, but Porter saw through it. To be truthful, right now, he was too. All Porter saw every time he opened his eyes was that photo, followed by his professional and personal life flashing before his face. But he felt safe to assume if she hadn't said anything by now, she knew nothing about the pictures. He had to believe that.

According to the records and her age on file, Kimani Turner was a minor when that picture was taken, so consensual or not, it was rape. And now someone was trying to blackmail him with it. Yes, he had a black mind. She was right about that, because his thoughts were on pure survival.

Maybe he loved her like she said he did?

I have no clue. I just know she's affecting me, and I need to get to the bottom of it. I just know that I have to protect her from what's coming. I just know from the moment I laid eyes on her . . .

Suddenly, with each exhalation he could hear through that receiver, with each heavy breath she took, darkness was lifting from his mood, fading to gray, to white, to yellow, until finally gold. As much as he wanted to fight it—

and he knew he'd better fight it—she was becoming the "sunshine of his life."

"I'm serious. I really think we should meet, Kiki. Where do you live? I'll come to you. We really should talk, because I think we have some unfinished business, so don't say no anymore. Just tell me where you want to meet?" he asked then, sounding nonchalant about the whole thing, as if it were an everyday request instead of the hardest motion he'd ever made.

Kiki felt faint. She rubbed the back of her hand along her forehead, etching it with what was left of the bread crumbs on her hands. She couldn't do this.

She had to do this.

She was going to die trying to do this.

Her heart, as if receiving a blast from a defibulator, was beating again because of this.

What a deep fantasy she had created in her heart over the years. And now she wasn't sure how she truly felt. Tommy told her it was a virtual crush, not even real. But in her heart she had grown to need Sean Porter, like air. She depended on him to creep into her dreams, and now she had a chance to make it real. Last night she had vented. Today she needed filling for the void left behind.

Chapter 36

Kiki pulled into the hotel parking lot. Porter was going to meet her at the restaurant and bar inside. She hadn't dated much, and so meeting men wasn't her strong suit. *Hell, why lie?* Outside of business lunches, Kiki didn't date at all. She'd not even had sex since that night at the frat party, unless you counted her dreams. If that were the case, she had sex all the time, and with Sean Porter in the starring role as her lover. With that in mind, one would think she'd be more comfortable with meeting him here today.

You are crazy, she told herself, despite the many times her therapist had told her she wasn't.

"Long term celibacy is normal in rape cases," he confirmed.

That's right, Kiki. It was rape. You were the victim, and he was the rapist. Never forget that! Never. How can you even think you love him? He abandoned you after taking advantage of you.

"Kiki!" Porter called, fanning her over to the table.

Her face, still stiff from the terrible memory that she'd just brought to the front of her mind didn't change in expression as she followed the uncontrollable draw to his table. "Hello, Mr. Porter," she greeted, sounding curt and distant.

Porter was taken aback. An hour ago she'd all but leapt through the phone eager to meet him. "Mr. Porter?" he asked, trying to catch her eyes. He used to be good at reading eyes. They were a mirror to a person's heart condition, but today, Ms. Kiki was avoiding that invasion into her soul. "How are you?" he asked.

"Concerned about this case, and wondering why we had to meet here, and why we couldn't do this Monday."

"Because I wanted to speak with you off the record."

"How far off?"

"Pretty far. I want you to give this case back to Peter to handle himself or appoint another attorney. I don't think you're ready. I think you're in over your head, and Peter's little extortion slash blackmail attempt today proved it."

"Wow! That was a mouthful." Kiki felt her face snarl up. She splayed her hands out in front of her on the table to calm herself. She was hoping her hands weren't shaking, hoping her feelings weren't showing too badly.

She then made the mistake of looking at him. And, dammit, if his lips didn't curve just slightly. He was smiling at her? She thought he would break into song any moment. At any second she just knew he would serenade her the way he did that night, wooing her, teasing her.

"What say you?" he asked flatly, sipping his water. The waitress had already been at the table.

Porter must have flown here, Kiki thought. She was instantly flattered. *Stay focused, girl.* "How is your family, Porter?" she asked, changing the subject abruptly.

His face twisted up. "Family? I don't have any family, unless you count my brother's grand-*dog*."

Kiki frowned. Was he making fun of her? "No, Porter, your family—your wife and kids and stuff like that there."

"Baby, I don't have a wife, and sure as hell don't have any kids," he popped off quickly, leaning back comfortably in his seat. He sipped his water again and then looked at the glass, as if wondering how the Scotch he imagined to be in that glass had turned into something so bland as spring water.

"No children?"

"Why do women always ask that?"

"I guess I was just trying to make conversation."

"Well, make a different one."

"Why are you so rude?"

"I'm not rude. It's just being private with my business. You're all up in my business, and I'd rather not talk about that."

"What? I asked you a simple question and you can't answer it?"

"Well, I don't care to answer."

"So you wish to omit that little bit of information."

"And you've never omitted."

"I've never lied, if that's what you're asking."

"You've never lied to a man about how old you were before having sex with him?"

"No man ever asked me how old I was before I had sex with him." Kiki's face was on fire now.

"You lied, Kiki! You lied, and you set me up. You and whoever your partner was set me up, and now you, for some reason, are trying to ruin my bloody career. Wasn't killing me enough?"

Kiki wasn't impressed with his dramatic outburst. "Lied? Killed you? Please, if anything, call that an omission."

"We can call it omission all night long if you want but"—Jutting forward in his seat quickly, he pointed his finger in her face—"omission is the same damn thing as a lie! And, Kiki, it's dangerous, the game you're playing. Okay, so we went there." Porter rolled his eyes wildly and flung his large hands. "And I almost wish I did remember, but I don't. So let it go."

"What? You're talking in circles. Look, omission is your client not saying upon arrest that he knew Lionel Harrison." Kiki was done with this conversation and tried to change it. "When in fact he actually had an altercation with Lionel Harrison and threw that man out of window and said he didn't. See how close the two are. But you see, Mr. Porter, I've never done or said anything that resembles either of those scenarios."

"Oh, will you stop trying to be a lawyer. It's a façade. It's fake; you're fake."

Kiki's eyes welled up with tears. "I'm not fake. It really happened. Sean, it happened. I know it did. And I have loved you ever since." Her voice was low and covert, but her heart was breaking, loud and painfully.

Porter slowly pulled the envelope from his jacket and slid it over to Kiki's side of the table. She looked at it and then him, while taking it from him. And he looked away and then back at her, biting his full lip.

Chapter 37

Porter couldn't think because he didn't know what to think first. She was breaking. He had won. He had gotten her to confess. But at what cost?

He watched her slowly open the envelope and peek inside. Her eyes widened and then closed before she dropped the envelope on the table and covered her face with her hands. He couldn't read her thoughts, but felt he knew what she was thinking. He reached for her hand but she pulled away.

"Please don't touch me."

"Kiki, wait. I wish I didn't have to show you those, but they came today. I had to know."

"You thought I was behind this?" Her voice cracked. "You are some kind of pervert. I think my father was right about you."

"Your father never liked me."

"What are you talking about? He adored you until"— She threw the envelope at him— "until that!"

"Kiki, somebody tried to blackmail me that night, and

that person also tried to kill me. Maybe it was your father." Porter paused. "I don't know."

"My father would never have done that. He was devastated at what happened." Kiki paused. "And when . . ."

Porter leaned forward. "What?" Kiki knew something. She had some information, just like he imagined.

"And when he thought you had died, he was devastated. But when you came to and didn't so much as call, it broke his heart. I didn't know it was you he was talking about. I had no idea it was you." Kiki cried now. Painful tears.

Porter could feel them way down deep. He reached for her hand. This time she let him take it. It was a natural moment, and he was glad she allowed the moment to happen. Her hand was soft and wonderful, just like he imagined.

Her lips were soft too.

Kiki pulled back immediately. Porter's hands flew up in surrender. "I'm sorry. I'm sorry," he sputtered.

Standing, Kiki grabbed her small handbag and slid her chair under the table quickly. "That was a mistake, Porter, just like the night we met—a terrible, terrible, regrettable mistake."

"I know. I know. I'm sorry." Porter looked down shamefully, feeling unmistakable regret. He was still holding his hands up in full admittance of his injudicious error.

"You are nothing more than an opportunist and a rapist, Mr. Porter. There I've said it, and now I can move forward with my life."

"Kiki, don't say that. Come on now."

"I have to say it, and I have to believe it. Your attempt at discrediting me will not work. I'm going to try this case. I'm going to win it. I'm going to show my father that he was wrong in caring more about you than me." Kiki stormed off, barely catching her falling tears as she hit the door of the hotel.

Chapter 38

Stopping at her car to catch her breath, Kiki looked back toward the door. She wanted so badly to go back in and tell him about Shayla. But Porter's disappointing resurgence was like ripping off the Band-Aid she'd put in place a long time ago. He wasn't offering her much by way of salve, only salt. She wanted so badly to show him how hurt she was and tell him how she all but shut down since the last time he'd touched her. But her injuries of the past and now the present, with those photos, took her thinking beyond reason. Beyond pain management.

"How could he do that to me? How could he be so evil?" She climbed in her car.

Just then he stepped from the entrance, having probably been delayed by having to pay the small tab for their minimal table service. He was looking around for her. Quickly she started her car and drove out of the lot before he could reach his car and follow her.

She'd done what her therapist had said would give her peace. She addressed her rapist. But it didn't work. She hurt more now than before. But one thing was true—they had made love that night, in that cold room, on that old mattress. They had shared what she'd never shared with anyone again.

"He was so awful. He didn't even want to talk about it," Kiki told Tommy, calling her from her cell phone while driving, catching Tommy on the job. Tommy always took Kiki's calls, and good thing too, because today was an emergency. Kiki needed repair.

"Well, what's there to talk about? You called him a rapist. What was the man to say? Deny it? It's obvious what happened. He couldn't deny it. You want a blood test. You want me to get some blood from him? I can do that. I'll kick the shit outta him, bleed him, and then we'll put it under the glass, get this matter resolved once and for all." Tommy nudged her partner, who laughed along goofily. They were both buzzing on a chocolate high, and neither of them could sense Kiki's agony through the phone.

"No." Kiki wiped her eyes. "I'm pulling out of the case. He won." Kiki couldn't mention the pictures. She knew Tommy's temper.

"What? Stop playin'," Tommy said, growing instantly serious.

"I'll talk to you later."

Kiki pulled into the Starbucks parking lot and climbed out of her car. Her mind was on so many things, she didn't notice Garret watching her, following her. She dragged in as if the weight of the world was on her shoulders and ordered a raspberry mocha frappuccino. "Of course, I want whipped cream," she whined to the barista after she asked.

Just then the door jingled, and Garret walked in. He smiled, and she returned it without thinking.

"Hello, Ms. DA," he teased.

Kiki forced a smile. "My name is Kiki, Garret. Today, I'm just Kiki, a girl needing to be taken to dinner."

And why the hell not? It was time to walk into a relationship with both eyes open. Sean Porter had humiliated her for the last time. It was over. The days of dream lover SP needs to end. *Lover? Ha! Just a nasty little encounter that wasn't about shit!* She tried to remember what Garret had called his encounter with Mr. Porter.

"Are you serious?" Garret asked, interrupting her reverie.

"Yes, I'm serious."

"Then maybe you should get cleaned up."

"What?"

Smiling warmly, Garret touched his lip and then pointed at her. She touched her lip and realized she had cream covering it. And the giggling continued.

Chapter 39

Porter had no clue what he'd done wrong. But he'd done it. Put his foot right into it. And what was all that talk about Judge Turner's feelings toward him? There was no love between them. Last thing he remembered, the judge was trying to have his P.I. license revoked. No, wait, I was never a P.I. Why would I think that? Why?

Porter was stunned for a moment. He tried to focus on his thoughts again. He hated when they crossed over this way. It was Bond who had just had a run-in with the judge. Turner had told Bond he would never make it as a P.I., not in this city.

Bond was furious. "You are not God. Just because you co-founded some whack-ass secret society so you and men like my brother can pretend to be above everyone else. I'm not impressed. You have my brother fooled. Yes, yes, you do, but not me. You're not untouchable."

"Is that a threat?"

"Hell, no! It's a promise. So watch your back. You say I can't be a P.I. Well, watch me. You got dirt, judge.

Everybody does, and trust me, I'm-a find it. You can run, but you can't hide."

"I'd advise you not to threaten me. I don't take kindly to that."

"I don't expect kindness. I kinda like it rough!" Bond squinted his eye, allowing a wicked curve to come to his lips. He slammed out.

Porter jerked awake, shaking his head free of the dream, the vision. "Bond? What did you find out? You had to have found out something . . . because the judge had you killed that night. I'm sure of it now. You knew that was his daughter. You knew she was at the party. Damn it, Bond, you took the picture, didn't you?" Porter sat up. "That's why we fought in the car. You didn't know it was me with her in that room."

Porter was on his feet now, stomping around his living room, thinking on his feet. "Bond was going to blackmail you with those photos until he realized it was me." He stopped in the middle of his diatribe, his finger pointed outward. "But if Bond took them, who sent them?"

Chapter 40

Kiki took a long shower as she thought about the night out with Garret. He was handsome enough, albeit a bit on the pushy side. "But then maybe it's just me. Maybe dating has turned into an aggressive sport," she thought aloud. "I'd never know from the sidelines."

Stepping from the shower, she heard the beep of her VM. She glanced at the phone. It was Peter. She wasn't in the mood to hear from him right now. Or for anything that had to do with the Watson case. Or her life. It was all going to change after Monday anyway, so to hell with it.

Tonight she wasn't a lawyer, but a single woman. A grown-up woman whose father had convinced her she had no right to raise her own child. Whose dominating personality had caused everyone pain. She would have to address all of his mess when she got back. She would have to tell him the truth about his reality. Which wasn't reality at all. She would purge her soul and tell Shayla the truth.

Tommy was right. So she had a one-night stand, big flipping deal. Okay, so she had a baby. Bigger deal, but still not the end of the world. Okay, so Sean Porter isn't the dream man she wanted him to be. "Like that is a surprise. Glad you found it out before you were old and gray."

Sliding into the new sexy lingerie she'd picked up on her way home, Kiki caught her reflection and burst into laughter. "Girl, you need to quit."

The doorbell rang. "Wow! Is Garret eager or what?"

Chapter 41

"I want off this case," Porter told Damian.

Damian seemed unmoved by the statement, until finally, sucking the air through his teeth and shoving his tumbler toward the woman who came from the house on to the balcony, where they sat. As if on cue, he shook his head slightly.

The woman was tall and slender, dark-skinned, and pretty. Well, Porter assumed she was pretty, judging by her taunt jawline, and high cheekbones. Maybe he could tell for sure, if she didn't have on those dark sunglasses. Upon closer examination he could see the remains of a black eye.

The woman's lip curved when she caught Porter looking closer at her. She took the glass from Damian's hand in a cautious snatch that surely was a sign of avoidance. It was as if she wanted to make sure she didn't give Damian enough time to swat, pinch, or otherwise touch her. Porter wasn't sure what was up with that, but at this moment it wasn't his concern.

"Why don't I believe you?"

"I don't know and don't care. It's the truth though."

"Why not just wait until Ms. Kimani surrenders the case? It's sure to come. It's just a battle of wills."

"Battle of wills? Damian, this is not a battle. It's due process. The DA—"

"Kiki." Damian said it as if he had exposed a secret that he wasn't supposed to know.

"Fine. Kiki and I have come to an agreement that due to some"—Porter paused— "unforeseen circumstances, it would be in our best interest for me to withdraw from the case."

"Why you?"

"Kiki—Ms. Turner insists on trying the case, so there ya go. It's her or me, and I've decided—"

"You mean, Peter decided. Sean, you drop the case, Peter will still blackmail her into resigning. You'll both be gone, and he'll take it over. Simon will get some idiot like, like Garret Lansing to get up there and bumble my brother into the penitentiary for the rest of his life. Is that what you want?"

"Well, no, but—"

"Well, it's what Peter wants. I assure you."

"Damian, you don't understand."

"I understand perfectly. He's blackmailing you with the past, and you feel trapped and overly protective of that little"—Damian caught his tongue just as the woman brought his refreshed drink from the house—"woman who has you by the balls. Or had you by the balls at one time."

Damian's laughter told Porter all he needed to know. Damian had seen the pictures.

"You son of a bitch, and that goes for Peter too. How did you get the pictures? Who's behind this?"

"Probably the same way you did. Little weird kid on a bike."

"What's the game? I mean, why all of this crap? Let Jamon do his time if he did the crime."

"It's not about Jamon. And Jamon is innocent, by the way; that's not it. This is about me. Peter wants me."

"When did the love die?"

"When I slept with his wife."

"Damn!" Porter moaned. He looked off and then caught Damian's wicked grin upon looking back. "Why does everyone find this so fuckin' funny?"

"If you were Bond, you'd understand."

"But I'm not!" Porter stood. "You took those pictures, didn't you? That night, you and Peter plotted, right?"

"And what sense would that make? Why would I do that? Never crossed my mind to get the goods on a straight-up brother like yaself. Now I can't speak for our lighter side of the family."

"Peter said he didn't do it. He said the same thing. Bond was his friend."

"And you believed him. You up there fuckin' the minor child," Damian said, putting emphasis on the *D* in child, "of the most prominent judge in the city—no, the state—and you think you had friends?"

"Who would care?"

"You really don't think it occurred to someone to maybe record that information for posthumous inquiry?"

"So someone knew we were going to die that night?"

Damian grinned. "Is that what you heard me say?"

Porter leaned forward. "That's what I heard you say, so unless you want me looking at you as an accomplice to murder, you better re-think your terminology."

"Oh please, Sean. I don't know anything about any pictures until the weird kid on the bike delivered them, and I sure didn't know anyone was trying to kill the two of you until you were dead."

"But I'm sure that's all changed. I'm sure you're loaded with answers now."

"Perhaps," Damian said, sucking his teeth and checking his manicure.

"And this information is going to cost me what?"

"Well, certainly not your life again. And surely not as much as it cost me. But it's all good. I've got your back this time, bro."

" Excuse me?"

"That night, it all happened so fast. You and Bond got caught up before either of you realized what was happening, I'm sure. We were all messed up. Next thing I knew, you and Bond were fighting. You two got loud, and it was more than clear what had happened. Well, walls had ears that night, and somebody had their own agenda."

"And killed us over what? Some pictures that Bond took." Porter realized clearly now that indeed Bond had taken the photographs. He remembered the argument, not clearly, but he remembered it.

"And now this fool is trying to kill you again. I was like, *Dang, don't you think once is enough*?"

"Damian, tell me who is trying to kill me, so that I can take care of it. Don't take matters in your own hands."

"Hey, Bond was my friend. I don't have many. Never have. When you came back, it made me realize that. I know you don't like me. But me and Bond, we had a special something. He understood me. And, well, I owe him this one."

"I understand you too. Is it Peter?"

Damian chuckled. "You don't understand me. Stop your guessing. Just do your job. Get my brother out of jail, and I'll do my part. Then, I promise, I'll go away."

"Damian, I can't turn my head to this."

"You already have. When you took that oath and became my brother, you turned your head, my man."

Chapter 42

Kiki wasn't prepared to be served tonight, but Garret had her sit on her sofa and took it upon himself to go into her kitchen, find glasses, a corkscrew, and make himself right at home, as if she was at his house and not the other way around. She thought they were going out, but he decided they would order in. It was fine. She wasn't really in the mood for another restaurant thing.

As Garret headed back her way with the filled-to-the-rim glasses, Kiki thought about Porter again, and the first time she drank with him. Although she was a virgin then, she wasn't new to underage drinking. The girls she hung out with had introduced her to that vice weeks before the party.

Kiki smiled at the memory of Sean that night. He was grinning like a Cheshire cat when she agreed to go to the room with him, and so immediately she knew he was planning something sexual. And she was ready.

Quickly grabbing her foot and sliding it from her shoe, Garret began to rub her feet.

Kiki pulled away awkwardly. "What, Garret?" she said, gasping in her surprise.

"You no likey?" he asked.

Kiki realized immediately she hated baby-talk, especially from a grown man Garret's age.

"No, uh, I no likey," she said, sliding her foot back into her shoe.

"Ahh," he sighed, recovering gracefully from the rejected foot rub by handing Kiki her drink. "Drink up."

Her stomach hadn't fully settled since finishing the fancy version of take-out dinner, and actually she wasn't in the mood for the drink. She had just hoped to enjoy Garret's company, to get her mind off Sean Porter for half a second, but she'd failed in both quests. Sean was right on the front of her brain, and Garret was getting pushy and becoming less-than-enjoyable company. She was past ready for him to leave.

"I will, later," she lied. She had no intention of drinking that wine.

Garret sipped his wine and smiled. "So tell about your big case. How are things going?"

"I really can't talk about it, Garret. At this point, it's all very confidential."

"Ahh! I bet if I was your man, I'd get the juicy details," he retorted quickly, getting in her face but not quite kissing her.

"Perhaps. But, Garret, you're not my man, and it's confidential." Kiki eased from the close proximity.

Sitting back on his side of the sofa, a smile crossed Garret's lips. "I got something confidential for ya." He reached in his jacket and pulled out a small manila envelope and handed it to her.

"What is this?" Kiki noted it was addressed to her father.

"Don't know."

"Really? Where did you get it?" she asked cautiously.

"Porter's outbox. I noticed who it was addressed to, so I figured, since I was seeing you tonight . . ."

Quickly she ripped open the envelope and moved it open with her fingers discreetly so that Garret couldn't see inside, despite his neck all but straining. What Garret had given her were more pictures of her and Sean having sex. These were different even from the ones Sean had shown her.

What? Did he have a collection? she asked herself, growling through gritted teeth.

"What is it, Kiki?" Garret asked, showing true concern. He reached for the envelope, only to have her push his hands back.

"This was in Porter's outbox?"

"Well, yes. I assumed it was law-related. I mean, with him having mentored under your father and all."

Kiki felt the hot tears forming in her eyes and fought them with all her might.

"What's wrong, Kiki? What did that bastard do?" Garret again reached for the envelope, only to have Kiki recoil. "I know they are trying to stop this case from going to court. Did it have something to with that? Is Porter playing dirty pool again? He's such a dog . . . always has been. I remember he and his brother used to work together setting people up. They were worse than ambulance chasers."

"You know him from before?" Kiki lost her voice to the mixed emotions that took her over.

Sliding his arm around her shoulder, Garret continued to attempt to console her. "Shhh. Drink your wine and tell me what that bastard did," he urged, moving back in her face, holding out her glass nearly up to her lips. "That bastard, Damian Watson, has him wrapped around his finger ya know, but I thought he was his own man. There are just easier ways to . . ."

"To what?" Kiki asked, gathering her wits quickly. Suddenly she realized that there was no way on God's green earth that she was going to drink wine from a bottle she hadn't bought or poured, especially not with a man who couldn't take no for an answer. Call it her post-traumatic syndrome, or just being pissed, but no meant no.

"Get that glass out of my face, Garret." Kiki bumped him, causing the wine to empty into her lap. She jumped up, pooling the liquid in her top as she held it out. "Oh my God!"

Garret's actions bothered her, and she wanted to know why he was acting shadier than usual. She'd known him for years, but tonight he was acting badly. Surely he'd seen the pictures of her having sex with Sean Porter—illicit sex—so why was he acting as if he hadn't?

"What's wrong with you?"

"I'm not a freak," she gasped, hurrying off to the bathroom.

"Freak? Why would I think that? Can I help you outta your wet clothes, baby?" she heard him asking, his voice coming closer to her bedroom door.

"Just sit down. I'll be right out."

Kiki pulled off the top and quickly squeezed the drops of wine from it into the glass sitting on the counter. There was probably less than an ounce squeezed from her blouse top, but it would be enough. She slid the glass into her medicine cabinet. "Tomorrow I'm taking you to Tommy for an analysis. If you come back clean, then we'll talk about what's what, Garret. But, for tonight, this date is over."

Then she slid the envelope into the bathroom's vanity drawer. "To hell with you, Sean Porter," she whispered under her breath.

Kiki put on her robe that hung on the door and opened the bathroom door, only to run into Garret, who had made his way into her bedroom.

She cleared her throat. "I told you I was all right," she said, quickly shutting the bathroom door behind her.

She wanted to move him out of the room, but instead he pulled her into a kiss. "There," he said, smiling at her once her eyes opened. "I hope that shows you how sorry I am for what Porter did."

"There was no need to be sorry, Garret. It was my clumsiness." Kiki moved past him and out of the area close to her bed.

Garret looked around at her pictures. He paused at the photos of she and Tommy, and then again at those of her father, and then he paused again at those of Shayla. "Shayla is such a pretty girl."

"Let's go back in the living room."

"Seriously, that little sister of yours is really cute."

"Yes, she is," Kiki said, fanning her hand toward the door, inviting him out.

Kiki's heart jumped nearly out of her chest when she came back into the living room. Porter stood in there tall and handsome, his brow curved downwards, as if he wasn't happy with what he was seeing.

"How the hell did you get in here?" she exclaimed.

"Tried the knob. Your door was unlocked. I walked in."

"Get the hell out!"

"Look, I saw your car, knew you were home, called and called. Got to the door, heard voices."

"God," she gasped, covering her mouth. Her eyes burned with mixed emotions. Suddenly she remembered she was in a robe that now hung open and exposed her sexy bra.

Both men took a moment to notice the pretty piece of lingerie before Garret cleared his throat. "Sorry, Porter. I didn't figure you one for working afterhours."

"You don't have to apologize or explain anything to him. Nothing was going on. I spilled my drink and was cleaning up."

"Why are you explaining then?" Porter asked, sounding curt.

"Well, I guess I feel stupid," Garret said, inching toward the door.

"For what? And you don't have to leave, Garret," Kiki said. She actually wanted nothing more than for Garret to leave at the moment. She felt the need to say something.

"No, no, I think leaving would be best." Garret waved over his head as he opened the door and headed out.

"Wait a minute," Porter called.

Garret turned, resting his hands loosely on his hips. The way his sport coat opened slightly was almost as if his posture was more practiced than a natural stance.

If Porter didn't know better, he'd say Garret was carrying a gun. "What are you doing here anyway? No, don't tell me. I'm really not interested in your personal business," Porter said, dismissing him.

Kiki smacked her lips at the implication of his last statement. "You can't tell my guest to leave. Besides, he was delivering a little present from you."

"Present? What?"

Kiki walked over to Garret and held the door open for him. "Garret, I think you should go."

"Are you sure you want to be alone with him? I mean, he might try something."

"Try something. Hell, she's already out of her clothes," Porter barked, motioning for her to close her robe, which she quickly did.

"Good night, Garret. I'll call you later." Kiki closed the door and leaned on it without turning around.

"I know, I know. I shouldn't be here," Porter finally said, "but we have to talk."

Kiki still hadn't moved from where she stood. "You black bastard, after I cuss you out and then try my best to beat your ass, you are gonna leave my house, never to return again. How dare you bust up in here."

"I didn't bust in, I walked in," he said, moving closer to her. "You sure have a problem with the facts."

"You always have a comeback."

"That's what makes me a good attorney."

"That's what makes you . . ." Kiki paused, unable to think of anything to say. Unable to do anything, but breathe in his air as he closed in on her. She swallowed hard, twice, in order to get the sudden lump that formed in her throat down.

After a moment of regrouping silence between them, he spoke. His tone was soft as a whisper. "I'm-I'm sorry I kissed you today," he said.

She looked at him. Her heart was throbbing. Did she really want him to be so sorry? Was she sorry? His strong jawline, his large hands, his pretty teeth. "You are?"

Suddenly he pulled her into a tight embrace. Kiki felt the instant heat of want from him and fought hard to resist it. Turning her head, she tried to avoid his hungry mouth, his lips that groped for hers.

"Don't send me away, Kiki. Don't do it," he threatened weakly.

Kiki pushed away from him, but he quickly pulled her back into his arms.

"We have so much to talk about. That night has come around to get both of us, and we need to be on the same page."

"Same page? Those pictures . . . Garret said you were sending them to my father," she said, her tone begging for understanding.

"That lying prick!"

Porter tore away from her and started for the door, but Kiki pulled his arm.

"Forget Garret. I don't know where he found the pictures. Apparently they're everywhere. It doesn't matter. My father probably already has a copy of them. Hell, he probably took them, as crazy as all this is. So many secrets," she said, allowing her own reflections to surface. "I'm so done with this whole thing."

Guilt suddenly covered Porter's face. It was an expression new to her, but she could tell he'd worn it before.

"I know who took them," he confessed.

"You do?"

He fanned his hand out toward the sofa. "Let's sit and talk.

Kiki looked around the living room and noticed now all the pictures that spoke to her life, a life she'd invented to replace the one that had been taken from her. And now here sat SP, the missing link to her existence. She wanted nothing more than to sit with him. It was a dream come true, or a nightmare in the making. She wasn't sure which, but she couldn't resist.

"Start from the beginning and tell me what you remember." Kiki could resist his warmth no longer and joined him on the sofa. Pulling the robe tightly around her, she took a deep cleansing breath, the first one in years.

Chapter 43

Morning came to find Porter in her bed fully clothed, and she, still in her robe and slacks, tucked close behind him. Opening her eyes slowly, glancing over his back at her clock, Kiki jolted fully awake. She shoved him hard, waking him. "Sean, wake up. Oh my goodness, wake up. We have to go. We have to see my father. I can only imagine what he thinks happened on my date with Garret." Kiki jumped from the bed and dashed toward the bathroom. "He hates Garret."

"Who doesn't? He's such a loser. Always has been. I remember in college. He was like the waterboy of all waterboys."

"You went to college with him?"

"Yeah, his father is one of the elders"—Porter put quotation marks around the word *elders*—"of our fraternity. Your father too. That's why getting an internship under him was like a major covet. You were the total shit if you could even get the time of day from him, let alone be favored. He was one of the few black elders, and a judge at that. No, he was a super judge." Porter laughed.

"Don't say that. My father has many flaws."

"And many good traits too."

"Well, he was crazy about you. I'm telling you, boy. Everybody knew he had a daughter, but nobody had seen you. It was as if he had hidden you away from the world. But then again you were just a kid. It would have killed him dead if he knew about . . ." Kiki hesitated. She thought about Shayla. How would she tell him? She weighed the moment. It still wasn't right. "I've got to shower." She headed into the bathroom.

"Can I join you?" Porter asked, sounding as if the comment came on impulse.

Kiki turned at the doorway of the bathroom and looked at him laying here. *Damn, he's beautiful.* He had aged like wine, with very few changes. It was amazing how accurate her dreams had been.

"Kimani, I'm sorry. I'm so sorry for saying that."

Kiki moved slowly back to the bed. "Sean, I've loved you in my dreams for fifteen years. I've all but prayed for a morning like this, the thought of waking up with you." Kiki bit her lip to keep from saying more.

Porter sat up on the side of the bed now. His dark eyes burrowed into hers, expressing what his words couldn't say. He wanted her, she could tell. And what she couldn't deny was that she wanted him.

What they had shared the night before had been beyond intimate. They had shared the past, filled the gaps that existed in their minds and hearts, at least for Kiki. She now understood why he had acted the way he did when they first met. She cried over the pain he expressed losing his identical twin brother. She could only imagine his loss. She laughed at his crazy stories about his life, and related to his need to succeed after a traumatizing experience.

The moment between them, shared now in her bedroom, took up seconds, moments, hours, days, years. It took them back to a time when this moment was new and the feelings between them fresh. He felt it too, she believed that.

Chapter 44

Porter couldn't believe it. Kiki took his hand and led him to the bathroom. She pulled off the robe and hung it on the back of the door. His eyes covered her body, stopping at her ample breasts squeezed into that pretty pink bra. Reaching behind her, she unhooked it, allowing it to free her full mounds, which immediately filled his large hands, his full lips.

She rubbed his head, as he crouched slightly to taste the nectar of her breasts. She cooed and purred, while he slid her slacks and underwear over her ample hips. Standing naked before him, she watched as he undressed. He saw his own beauty in her eyes, and it made him smile. Together they were like a soft-serve ice cream, the swirly kind, and he couldn't wait to wrap himself around her.

As Kiki moved within inches of him, his body instantly reacted to her, rising thick and hard.

"I've not had sex without a condom, since you and me apparently—"

Kiki put her fingers on his lips. "I've not had sex since

the night, since you and me apparently . . ." She turned on the shower water.

Porter's mind spun, almost at a dizzying speed. *"She was a virgin?"* he heard Bond ask? *"You popped her fuckin' cherry? You don't think Judge Turner is gonna pop your fuckin' license to practice law anywhere on earth? Are you insane?"*

"But I believe when I fall in love this time, it'll be forever," Porter said, not realizing Kiki could hear him.

"Oh my God, Sean," Kiki cried upon hearing his soft song, wrapping her body around his.

Kiki was tight, tighter than he remembered any woman ever being, as he pushed his way carefully, gently, but with determination, inside her, holding her leg just high enough, and pulling her hips back just far enough to make entry easy from behind. She gasped and groaned but allowed him into her warm, silky cove, her belly sucked in tight.

First slow, and then fast, and then faster still, until they had a rhythm that felt good to both of them.

He fondled her firm breasts and hard-as-a-rock nipples. "Is it good?" he asked, just making sure. "Is it good, Kiki?"

Her eyes were closed, and her face scrunched up, but she said nothing as he worked on raising her pleasure meter. Deeper and deeper, slow, quick, slow, slow and deep. She groaned with each new stroke, until her moans were guttural and primal sounding.

He knew he had found her heaven when she trembled slightly. A mild orgasm, he was sure of it.

Pulling from her, Porter turned her to him. He crotched down to her heat, swollen slightly from the friction they'd made so far. He buried his tongue between the folds, lapping at the head of her clit that toyed with him, ducking and hiding so as not to be bullied around by his brutish tongue. He enjoyed a playful clit, and hers seemed childlike and innocent to the game. Grabbing her hips, he sucked on her gently, causing her to squeal and call out his name, while hanging on for dear life to his ears. She came again, moist, hot and sweet.

Slowly he slid her down the wet walls of the large shower, so as to mount her missionary-style. The water spray was just the right temperature to keep his passion alive. He wanted to go deep, to become one with her. He wanted to remember the first time they had done this.

Her hips swiveled as she sought comfort while receiving his endowment. She was much smaller than him and easily curled around his frame. They were a perfect fit. She was amazing.

Kiki bit his chest as her orgasm built.

Porter pulled at her short hair and kissed the top of her head while the water pounded against his back. He'd not had sex in over six months, yet his orgasm would not be rushed. The pleasure of Kiki's body was too wonderful to hurry through.

But the fact was, there was no way he had been inside her before. There would have been no way he would have ever forgotten this.

Deeper and deeper he went with hard thrusts that caused his voice to escape in guttural growls and pants. "So good," he moaned.

"It hurts SP. It hurts so bad," she cried.

"She was crying? Damn," Bond said, getting into the story.

"Stay with me, girl," I said to her. "I'm almost there. Stay with me."

Bond listened when he shared that part. It was as if he wanted to feel the virgin's orgasm too. They had gotten over their argument about the pictures, taken through that open window. Bond had used a Polaroid, and so he had them with him. He had taken eight, maybe nine, before even really looking at them. He was a good photographer and caught all the angles of Kiki's face. He'd been paid to catch her in a compromising position and he'd caught her in several.

"But, I swear, I didn't know it was you until I had taken the pictures. I really wasn't looking. I was mostly looking at the girl. God, she was beautiful."

"Who told you to do it?" he screamed. "Who, Bond?"

"Oh God!" Kiki screamed, pushing against his chest, interrupting the memory. She was cumming again, violently this time. She cursed him, begged him, and swore her love to him.

Porter pulled her hair, harder this time, forcing her face from his chest until he could see it clearly. The ecstasy on her face brought back the memory of that night for sure. He remembered this look on her face. Yes, they did share this moment before.

Kissing her, he felt his release building. "Stay with me," he pleaded.

Faster and faster, he worked with her, deeper and deeper, until finally the fire came from him deep into her womb. The friction of her body tightening around his without a condom was beyond intense. She cried out in ecstasy, his baritone accompaniment following in harmony.

"She's a judge's daughter. She's fifteen," Bond said. "You just fucked your career down the toilet. I sure as hell hope it was worth it."

"Not if nobody finds out."

"And they won't, thank you, not as long as I have these pictures."

"You gonna destroy them, right?"

"Yeah, as soon as we get home."

"Well, shit, give me one of them."

"You're sick as hell."

"No, I'm not." Sean laughed. He pulled one of the photos from Bond's hand and tucked it into the breast pocket of his jacket. "What about the money you got paid?"

Bond frowned. "Fuck that loser. Little perv got what he deserved—nothing. Nothing from nothing leaves nothing, right? Don't nobody blackmail my brother."

Sean grinned. "Kiki." He sighed, eyeing the picture once more, before glass shattered. The gunfire blasted. The car swerved, rolling over and over, throwing both of them from it. Blood covering his face, he said her name, before he closed his eyes in death.

"Shit," Porter groaned as he pulled away from her. The memories were pouring in like the water pouring over his shoulders onto Kiki, who lay beneath him.

"What's wrong?" she asked, as if sensing his despair, her voice just about an undertone.

"I'm so sorry, Kiki," he whispered in her ear. "I'm sorry for all you went through."

"I have something to tell you," she said softly. "I have a child. We have a child."

Porter's breath stopped in his chest, and his heart raced downward toward his stomach.

Chapter 45

"Tell you what," Kiki said as they walked up the driveway to the front door of Frank's house. "I'm gonna make breakfast. It's always easier to talk when everyone is eating, ya know."

Kiki had been babbling all the way there. Porter was beyond nervous and had said nothing. Seeing Judge Turner again was one thing; he hadn't fully accepted his feelings about the judge yet. And now seeing him under these conditions, he really wasn't feeling this at all

"Kiki, can I say something?"

"No." She chuckled playfully, noticing her father's car parked just as she had seen it when she'd stopped by the day before. "That's too weird. They're here. I wonder why he's not answering the phone. He must really be mad. I usually check in. You have to understand, my father hasn't changed much at all. Well, you know him. You know how he is." Nervously Kiki giggled, before pulling out her cell phone and calling again . . . for the tenth time.

"Kiki, what are you going say? I mean, you can't just walk in there and blurt it out. What are we gonna say? So much has happened. Last he knew, I was dead. I mean, I can't just walk in there and tell him, tell your daughter. I can't do this."

"Stop sweating this. Remember, we're the ones who have had all this therapy. We're supposed to be experts at this kind of stuff. It's called a breakthrough. It's supposed to be a good thing. If nothing else, I've learned that sometimes you just gotta jump in and do it."

As she reached the door, she put her key in the lock, but the door opened on just the pressure of her slight push. "What the hell?" she exclaimed. "This isn't right."

Porter moved past her to enter the house first. He called loudly, "Judge Turner!" His gut was reacting.

Chapter 46

"Shayla! Daddy!" Kiki hurried into the house, her heart racing.

She was panicking as she immediately noticed the unnatural condition of the living room. The TV was on, not like him. Shayla's iPod was lying in the middle of the floor, earPod missing, not like her. The automatic coffee pot had made coffee a full pot that sat, cold and untouched. Something was wrong. Beds made, bathroom's unvisited.

"This doesn't feel right," Kiki told him as they both stepped back into the living room from opposite directions. "My father is a creature of—"

Kiki had bent to pick up Shayla's iPod, but Porter stopped her.

Suddenly, she noticed Shayla's insulin pack and syringe on the coffee table. She moved closer to it. "Sean, that's blood!" She screamed at the sight of the bloodstain on the back of her father's favorite recliner, which was overturned. "Sean! Shayla is missing! My God, my daughter is missing!"

Kiki again reached for the insulin, but Porter grabbed her hand.

"Don't touch anything, Kiki." Porter flipped open his cell phone and called 9-1-1.

"Call Tommy!" she screamed.

Chapter 47

He stood silent while she tried to speak to the detective. Tommy was on a call and would be there as soon as she could. Kiki's voice was shaky and less than confident, no matter how hard she tried. "I, um," she stammered. She could barely think, let alone, recap the hours since she'd last seen her father and daughter.

Porter rubbed her shoulder for comfort. "Just tell them everything." Porter spoke clearly, trying to say more than just words.

Kiki nodded, her lip buckling just a little. "I stopped in around six p.m. yesterday to tell Shayla and my dad that I had a dinner date so that Shayla wouldn't come home and me not be there and—"

"Dinner date? With who?" The detective pointed his pen at Porter. "You?"

"No, no," Kiki interjected. "His name was Garret."

"You don't know his last name?" the detective asked, his tone reprimanding.

Porter changed his body language to take on the challenge, but Kiki stopped him before he spoke.

"It wasn't a marriage, detective, it was dinner," Kiki answered quickly. "Lansing is his last name. Anyway, we ordered in from Singer's."

"Nice place."

"Yes, that's why we chose it. After dinner, Mr. Porter showed up."

"Was Mr. Lansing still there when you showed up?" the detective asked Porter. "About what time was that?"

"Yes, Mr. Porter came in, and Mr. Lansing left," Kiki answered for Porter.

"You just walked in and he walked out?" he asked, directing the question toward Porter. "So what time was this?"

"You know, this line of questioning is getting off track. I know where you're going with this. Let's keep our focus here, shall we? It hasn't been twenty-four hours, I realize that, but my father is not known to just take off with my daughter. Even if he did go out for the night, she's diabetic and he wouldn't have left without her medicine." Kiki pointed at the medicine preparation on the coffee table. "So let's get here"—She then pointed downward where she stood—"and not into my personal life way across town."

Again Porter tried to calm her by tightening his grip on her shoulder. "I got there around ten," he said. "She had left the door unlocked, and so I walked in,"

"Is that common, I mean, you two seeing one another?"

Kiki groaned impatiently, "Years ago, we used to . . . we—"

"We're dating," Porter answered flatly, saying no more on the subject and urging the detective, seemingly through telepathy, to do the same. The detective's mindless shrug showed he must have picked up on Porter's vibe.

"Where did you go when you left Ms. Turner's place?"

"I didn't leave," Porter said, sounding cold and less than friendly to the detective.

"Ah!" The detective's head went back in a knowing gesture. "Okay, so this Garret guy, did you and he have any words or . . ."

Kiki's mind drifted, not even caring about the "man thang" playing out in front of her. She was too busy thinking about Shayla and her father. How scared they must be. How scared she was. Was this more punishment for making a wrong choice? She'd chosen wrong and got her daughter. Was the same choice now going to lose her the same? She looked at Sean Porter, the man she loved. He was by her side this time. She couldn't be wrong about him this time.

"So, yeah, the evening was way past over when I arrived and walked in," Kiki heard, rejoining the circular nonsense going on between the men.

She thought about the photos and what Porter had told her about his brother, and about how he died that night. She thought about what he suspected was going on with this case. That was enough. She broke away from Porter's arm and ran outside. The men followed her.

"I need to talk to Damian Watson!"

"What? Why?" Porter asked.

"He did this? Can't you see?"

"You think Damian kidnapped your father and your daughter?" Porter nearly choked on the last two words.

Detective Schultz was starting to feel over-thought and over-reasoned. He hated working with attorneys; they never knew when to leave a case to the cops. "That's a bit of a jump, don't you think? I mean, how did we suddenly get Damian Watson, the attorney, right? How did he come into this?"

"Of course I do. That would explain why Garret got outta there so fast. Garret had to be thinking that you were there to do something to me. You work for Damian. He must have known something was up. He's been stalking you and probably knows more about your business with Damian than you do. He all but said you were in cahoots with Damian when he gave me the pictures."

"But I'm not in cahoots," Porter defended. Actually, he felt more like over a barrel.

The detective struggled to follow. "You work for Damian Watson? I thought you were with Simon? What pictures?"

"But if he really thought that, why wouldn't he stay and try to stop me? Or help me? No, he's an opportunist," Porter stated flatly, trying to stay on top of Kiki's next move. He knew it would be an impulsive one, and he wanted to keep her from acting foolish and causing more problems.

"Because he's a lil' bitch!" Kiki yelped.

"True but—"

"Take me to Damian's!" she screamed. "No, wait," she blurted, making a quick mental U-turn. "Damian can't possibly be that stupid. You take me to the jail. I'm going beat the hell out of Pee Wee Watson, and he gonna tell me what happened to my daughter. He's gonna tell me everything. He's gonna tell me why Peter is acting shady, why his brother wants me and you off this case." Kiki was now deducing some of the information he had shared with her the night before regarding Peter's request that one of them resign the case.

"No, now stop. Jamon wouldn't know. Stop it. You are really reaching here, thinking out loud for the most part," Porter said, attempting to compose her, wrapping his arms around her.

As the neighbors slowly started to look out their windows, the detective straightened his notepad to take down more information. "Why would Damian Watson be behind this? I didn't realize he'd been arrested."

Looking around, Porter knew he needed to protect Kiki, who was falling apart for all to see. "He hasn't yet. Let's all get back in the house," Porter ordered, taking control of the situation. This wasn't Harvey's, and even if it was, this was twice she'd shown her vulnerability. Porter half-wondered if she was being followed, and if so, this was not what the stalker needed to see or hear.

Growing hysterical and fighting him, Kiki all but needed to be carried back to the house. Porter hurried her feet to walk in the opposite direction of her passion.

"Okay, so I think I have a great place to start. Thanks for all your information," the detective stated, shaking hands with Porter, who had walked him to out to the lawn. The detective had asked plenty of questions and had a lot to go on, short of true solid evidence that a kidnapping had taken place. It had been less than twenty-four hours, and there had been no call for ransom. Porter turned back through the bay window to see Tommy Turner comforting Kiki in the kitchen. She had arrived on the scene about an hour earlier.

"We're not going to wait twenty-four hours, Mr. Porter. I can assure you of that."

"I should hope not. Because Ms. Turner's daughter, Shayla, uh, my uh"—Porter stammered, swallowing hard, unable to say the words—"she's on insulin. We can't wait. If that was her last injection, it's been nearly twelve hours."

The detective agreed with a nod and walked off toward the photographers who had come to take photos of the newly developing crime scene.

Walking back in the house Porter noticed how quiet it was. He noticed Kiki and Tommy in the kitchen. No one seemed to feel as if they could sit or do anything other than stand around ready for the next thing to happen.

"Kiki, we're gonna find them. We already have some great leads. I mean, it's not like Damian didn't live a scarlet trail. Damian wanted us to know he was behind this. He wanted it. All we have to do now is wait for him to make his next move," Tommy explained. "And I promise you, I don't need to wait on the department. Even my partner said he would help us if we just wanted to go find him, beat the shit outta him, and bring Shayla home."

Porter joined their conversation. "How do you know it's Damian? Why are you assuming like this?"

"What?" Tommy asked, nearly screeching her voice. "You know it's Damian. He has his brother arrested for murder. He wants her to drop the charges. Who the hell else is it?" she asked, gritting her teeth, ending her question with a low-sounding growl. "We went out to the house. They've cleared out like rats." Tommy spoke softly so as not to send Kiki over the edge again. She all but had to slap her face to calm her down when she first arrived.

"I still think you are jumping to conclusions here."

"You're full of it, Porter," Tommy told him.

"What?" It was almost too much. His head hurt like hell. Kiki had stepped from the spiritual world and caused reality to come crashing in. But this was no time to lose focus on the mission and the present. "Never mind, you're being emotional. Excuse me for a minute," he said, moving from in front of her confrontational stance. He glanced around the living room at the pictures of Shayla sitting all around. He had to admit that she was indeed a Porter. He was certain of it.

Tall, smooth brown skin, she looked just like him. He looked closer. *But maybe she actually looks more like my twin brother.* Considering how identical they were, he found his thoughts funny. They were so much alike in so many ways that even their mother made mistakes sometimes. The only separation between them was internal. And the fact that their bout with the mumps had left Bond sterile.

Porter smiled at his memories of Bond. *My twin, so alike, yet so different.* He sat down the photo of Shayla that had found its way into his hand. *Bond was such a clown, unlike me.*

Turning now, he looked at the two women, Tommy and Kiki. They looked sort of alike too. It was true. Despite the fact that Kiki was petite with brownish green eyes and dark hair and Tommy was a bit taller with bluish green eyes and sandy blond hair, they favored each other. The nose, the lips.

Before long, Kiki moved up behind him and hugged him around the waist. "What does he want, Porter? What does whoever has Shayla want from me? From us?"

Pulling her around him so as to hug her back, Porter looked over her head at Tommy, who had moved into the kitchen, standing there with eyes closed, head turned up toward the ceiling, clearly deep in thought. "I'm going to the jail to talk to Jamon. Maybe Tommy is right. Maybe he knows something. And if he does, I might have to spend a little time there . . . beating it out of him," Porter said, showing Kiki his convictions. "Because, if Damian is behind this, I need to know why he felt the need to usurp me this way. I told him I had this under control."

Tommy came from the kitchen. She'd misunderstood. "This?"

"The case, Tommy. Get off my back, okay. You seem to be looking for something to nail on me, but girlie, this it isn't this."

"Riiiight, like I'm falling for that one. I don't want you out of my sight. For all I know, we're giving you way too much credit here. For all I know you're about to bolt, just like you did after raping Kiki. Who's to say you didn't send out those sick-ass pictures just to shake everybody up? To cause Kiki to want to bow out of the case so you and Damian could go off to 'perv land' and live happily ever after. I don't believe you and your little memory-loss thing. I think it's selective, Mr. Porter. And don't ever call me *girlie* again!"

"Then stop acting like one."

"What choo tryin' ta say, man? Do you know who you're talking to? I will have you investigated—like right now."

"Do it! Do ya thang, *woman*, do ya thang." Porter got up in Tommy's face.

Tommy was tall but not as tall as Porter, but right now they looked like a match, if they were to come to blows. Her hair was flying as she spoke, her eyes blazing with acrimony. She was transforming right before his eyes. Maybe that was why Porter called her a *woman*, to make sure he remembered that, just in case she swung on him.

Kiki groaned, "Oh my God! Just stop it. Please." She moved away from the two of them and flopped on the sofa, burying her head in her hands. "I don't care about any of it, Damian Watson, Pee Wee Watson, the pictures, Peter, you, him. None of it. I care about this," Kiki announced, spying Shayla's syringe and holding it up.

After a moment of regrouping silence, both Tommy and Porter huffed, re-capping their emotions. "I'm sorry, Porter," Tommy mumbled. "I was outta line."

He nodded in acceptance of her apology. "No, you weren't. You were speaking your mind. You're entitled. You've been the only real friend Kiki has had, and I'm sorry for blowing my stack. We're all tense. It's okay. A real friend would do just what you did, and you're right in having me investigated. Hell, I need to have my own self investigated . . . several times." Porter chuckled slightly.

Taking a cleansing breath, he then looked at both the women. He could see the tension growing on their faces. He needed to get to the jail. But what he didn't need was

Tommy tagging along, tying up Jamon's tongue. "I need to step outside for a minute."

Porter walked down to the driveway. He climbed behind the wheel and started the ignition. Kiki ran to the window, only to see him getting out the driveway. His heart tightened. He'd explain later.

Chapter 48

Jamon sat down nervously, hesitating to take the phone off the hook. "What do you want? Why you looking all tense?"

"What do you mean, what do I want? I'm your attorney. I'm here to confer with you. And don't worry yourself about how I'm doing. I'm doing my job. Worry about yourself," Porter told him.

"Dame told me not to talk to you anymore. Says you punked us and that you weren't to be trusted anymore. He told me about you and that trick DA."

"Now what does that mean? And when did he tell you that?"

"Well, he didn't, that other guy did, but—"

Porter felt his eyebrow rise. "Other guy?"

Jamon went on, trying hard to gather his courage and nerve. He sat up straighter, as if feeling a little safer to speak. "Yeah, the one that's gonna take over the case when Damian fires your ass on Monday. He told me what you and that bitch were up to, and you know what?"

"What, Jamon? What do I know?" Porter noticed that

Jamon looked as if he'd been holding his own in the system. No bruises. No problem with the population harassing him for being the little punk that he was. He was impressed.

"He told me that I could press charges. And I am. I'm gonna press charges against you for impro-impropri—"

"*Impropriety*? Is that what you're trying to say? You should go for conflict of interest. That one might work better because most definitely my interest in you has become gravely conflicted."

"Yeah, I figured that, when the girl and that old man went ghost. Yeah, I figured." Jamon laughed before realizing what he had said.

"So you know about that? It's hella early in the morning, and you already know all there is to know. So you tell me this, Mr. I Know Every Fuckin' Thing—Where does Damian have them?"

Jamon grew immediately serious. "Damn, I didn't tell you that."

"Sure, you did." Porter stood. "And that's all I needed to know."

Jamon's eyes widened in growing fear. "All you need to know to do what?"

"Get a warrant out on Damian, have him picked up for kidnapping. Oh, and maybe for murdering Pepper Johnson, since you told me that too."

"You can't do that."

"Sure, I can. You just told me that you were a coconspirator to a plan to kidnap the daughter of former Superior Court Judge Frank Turner in exchange for a plea bargain. It's called blackmail, extortion, kidnapping. Oh, and endangering a minor. Let me see what else. Well, I'm not even gonna go into how you know he'd killed Pepper." Porter spoke knowing Jamon didn't know the actual parentage of Shayla, which was clear from his response.

"Dame's not gonna do nothing with them. It wasn't even his plan. He just wanted me out and you were takin' too long."

"As a matter of fact, I think I'll tell the press. No, better yet, I'll tell Damian himself what you confessed to me when he calls me." Porter pulled out his cell phone. "No, wait. I got him right here on speed dial. Let me just—"

"Wait!" Jamon jumped up.

The guard stepped forward, but Porter signaled for him to relax. "Talk to me, Jamon."

Jamon started spouting like a badly taped faucet. "He said he wasn't gonna do the ransom thing."

"You better sit down and listen to me, you little shit."

"Okay, okay," Jamon huffed and puffed nervously and sat quickly.

"You better tell me where Damian is, and you tell me right now."

"I don't know."

"You tell me, or I'll make sure Damian knows that you implicated him in Lionel's and Pepper's murder."

"He won't believe you."

"Oh yeah, he will. He knows what a punk you are. Hell, that's why he wanted you out of here so fast. Didn't want you in here turning tricks for favors. But after I talk to him, he'll let you go. He'll let nature take its course on your ass."

"I don't do that no mo'," Jamon groveled, losing his grip on bravery.

Porter held his poker face. He'd been bluffing, but apparently Jamon had several secrets of his own. "Tell me," Porter demanded.

"I did. I told you all I know."

"The guy who came in here, what's his name?"

"Dunno."

"White or black."

"White."

"Fine then, Jamon. You have a good night." Porter hung up the phone and stood.

Jamon began to call out to him, begging for mercy from behind the soundproof glass. "I don't know, man! I don't know! Don't just leave like that! What's gonna happen next?"

Before walking out, Porter made sure Jamon saw him whispering to the guard at the door, who smiled at Jamon hungrily. All Porter said was, "Look at that punk like you wanna beat his ass."

Chapter 49

"Yes, the prescription refill is standing," Roxi said, wording herself carefully, trying not to look suspicious, trying to look like a concerned mother. *Hell, you'd think looking concerned would be easy, considering I have a son that poor little girl's age.* She shoved her hands in her pockets to keep them from shaking. *Last night was rough. Damian showed that poor man no mercy, hitting him in the face like that, humiliating him in front of everyone. Why be so mean? Just because your father was a prick and beat you?* Roxi's mind wandered. *And that woman, Kimani Turner, she was just trying to do her job. All this was so very wrong.*

"Yes, here it is, insulin." The young girl behind the pharmacy window smiled.

"Yes, that's it, all right." Roxi grinned excitedly and stepped forward to grab it.

The girl pulled the prescription dosage back slightly. "Now I'm just going to need to see your ID."

"My ID?"

"Yes, Ms. Turner. You've never filled at this pharmacy, and so we'll need to see your ID."

"Isn't it on file or whatever? I mean, my sister needs her medicine." Roxi was gonna get loud. She couldn't help it. She was on the verge of losing it and had been for days, weeks, months. She needed to get out of all this mess. She needed to walk away right now and not look back.

"Look, I'm an attorney, and I forgot my wallet. You can call my job."

"It's Sunday, ma'am, and we don't work like that."

Roxi thought about pulling a gun on her, but that wouldn't help. Besides, she didn't have a gun to pull out. If anything, someone probably had a gun pointed at her at this very moment. "Well, shit, I should have called it into my regular pharmacy then." She looked around. "I get so much better customer service there anyway."

The girl, reading the form in front of her, smirked at the comment while. "Well, they do have the same standing refill order at the West Side Pharmacy."

"West Side Pharmacy? Okay, cool." Roxi rushed from the window. She headed for the door and didn't notice the girl pick up the phone.

For a second after leaving the counter, Roxie thought to keep on going, but one of Damian's goons met her before she made it out the door. The thought of running past the car and onto the city bus stop was out of the question now.

"We have to get it at the West Side Pharmacy," Roxi told the driver as soon as she slid into the back seat. "She always gets the stuff there. I'm gonna have to show ID here."

"Why did that fool grab a kid anyway? I thought he was supposed to get the lawyer, not some damn sick kid and an old man," the driver griped.

"I don't know," the other goon said, "but let's get over to the West Side Pharmacy. Them white folks be shutting up early on Sundays."

Dana felt good and bad about her life at this moment. Porter was a chance to step out of the norm and maybe see what the real side of life was like. Maybe even have a chance to be real family. He didn't know it yet, but she was in love with him. One kiss and she was smitten. Sure, he'd called only for Kiki's phone number, but still . . .

Getting married to a successful attorney, getting her child back from her mother, who was now raising both her and Roxi's children, yes, it would be divine. Having another baby was risky anyway for someone like her, with her history of drugs and such. For a man like Sean Porter, though, she'd take the chance. But then again it had been years since she'd lived a risky life. She was much healthier than when she'd had her first child. She pondered a fantasy life with Sean Porter for a moment.

"Let me stop. It's always somebody else's life I'm living," she mumbled, squeezing and sniffing the mangoes. Dana made a point of shopping on the West Side because of the produce. It was always fresher over there.

Just then she noticed Roxi. Her face was tense as she and the man she was with, who seemed to be bum-rushing her, headed toward the exit door. "Roxi!" Dana called as they exited.

Roxi heard her name called again when she reached the car. "Oh my God, it's my sister. I've got to talk to her." She handed the goon the prescription bag.

The goon looked at the bag and quickly tried to make an executive decision, which wasn't his strong suit. "Well, you be quick," he said.

"No, man," the driver insisted, catching the bag that

was tossed to him through the window. "We got the shit now, so we need to get outta here."

"Roxi, I know you see me." Dana approached them. "What is up? Is that yo' man?"

"I have to go to her," Roxi explained. "It's my sister."

"You be quick, I said. Tell her you was pickin' up some pads or sumthin," the goon outside the car with her growled.

Roxi frowned. "I know what to tell her, damn. You need to get in the car and wait, or she's gonna keep asking questions."

"No. I'm gonna stand by you right here."

"Ugh, fine. Hey, girl." Roxi, her arms extended, moved from the goon to greet her sister.

Dana looked at her sister's arms outstretched to embrace her. *Since when?* Dana thought, frowning up.

"Where's your car?" Roxi whispered upon the embrace. "We gotta run like fuck—right now!"

Dana's eyes widened, and without asking questions, her brain put her feet in motion. Instinctively she grabbed the fabric of Roxi's jacket. "Shit!"

As they both ran, shots rang out over their heads as they ducked and weaved. Screaming and running, the parking lot immediately turned into a wild, frenzied scene.

Chapter 50

The hours were ticking. Kiki paced the living room. The detective hadn't returned with any news, and she was going nuts. Stretching, she ran her fingers through her hair and swung her arms for circulation.

"Kiki, you need to lay down or something," Tommy told her. "You're gonna make a ditch through your Daddy's carpet. And you know he'll throw a pure *D* fit."

"I know, I know. I just can't think. I can't breathe." Kiki tugged at the neckline of her top. "It's been long enough to classify this as a 'missing persons' now, hasn't it? Besides, they know it's a kidnapping."

Tommy clearly felt Kiki's tension and joined her now in the pacing. "Kiki, they know, they know. With what you told Detective Schultz and what Porter told you over the phone, they know."

"But Damian hasn't called. Nobody has called. No ransom notice, nothing. Maybe it's not Damian. Maybe Jamon was lying to try and make Damian look powerful. Maybe it's some weirdo freak that's been watching my father's house or some old client he pissed off. You know how my father can anger people. Maybe somebody was after Shayla. What about that boy? Isaiah? Have you questioned him?"

"Kiki!" Porter raised his hand to silence her.

Both women stopped dead in their tracks.

"Damian is behind this—Porter confirmed it. Maybe he was too, until he realized he was Shayla's father. I don't know. Let me try to believe him." Tommy shook her head. "It's just hard. Something about that guy just doesn't ring true."

"Well, Tommy, I love Sean Porter. For me, he rings true, he rings real, he rings my bell," Kiki said, still holding a serious face. "I believe he's going to find Shayla. I want to say I believe he didn't know about Damian's plan, but either way, he wants out now. He wants to get our daughter back."

"And that's all it takes—Oops, I was gonna kidnap your daughter and wow! found out she was mine, and so changed my mind? Is it that simple?"

"No, hell no, but Tommy, right now, all I want is Shayla and my dad back. If the devil said he'd help me, I'd be like, 'Go for it, buddy.' "

"Let's get out here. Nothing is gonna happen here. We know who's behind this. Ain't nobody gonna call here. We need to be at your place."

"Yeah, and I need to call Peter."

"Peter? Why would you call Peter?" Tommy asked.

"He's my boss. He needs to know I'm resigning this case Monday morning."

"Aww, Kiki, no!"

"I'm sure that's what they want to hear. I can't risk Shayla and Daddy's life this way. I'm going to tell Peter. I already told Sean."

"I think all this bullshit is covering over something else we need to be addressing," Tommy thought out loud.

"What else could it be? My child gets kidnapped just days before Damian's brother was going up on murder charges. If the pictures didn't get my attention, this sure as hell would."

"Wait—who know the pictures didn't get your attention? Technically, you didn't get any pictures. You said Sean got pictures."

"Yes, he showed me the courier stamp. Garret brought me the pictures by hand with my dad's address scribbled on them. He said he got them out of Sean's outbox. He said Sean was mailing them."

"I want to see that scribbling."

"Why?"

"Just a thought."

Chapter 51

Damian Watson's house was under surveillance. Heavy manpower was now devoted to the mission of taking him in for questioning on this matter. It was pure luck Porter wasn't under suspicion. But Porter knew he only had a short time before they would start looking in his direction.

Both Peter's and Damian's phone rendered him no answers, and so he was left to wander the street. Bond had been a wonderful detective, could have been one of the best, and Porter regretted now not paying attention to the way he worked.

Porter found himself in the alley where Lionel came from the window. He parked and got out of the car. Looking up, down, and all around, he wondered why he was there. This alley was dirty, as was the neighborhood, The Palemos. What a place!

Porter had grown up on a street much like this. So growing up poor and ending up at a prestigious law school like Stanford Law School, located not too far from there, was a great leap.

He began looking around the location where they'd found Lionel's body. Picking up an empty bottle of Hennessy, he tossed it into a dumpster. "Yeah, these streets coulda been my life—like Bond. But he loved the streets." Porter looked up and around, as if sizing up the incident and how it could have gone down. "Not me, boy. And look at me now, a rapist, a father of a teenage daughter I didn't know I had. In love with a woman that I don't even know, and on the brink of being disbarred. Wow! I've come far."

"Well, that's the window he came flying out of," he mumbled, changing his own subject.

Just then there was a rustle.

"Who is it?" he called, ready to take whoever or whatever on. The "whatever" kind of un-nerved him though. He'd heard about the size of the rats in the Palemos and sure didn't feel like meeting up with one of them right now.

"You looking for me?" The small, dirty man creeped from one of the doorways.

"No."

"Uh, because I was told the cops have been through here looking for whoever saw Lionel go out that window. I saw it all, but I been sick. I been laid up since . . . hell, since the day it happened."

"Why didn't you go to the police once you found out someone was looking for you?"

"Told you. I was sick," the man explained.

Porter reached in his pocket. He pulled out his wallet and handed the man twenty dollars. "There. Will that help get your medicine?"

"Yeah, a little."

"What did you see?"

"I don't remember all of it."

"You best remember twenty dollars worth."

Harry's eyes widened a little as he resized Porter's

stature. “I saw them two young niggas throw Lionel out that window up there. One of them just picked him up and threw him out like he was garbage. It was sad too. Lionel screamed and hollered all the way down. Almost gave me a heart attack when he landed right by me. I had to get up outta there with a quickness. I ran faster than I had in a long time. Bet that’s what got my pressure up, all them cops rushing in and disruptin’ my life.”

“Did you see where the boy that got away went?”

“Well, yeah. After I made it around the corner, and he was coming out the alley over that way, headed toward Mather Street.”

“Wow! You musta been looking to see where he came out of?” Porter said.

The man looked around and smiled sheepishly. “I used ta play sports. I’m kinda fast when I wanna be.”

Porter was having a hard time believing his story. “What else you see?”

“I saw a murda . . . second one that day.”

“Reaaaaally. And who else by chance got knocked off?”

“Little nigga that was runnin’. I knowed it was him in that bag them big guys brought out because everybody came out but him.”

“What’s your name?” Porter said, reaching in his wallet for another twenty, or two.

“Harry. You want me to testify?” Harry’s hand went out quickly to receive the money. “I mean, I’ll do it, but I could use a new suit and a place to sleep tonight.”

“I might be able to arrange something.”

The man grinned when Porter quickly headed him toward the big, shiny, comfortable-looking car. Harry was going to be making a trip with them to Mather Street and then to a secured hotel to stay for a while.

Chapter 52

"This was supposed to be simple. I just needed Kimani Turner to drop the charges. Now it's complicated. You all are fucking idiots!" Damian yelled, stomping his foot into the goon's face.

He had just walked in the room where Frank and Shayla sat. The look of surprise was written all over his face. Frank saw it clearly.

Shayla jumped and turned her head into Frank's chest at the sight of the goon's busted nose. "Don't say fuck," she mumbled.

Frank tried with all he had inside him to maintain his cool. It had been so long since her shot, her sugar was dropping. Who knew what she might say next?

Apparently the goons coming back with the prescription earned them no rewards, especially since they'd come back without Roxi. Her absence had complicated this situation yet further.

Frank made sure he remembered the woman's name. He was trying to remember everything he heard, but the conk on his head wasn't making that easy. Clearly, the woman had made her escape, and now she was free, unless of course, Damian's reach went further than she thought. He was always a wily one, able to pull rabbits out of his hand on demand.

Frank thought back to his days on the bench. When Damian stood, his mood dropped two notches. Lies, lies, and more lies came from his mouth constantly. The thought that Sean Porter had ever called Damian Watson *brother* just irked Frank to no end. The body of elders wasn't all in agreement when taking Damian into brotherhood. Poor and streetwise, he was a hustler with few scruples. Frank saw that too.

Sean Porter, on the other hand, was a lad Frank liked right off, unlike that scamp of a brother he had. Bond Porter rubbed Frank's nerves raw. He wasn't vicious like Damian, but he was cocky as hell and so full of hot air, he could have floated. Maybe it was jealousy. Bond was a free spirit, and no one had ties on him. No one controlled him. He could care less about the fraternity. Called it a bunch of bogus bullshit—boys in matching tutus and tights, he called them. That day they fought, Bond challenged him, saying he'd get the dirt on him. Frank hid the fact that he was indeed shook, for he had secrets, one big one he'd hid until now—Tommy Turner.

Frank was rethinking his life. He could only imagine what Damian would do to that woman Roxi. Frank would thank her with all his heart.

Carefully Frank thumped the syringe loaded with the insulin, squeezing out the air through the top. He needed to concentrate now. "Give me your arm, baby."

Shayla stuck it out without moving her head from his chest.

Frank closed one of his eyes, trying to see without his glasses, which had been broken when he was hit upside his head,.

"Owwww!" Shayla yelled as he poked her.

"Shhh, baby. Damian is already tense."

Damian growled, "Shut her up! She's old enough to do that herself anyway. Why you baby her? That's your problem, Turner. You come off as this biggo hard-ass, but yet you're just a softy. Me, on the other hand, I don't play such games." Then he stormed out of the room.

The busted-up goon dragged to his feet, holding his nose, while his partner gathered paper towels for him from the bathroom. He was certainly bigger than Damian in mass, but apparently not in brain muscle, because he hadn't figured out how not avoid physical abuse from a man with Damian's size.

Frank knew in his own heart that, if was twenty years younger, Damian's ass would be taken down, no questions asked.

Chapter 53

The stain blood makes is unmistakable. And there was plenty here, old, dried, and not going anywhere. Porter all but smiled to himself. Bullets from a Damian's Luger had done the job, Porter was sure. Why? Why he had killed Pepper, Porter didn't know or care. Damian was going down, and Peter too, if he could pin any of this on him. He'd had enough. Loyalty had met its match this year, or maybe Porter just didn't have as much as he used to since losing his brother because of it. It was clear to him now that the accident had occurred because of his brother's loyalty to him. The conundrum was one he'd ponder the rest of his life.

"So where to now, hotshot P.I.?" Harry asked.

"I'm not a P.I., I'm a lawyer."

"Wow! I'm usually pretty good at guessing. Maybe you should change your career."

"Or you should change your guess."

Both men laughed.

Chapter 54

Again Frank looked around in hopes of figuring out where he was. The room, abandoned and sterile, with only two folding chairs and a dirty, ill-stocked bathroom gave nothing away, not even which side of town they were on. They had blindfolded him last night during the ride, and he didn't hear any outside sounds or clues to indicate where they were going. They had driven for a long time, of that Frank was sure, so he was more than certain they were out of the city. Or maybe they had driven in circles to confuse him.

It wasn't as if he was into all this espionage. He just wished he knew what this was all about so that he could know if he and Shayla were about to die or not. But he didn't have much of a clue, except that Damian was pitching a fit about the woman not coming back and alluding to the fact that having him and Shayla wasn't in his plans. But there was no mention of letting them go either. If anything, they were talking about moving them.

But Frank wasn't about to go anywhere. Not until Shayla had her needs met. She had to wait too long to get her shot, and now these people weren't feeding her. Since they had been nabbed Saturday night, they'd spent a cold night on cold concrete and then fed McDonald's, as if that would make it all right. A McDonald's kid meal and some milk to go along with it wasn't enough for Shayla. She needed more than that. It was afternoon already. She was nearly a grown woman. Couldn't they see that?

Actually, it was the first time Frank had seen it. She looked much older than fifteen. Kiki was the same way. Why he acted as if her having sex was so bizarre was beyond him now. He glanced over at Shayla, who sat staring into space, her knees pulled up to her chest, as if a lot was on her mind. She was hanging in, and not complaining, but she needed better care. Yes, she was no child; she was nearly a woman. Hell, she was born when Kiki was her age. Frank glanced at his precious daughter. No, his granddaughter. He thought about Kiki and all he'd taken her through over the years.

As if reading his mind, Shayla glanced over at him. "Where's Kimani?" she asked quietly, locking her eyes on his, no doubt finding a way not to be caught looking at any of the men in the room. She was a bright girl. She watched a lot of TV and probably knew being able to identify these men wouldn't be a good thing.

Frank tried to smile. "She's is looking for us, baby."

"And she'll find us too because Sean is helping her, I'm sure."

"Sean? Porter?"

"Yes. SP is helping her. Kiki is in love with him. She dreams about him all the time, calling his name and all that."

"She's in love with Sean Porter?"

"Yeah, once she realized that's who SP was. She loves his dirty drawers."

Frank knew the insulin was kicking in, and so he expected the giddiness that sometimes came when she was a few hours behind on a shot. He pulled off his robe now and put it around her shoulders. Thank goodness for night-time TV and a good recliner. He wouldn't have been in his robe, had it not been for those two things, and Shayla would be freezing right now.

Sean Porter? When had she met him? He had never brought him to their home. He'd purposely not had any pictures in his office of his family. He never wanted anyone to have an edge on him. It was bad enough that brother of his had gotten all in his personal business, but Bond Porter was another story. And he was dead now, so nothing he knew would ever come to light. But back to Sean Porter and Kiki. He glanced at Shayla, and sure enough, his mind went there. *Nah, impossible. My sugar must be low now.*

Chapter 55

"You were smart in coming home, Ms. Turner. We've been doing about all we can until they make contact, and by the looks of things, if the kidnapper really is Damian Watson, he might not make contact until after the arraignment Tuesday."

"He's the devil, and I'll be dead by Tuesday if I haven't heard anything," Kiki promised. She was nearly spent, having gone over the case again and again in her mind. She and Tommy had rushed back to the condo and double-checked Porter's handwriting from the notes he'd made on the case file against those on the envelope that Garret had claimed he'd addressed. They didn't match.

Instantly Kiki remembered the wine sample. "Suspect everyone," her father would say. She pulled the small glass from the cabinet and handed it to Tommy. "Don't ask. Just see what's in it," she'd said.

Tommy had just nodded, and was at the lab now, getting one of her colleagues down there to check it out.

Kiki was nervous and antsy. She'd called Porter more than once, only to have the phone go to voice mail.

"Well, Ms. Turner, in this case, no news is good news. I guarantee," the detective told her.

Kiki nodded, looking around her living room at pictures of Shayla and her father, her friends, and Tommy. She missed Sean. She hoped and prayed in the end he would be worthy of finding a spot in her gallery and in her heart. *Maybe his picture will replace that one*, she thought, noticing the one she had of her and Garret, taken at her graduation. She suddenly found the picture strange and ill-fitted for her collection. But Garret had been a friend, albeit a friend that had all but forced himself down her throat, and was there for her when it mattered.

After the detective left, Kiki went into her kitchen. She hated that stress made her eat. But she'd worry about that later. Right now she wanted something.

"Ahhh, soup," she said, noticing her leftovers.

Just then there was a knock at the door. She rushed to it, only to find Garret there. His smiled was warm, and she welcomed him in despite the questions she had in the back of her mind.

"I'm just making lunch," she said. "Want some?"

"Sure." He went with her back to the kitchen.

Kiki pulled the large pot from the fridge and sat it on the stove. She then noticed him staring at her. "What?"

"So you're just not going to tell me?"

"What? What can I tell you that you don't already know?"

"About Shayla."

"See, you already know," Kiki said, sounding less than enthusiastic.

"What are the cops doing?"

"They can't do a whole lot right now, so we're doing what we can ourselves."

"We?"

"Me, Tommy and Sean."

"Seeeeaaaan, oh I see. I gather our date ending was a great re-start opportunity."

"You saw the pictures, Garret. Okay, you saw them. What of it?"

"That guy . . . always on top, if you pardon the pun. I'm just saying, he's gotten away with whatever since day one. Golden boy, from head to toe, always winning favor. Now he'll find the judge before the cops and save the day and all that."

"You sound jealous. This is nothing to be jealous of."

"Oh, there sure as hell is. I mean, Sean Porter took my life."

"Excuse me?"

"Never mind."

"No, explain," Kiki said, holding the ladle, hand on her hip, as she took a stance of irritated inquiry.

"Can I take that to go?" Garret asked.

Kiki stared at him and then at the soup. It was an odd request, but the day had been less than normal anyway. "Sure, because I think I need some time by myself. I'm like . . . totally misunderstanding you right now and I need to like . . . not hear you anymore."

"Well said." Garret watched as she scooped an extra helping or two and put it in her Glad container.

No sooner than Garret left and Kiki sat down to her soup, Porter walked in. She'd not locked the door again. A bad habit she'd apparently just picked up.

She jumped up from the counter, spilling her lunch all over the place. "Where the hell have you been?"

"Calm down. Why are you screaming at me? I've been looking for Damian."

"Oh, you don't know where his friggin' hideout is?" she snapped, instantly regretting the innuendo.

"I'll let that go, Kiki. I was just checking in to make sure you were holding up all right."

"No, I'm not all right. What if he kills my father and my sister . . . my daughter?" Kiki was trying hard not to panic.

"Damian is not stupid. He's not going to kill your father or your daughter. I'm sure he wasn't planning to kill you. He was just buying time."

"How do you know? How do you know? Was this your plan, Sean? You and Watson's plan? Let's keep the cute little lady busy so we can rape justice one more time? Was it a plan? Well, it backfired! It backfired, because you didn't help him get me. You helped him get Shayla! And Shayla is your daughter too. Is that how you know he won't hurt them? Is it because you have a personal stake in this now? You know, I've not once heard that you're backing off this case!"

"What the hell are you talking about?"

"Are you ready to win? Because I'm sure as hell getting out of this as soon as I get my family back." Kiki lost it and began swinging on him.

Blocking her easily, he wrapped her arms around her body like a straight jacket, pulling her to him so as to be able to speak in her ear from behind her head.

"Kiki, I love you. I would never hurt you. I'm a good person. I'm not a criminal. I didn't know you were fifteen that night. I didn't know you had a baby. I didn't know you needed me all this time. I didn't even know if you were truly real, or I'da been here. I'da been right here, girl."

Kiki began to weep bitterly, but Porter just held her tighter.

"I know you're scared, but you can't start doubting me. You're my angel, remember? You dropped out of heaven just for me. I would never hurt you. I will love you until the day I die—again," he added.

Turning to him, Kiki held his face and stared into his eyes. She looked for the truth everywhere on his face, his beautiful face. He kissed her once, twice, and a third time with a passion that brought her love down and trembled her knees.

"We are going to find her . . . together," he promised.

Kiki pulled from his embrace.

Just then Tommy came through the door. "Got something interesting to tell you. Hey there, Porter," she said, addressing them as if they were long-lost friends. "The wine had enough roofy to knock you out until next Thursday."

"Wine?" Porter asked.

"Rohypnol?" Kiki asked.

"Whoa! Now y'all sounding alike. Pretty soon you gonna start looking alike." Tommy chuckled.

"Garret brought wine last night. He poured it and drank some, but I didn't. It caught me funny the way he was acting, pushing the wine in my face. Just like today. He was just here and—"

"Lansing was just here?" Porter asked.

"Yeah. He wanted soup . . . to go."

"Why would you test the wine you had with him last night?" Porter asked, trying to piece together what she was saying.

"I dunno. I guess because I always suspect—"

"Everyone," both Tommy and Kiki said at the same time. Frank had taught them well.

Together they all headed out toward Porter's car.

Kiki screeched when she saw seeing Harry in the back seat, "Who in the hell is that?"

"Oh, umm, it's Harry. He's a witness. I'm gonna put him up in a hotel until this mess is over with. We sort of"—Porter grinned—"have a deal."

"God, Porter! Can you say *depreciation*?" Tommy teased, walking around the car to the other side, her face twisted up as if she could smell Harry from outside the car.

Chapter 56

Reaching Garret's apartment after getting Harry set up at the Motel 6, the three of them climbed out of Porter's car and headed to the door.

"So if he's not home, what then?" Tommy asked.

Porter just smiled and knocked hard on the door. There was no answer.

Tommy again looked at Porter and shrugged as if unsure of what to do next.

"Stand right here." Porter pulled Kiki in the view of anyone who may have occasion to venture down the steps.

"Porter, what are you getting ready to do?" Tommy asked.

"Break the law. What else?"

Sighing heavily, Tommy turned her head, as if that would be enough to free her from being an accessory to breaking and entering.

Inside the stale apartment, the three of them walked in together, almost scared to separate. They wandered into the kitchen.

Tommy pulled on a pair of gloves, and started opening cabinets.

Porter snickered, "And you wanted to know what I was capable of."

Tommy looked at her hands. "Oh, these? I just happened to have a pair." She smiled.

Just then they both heard Kiki's loud gasp of horror and rushed into Garret's bedroom. Porter thought perhaps Garret was in there dead. Tommy didn't know what to think. But as they all stood there staring in an amazement, they suddenly had an answer to the mystery of Kiki's mortification. On each wall, on the ceiling, on the closet doors, were pictures of Kiki during different stages of her life.

She took one of the pictures off the wall to get a closer look. "This is my graduation. I have this picture in my house," she whispered, unable to find her voice.

"This guy is whacked out!" Porter gasped.

"Beyond whacked. This is crazy." Tommy's eyes stopped on a small group of photos stuck to the ceiling right above where he would probably lay his head. She stepped up on his bed and pulled down one of the pictures. She handed it to Porter. "Recognize this?" she said, her lips tight with disgust. "Know anybody with a Polaroid?

Porter took the picture, turning it this way and that, his heart pounding. He noticed the bloodstains on the edge, faded by time and buried memories. It was Porter's blood. His head swooned as Kiki reached out to hold him steady.

"Sean, what is it?"

"Kiki, my brother took this picture. This is the original Polaroid. What is Garret doing with it? When did he get it? When he killed me?" Porter's voice cracked slightly. He was losing it but couldn't stop himself.

Tommy tried to stop him but couldn't. He was like a bull, ripping at the photos, crying and remembering.

Chapter 57

Just then Garret walked into his makeshift office without knocking. He had the goons find a desk and other items that would make his life easier while getting through this weekend. And he purchased a new cell phone in another name. He had to make sure Monday went just right. He'd spoken to Peter and knew they had changed the meeting with Judge Hewlet from Tuesday to Monday—tomorrow. He was ready. With both Porter and Kiki gone, he was ready for whatever.

Here was a cocky Garret, looking as stupid as you could imagine. He even had a gun stuck in the front of his belt. Damian would have laughed, if it wasn't so pathetic. How much longer he would tolerate this imbecile, he wasn't sure, but he hoped not too much longer.

"My father informed me that the DA has had an"—Garret chuckled—"upheaval among the staff over there." He chuckled again, making quotation marks around the word *upheaval*. "Anyway, they changed up the program, and now they're planning a meeting with the judge for tomorrow morning after being fully informed about Mr. Porter and Ms. Kimani, thanks to yours truly." He winked, pointing to himself. "My father is planning to fire Porter for his omission of personal involvement with the DA's office, and he is releasing the case back to me." Garret wriggled while he spoke. "Porter put this case in jeopardy by his little conflict of interest with Ms. Thick Booty. He should have known better than to climb in bed with the enemy, and she is the enemy now."

Damian noted that Garret did not greet him with so much as an ounce of respect. "Well, look what the cat dragged in."

Garret looked around, unsure of how to read Damian's tone. "What? Who? Me?"

"And so now you are saying Kimani Turner is the enemy? I thought Sean Porter was the enemy. Do you really know who your enemies are, Garret?"

"Of course, I do. Kimani Turner is the biggest. Yeah, she had her chance to go with a winner, but instead, she went with that loser, Sean Porter." Garret licked and then bit his bottom lip.

Damian could smell the emotion filling the air and he didn't like it. Jealousy was a weakness he had no time for. His hand rose to the bridge of his nose to hide the wicked smile he'd donned. Ms. Thick Booty, as everyone seemed to be calling her these days, had changed many men's lives. Just last night, he'd thought long and hard, forcing his mind back to that night. It was the night Bond Porter used his best skills, his greatest talents and assets, and as a reward, he was run off the road and shot in the head for his trouble. Now this fool had the audacity to even imagine that he could replace him.

"Some bitch thought he could fuck with my life again. Ha! No. He's done nothing but take, take, take." Garret pulled out the gun and flailed it around.

Damian didn't move, as if daring him to aim it his way.

"Now I'm taking back, jack! Last time I needed M & M, but not this time. I got DW on my side, and this baby," he said, continuing to play with his new toy.

Garret was weak. Porter would not have shown his hand so easily. Damian liked that in a man. True, Sean wasn't Bond, but he was all right. "So you're going to be there Monday to watch the show?"

"Yes, of course, I am. I wouldn't miss Porter getting fired and disbarred to save my life. And you know what comes after bad . . . all but good. I can see Kimani falling into my understanding arms right now."

"I thought she was the enemy—never mind." Damian shook his head in confusion. Understanding a jealous man was nearly impossible. His mind ran to Peter, who had nearly lost his when he found out Damian had violated his bed. *But it wasn't as if it was rape.* "Then what about the judge and the girl?" Damian asked Garret.

"To hell with them! Do what you want with them."

"Interesting. So what I want is what you want, huh? You just bring your junk and leave it for me to clean up, huh?"

Garret chuckled. "Sure, Dame," he answered mindlessly, fiddling with the gun.

"Would it make you happy then if I just killed the judge? One of my frat brothers?" Damian asked. "And not just any brother either, a founding father."

Garret was finding it hard to read Damian's tone.

"Come, Dame, you know I'm not into that 'Grand Poobah' shit."

"Oh, that's right. You couldn't get in the fraternity. That's why you couldn't intern with Turner, because he only wanted the best."

"He's a clown. He was then, and he is now."

"So you want me to kill Frank, the girl? What? Porter too?"

"Yeah, since that nigger can't seem to stay dead. Sure."

Damian, lip trembling, wanted nothing more than to shoot Garret with his own gun right now, but he needed him. When this was all over he was going to need him. He needed someone to prosecute for all this. "How about I have Sean have an accident on his way to the courthouse? I mean, as he's leaving Kimani's bed and 'thick booty' as you call it, feeling confident that he's got everyone cajoled, and tricked. I mean, Kiki is off the case now, for sure, and if she's been sexed just right, she would even deny the photos are real, therefore leaving Sean Porter untouchable. So he could just try the case, bouncing Peter's sorry ass all around the courtroom and—"

"That's not going to happen!" Garret snapped.

"What? Waking up with Kimani Turner, or sexing her just right?"

"None of it! Sean needs to not get there on Monday. I've had it with Sean Porter, and if I have to kill him again, I will!"

"You're serious, aren't you?"

"Mos def." Garret pointed the gun again excitedly.

This time Damian's trigger hand tingled involuntarily.

"A little judge-bribing and or relieving the world of a couple of thugs, whores, and crackheads is one thing, but bumping off an officer of the court is quite another. And I'm sorry, but I don't want that. I never did. I would never take the life of a frat brother . . . ever."

Garret, not thinking clearly, hadn't even heard Damian's threat. He wasn't a Frat Brother and therefore fair game. But he was being dull-witted about the entire situation he was in. Maybe it was because he had never pledged loyalty to a brotherhood. How in the world could he possibly understand loyalty? How could he know that Damian would see him dead long before he would touch a hair on Sean Porter's head?

Chapter 58

Instead of heading back to Kiki's condo, Porter turned onto the expressway. Kiki noticed immediately and sat forward in her seat and looked around anxiously. She'd been on edge since Porter had exploded in Garret's apartment. She had advised Tommy to get out of there just in case. There was no sense in ruining a totally good career over a thing like that. Her days as an attorney were already numbered, and if they had been found out, or if Garret decided to press charges, Porter's would be too. The pictures were no definite confession that Garret had killed Porter's brother, but it was definitely circumstantial.

Once the lab came back with the results of the blood sample on them, at least that would take Porter a few steps closer to unraveling his twisted life. Tommy called her partner, Keliegh Jack, who was quick to pick her up from Garret's place, no questions asked.

"Where are we going?" Sean finally asked.

"Calm down. We're going to my place," he answered.

"Sean, please stop telling me to calm down. I'm very

calm. I just wanted to know why we weren't going back to my place."

"We will. I just needed to stop by my place for a minute. I needed a break, okay!"

Kiki pushed herself back into the plush upholstery of the passenger seat, forcing herself to accept its comfort. She turned on the radio, and smooth jazz poured out.

Sighing heavily, Porter reached forward and shut the radio off. Then he slid in a CD. The upbeat tempo of Stevie Wonder's *Talking Book* CD poured out.

Kiki didn't fight him and enjoyed the memories Stevie's lyrics brought to mind.

"Kiki, I have to think. I need a minute to swallow everything, dig? I'm not mad at you or anybody." Porter spoke in a low voice, merging in and out of the mid-morning traffic.

Finally he exited the freeway and was driving through a beautiful neighborhood in Pinole, not far from Hercules. Kiki had to admit she was impressed with his choice of living spots. She'd eyed property here, but it was too far from her father.

Thinking of her father again dampened her spirits. It was true; they needed a minute to regroup. This whole thing was getting too heavy.

Garret, a murderer? Why would he do something like that? But then again, why would he paper his bedroom with photos of me, Kiki thought, *with the most graphic right above his head? Perfect for all sorts of self-indulging, and possibly kinky activities.* She shivered slightly.

"Tell me what you're thinking," he requested, pulling into his driveway.

Kiki just sat forward, looking toward the front of the house. She was thinking she needed to change her thoughts, to focus on this house, his home, and it being the way she'd expected her dream man, Sean Porter, to live. She was thinking he was all she'd expected him to be. Every second with him was dreamlike, and she couldn't' wait to share him with Shayla. Life would be perfect then. That's what she was thinking.

Looking at him, she reached for his ears and pulled him gently into a kiss. It wasn't filled with passion, so much as gratitude, love, and forgiveness. It tasted like memories of long ago all culminating into the now. As she kissed him, a tear rolled down her cheek and ran in between their lips, adding to the flavor of the moment.

"I was thinking about how much I love you."

The large bay window showed a few of the furniture pieces—large and heavy woods, and the gardener was mowing the grass and seemed to be paying Porter and Kiki no mind as Porter got out of the car, opened her door and let her out.

There was a high fence closing off the backyard, but she could only imagine that he owned a large dog, probably a German shepherd, Shayla's favorite breed.

"I'm thinking that all of this is going to be hard to work through. You, me, Shayla, I'm thinking we're up against crazy, crazy, crazy odds," he said.

Kiki chuckled out of nervous habit more than any humor in his statement.

"And I'm just not sure I can do this. I'm not sure I can get over this. I'm not sure I know you or . . ."

"Or love me?" she asked.

Porter stared at her, long and hard, as if taking her in. As if again, running her through the rooms in his internal home, trying to find an empty one where she and Shayla might fit in. He swallowed hard, as if removing the lump in his throat. He was hesitating, and it hurt her heart. The way he locked eyes on hers lost her in their dark pool. She swam in them for a while instead of counting the seconds it was taking him to form words.

"I don't-I do-I do love you. As crazy as it sounds, I really do."

"Then we'll work it out. First we have to find Shayla and Daddy. Then we have to find Garret. My guess is, they will be in the same place," Kiki said, sounding confident and ready to take on anything. There was no way she was going to lose this chance. She was prepared to fight whoever, whatever, whenever to have her dream. She would fight to the death to have the love she'd dreamed of so many nights. "Because I believe when I fall in love this time . . ." she whispered.

Porter pulled her into an embrace, tenderly kissing her forehead. "It'll be forever, girl," he said, moving his lips on against her skin.

Kiki's eyes welled up with tears, and they were silent for a moment, standing there by his car, being ignored by Sam the gardener.

"I'm going to just grab a few things. I just can't be in this suit a minute longer," Porter explained, ripping at the shirt buttons.

"Okay, I'll just wait down here," she answered, already meandering around his living room, listening to the click of her heels on the hardwood flooring. She noticed the picture on the mantel of Sean and his brother Bond. Mirror twins. One twin was sweet and caring, the other trouble on wheels. She could tell which was which by the pose they were striking in the photograph. The thought of the two of them made her smile sadly. It was clear that Porter missed his brother very much.

Kiki ventured into his kitchen, peeking into Porter's poorly stocked cabinets. Although his home spoke of his success in business, it said little about his life. It was clear that no one was caring about him as a man, and it yelled out *loneliness*.

She noticed the insulin in the cabinet. Her heart leapt. She pulled the vial from off the shelf and examined it. Shutting the cabinet, she was startled by Porter standing there.

"I just grabbed some sweats. You ready?" he asked.

"How are you dealing with your diabetes?"

"Just fine. I don't have it. Why?"

She held up the vial. "Why do you have this?"

"Oh, I had to see my doctor in Atlanta for a physical, routine stuff, and the quack gave me a ton of prescriptions. He just sat there reading a chart and writing prescriptions. I wasn't paying attention. Got them all filled, and one of them was insulin. I was like, 'Why in the hell would he do that?' My God, I'm glad I read the damn thing. Coulda killed me. Said my history said I had developed onset diabetes. I'm like, 'Do I look like I have diabetes?' But it's just like the accident report. It said I was driving. I couldn't have been driving. I was too smashed too drive. I think they got their wires crossed."

"Strange."

"Yeah, it is. But when you have an identical twin, you get used to stuff like that."

"So Bond had diabetes?"

"If he did, he didn't tell me. I got checked again when I got here. I had to take another physical as part of Simon's little hiring process. I don't have it, period. "

Just then her cell phone rang. It was Tommy.

"Just checking in. No luck on finding Damian yet. He's left no signs of life at his place and no traces. Not even a credit card purchase has been made since Friday morning. His phone was traced, but that led to a dead-end. He hasn't been to the bank in over a week. His secretary is on vacation, so she didn't have a clue anything was even going on. Nothin'. He just up and got ghost. This was very well thought out."

"Apparently. But we're not through lookin' for him. I want Garret Lansing. He's got Shayla, and so he's going to have to make a move on her insulin, if he doesn't want more complications."

"Shayla's health is definitely a complication."

"Yes, it is, and unless he wants a murder charge attached, he's gonna consider her health. He's got to." Kiki glanced at Porter out of the corner of her eye.

Tommy was quiet for a moment, as if hearing her loud and clear through the silence.

"How's Porter holding up?"

"Fine. Why?"

"Just asking."

"You never just ask stuff."

"Because he's gonna freak out when he finds out that he was right. The photos are clearly fifteen years old, and the bloodstains on the pictures were his own."

"Cheesus!"

Porter noticed Kiki's gasp. "What's going on?"

"Nothing, Sean. Tommy was just giving me the lab results on the photo."

"And they were my brother's, right?"

"Yes," she lied. "They were your brother's."

"Bastard."

Chapter 59

The door opened, and Garret walked in. Frank was stunned to see him but quickly shook it off. *Of course he would be involved in some mess like this.*

"This will be over Tuesday, Judge."

"I'm retired."

"Why are you doing this, Garret?" Shayla asked.

"Uhhh, let's just call it *billable hours.*" Garret chuckled, half-quoting one of Frank's favorite law jokes.

Frank instantly regretted his life as a young man, taking the law so lightly, breaking the rules every chance he could. But still even with that, he would have never done what Garret Lansing and Damian Watson were doing here this day. Sure, back then Frank hadn't learned fully the importance of being earnest and honest. Not until way after mistakes were made and the damage was done to his life, wife, and family did he stop and take account of his actions and decide to pay back what he had taken.

Maybe it was the sobering hit he took when Kiki came up pregnant and his wife's diagnosis of breast cancer that took her from him so quickly that brought him down from his high horse. His life was a shambles after that. Thank God for Kiki and her strength and quiet unspoken forgiveness.

"If you think that was the answer to the question you were just asked, then you really are the chump I thought you were."

"Shayla doesn't think I'm a chump. Do ya, sweetie?" Garret leaned close to Shayla and touched her cheek, and she recoiled.

Frank slapped his hand. "Don't touch my daughter. Don't you even think about touching her, ever."

"Don't you mean *granddaughter*?"

Frank's lips pursed abruptly tight, so tight that Shayla noticed.

"Garret that was uncalled for. Now get us outta here," Shayla said, thinking Garret was just being rude about her father being older than most of her peers' fathers.

"Uncalled for? Ohhh, then you didn't know. You don't know what a whore your mother was. My God, you don't even know who your mother is."

Shayla turned her head away from him. "Stop talking."

"Or what? You and your grandfather are gonna fight me? He can't even see, Shay, baby." Garret thumped Frank upside the head and then turned to the bemused Shayla. He had stumped her for sure. "Oh, did I tell you something you didn't know, baby? Are you mad at me now? How can Garret fix it?"

"You're crazy."

Shayla started to get up from where she was sitting, but Garret grabbed her arm and slammed her back to the floor. "Your daddy was putting some ugly on that shit too. I bet that's what made you come out so purdy?"

"Don't talk to her like that!" Frank screeched. "She's just a child."

"So was her mama, from what I saw. Whowee! Girl

knew how to throw a party." The young man laughed at Frank and tauntingly pulled the photograph from the inside pocket of his sports jacket.

Turning back to Shayla, he touched her face again before shoving the picture in her face. She cringed and turned her head, but he jerked it back. "Do you know how to party like this?" he asked Shayla again, sounding eerie and cool.

"What is he talking about, Daddy?" Shayla asked Frank, her eyes nearly bulging with question and wonder. She was scared now, and Frank had had enough of Garret Lansing.

Garret looked at Frank. "What? What did I do? You haven't told her about her big sister? Shame on you."

"Daddy." Shayla was showing panic now. "What is he talking about? That's Kiki in that picture."

"Nothing, Shayla. Don't listen to this pecka."

"Daaady," Shayla said, cowering a little now and tucking deeper into Frank's arm. She was scared, and of what, she wasn't completely sure. Garret's words were sickening her with both fear and disgust.

"Come on now, tell her." Garret punched Frank in the chest. He began to laugh. "Damn, Judge, your pride is still thick. Good for you. Stand up for your boy Porter. He didn't deserve your loyalty but whatever."

"Get outta my face!" Frank all but spat out the bile forming in his throat. "You never deserved anything. You figured just because you were white, you could just waltz into an internship and have it. No! It's not a color thing for me. You had ta earn it."

Garret looked at the both of them, the young girl and her grandfather. "See, that's what I'm saying. You're such bad judge of character—pardon the pun. I'm here to tell Shayla the truth. I'm about the only one who is. I'm not here to be bashed by some old beat-up loser like you. Oh well . . ." He stood but left the bowl of soup on the floor. "I'm sure you'll love the soup. It's your mother's best recipe," he said, directing his words down at Shayla. Then he turned and headed out the door.

Chapter 60

"Hey, guess what? We've had a break!"

"We have!" Porter shot up in almost one fluid motion from where he and Kiki were sitting cuddled on the sofa in her living room.

"Kiki tried to get a prescription for insulin re-filled early this morning."

"Did they give it to me? I mean, her. Please God, tell me they gave it to her!" Kiki yelped

Tommy, shaking her head, looked at the floor and then back up at her.

Kiki sighed.

"But, listen, I'm hesitating because it's not all bad. She didn't have ID, but the girl said she told her that you normally fill at West Side Pharmacy, so we hurried our little asses over there, and guess what? I picked up some insulin from West Side Pharmacy."

Kiki jumped up and down excitedly.

"Yeah, but there was some shooting, and the woman got away, so we don't know if she still had the prescription or not."

"Okay. I'm out!" Porter said, sliding on his shoes and rushing out of the room.

This time Tommy didn't try to stop or go with him; it was as if she sensed his continued determination to prove his innocence and non-involvement with Damian and Garret Lansing.

"Sean, what are you going to look for?" Kiki asked.

"Whatever I find," Porter answered, looking at Tommy, who gave him a crooked grin. Giving Kiki a peck on the cheek, he hurried out of the condo.

"Be careful," Kiki told him, stroking his arm as he slid out the door.

He grinned excitedly, looking like many rookies Tommy had seen on their first chase, as Kiki closed the door behind him.

The officers staked out in her condo barely noticed the disruption the three of them—working on the case—had caused.

"Did I forget to say that we cleaned up the area, and there is nothing to find?" Tommy explained, turned her attention back.

"So Sean is rushing over there for nothing, huh?" Kiki asked, trying not to find humor in Porter's actions.

"It'll keep him busy for a minute," Tommy added, sounding just as tongue-in-cheek. "Anyway, the woman had a companion. We're not sure of all the who's and what's. We just know she came with one group and left with another."

"Well, thank God, she got away. That means Shayla more than likely got her insulin."

Kiki sighed heavily, pacing the floor for a moment or two before heading to the kitchen. The news had perked her up a bit, even though it wasn't all that good. There was still no way of knowing if Shayla had been medicated, but Kiki was certain of it in her heart.

"Did you hear about tomorrow? Me and Sean are supposed to face the judge tomorrow in his chambers." Kiki urged Tommy to accept a cup of tea.

"Sounds good," Tommy said, as if hiding an alternate plan she wasn't sharing.

"Do you think we are going to get them back?" Kiki asked, noting Tommy's stymied words.

"Of course! Damian has left more trails than a hooker on the rag," Tommy blurted.

Kiki let her words settle a moment. And she burst into laughter for the first time today. "God, Tommy, that's gross."

Chapter 61

"You ever done anything you regret?" Frank asked the goon who looked through his cards for any two that went together.

This game was complicated, but the old dude had shown him some tricks to learning it quickly. *He's all right. I hope we don't have to hurt 'em. The girl neither. She's a sweetie.* The goon watched Shayla sitting by herself, fiddling with the small hairbrush she apparently had in her pocket.

"Yeah, I done plenty," the goon answered, turning his attention back to Frank.

"What were you thinking before you did it, the thing you regretted?"

"Nothing. I just did it and then thought like, Daaayum! that was wrong." He laughed, shaking his head. "Then I felt bad for a minute and then I got over it."

"What about this situation? How do you feel about holding me and my innocent daughter hostage? I mean, your friend, I'm sure he's regretting it," Frank said, referencing the other goon, who had yet to return since his nose was broken by Damian after that woman got away.

"I don't feel nothing about it. We haven't hurt you or her. It's just like a temporary detainment. I'm sure you understand that, Judge."

"Oh, so you know I'm a judge?"

"Former. That's what that white guy said."

"True." Frank laid down a card and swiped up another one from the desk. "But former or otherwise, I know that you're going to do a lot of time for what Damian and Garret are doing to us."

"No, I'm not."

"And why do you think that?"

"Because I'm going to plead insanity."

"Reaaallly?"

"Yes, sir. I'm gonna starting cryin' and pissin' like a little bitch when the cops bust up in here." The goon laughed heartily.

Frank chuckled at the thought of his defense. "Or you could help me and my daughter get outta here, and then I could use my connections to make sure you walk away from all this. You could live on to regret another day."

"Well, Judge, I'll have to ponder that for a while, but for now. I've been hearing nothing but connection this and connection that for months, and the only hookup I've had is this here game you invented. The one I think I just won!"

The goon threw down his cards, only to have Frank lay his on top calling out the winner's call.

"Makahaka! I win!" Frank corrected. "Unfortunately when you allow someone else to make the rules, you can always count on losing," he explained, hoping the goon got the message.

"Damn! You're good, Old Man."

The goon's phone rang,and he answered it. Glancing up

at Frank, he spoke in short sentences now. "Yeah. Yeah. Okay," he said, before standing tall and ready to obey, like an ignorant solider off to fight a war he didn't understand but felt compelled to participate in. Hanging up, he looked at Frank and then over at Shayla, a little apprehension in his eyes. "We gotta move you."

"Why?" Frank asked.

"Ain't my game. Don't know all the rules. Now let's go."

Chapter 62

Porter wasn't sure what he would find when he pulled into the parking lot of Von's supermarket. But there had been a shooting, and so he figured the police had to still be there. He wanted answers. Kiki's place was suffocating him with all those people crowded in the living room, and Tommy was being vague, too vague for him, so he needed to get outta there. One more "sort-of lead" was going to make him crazy.

Monday was too far away.

Suddenly his phone rang. It was Dana.

Look, Dana, I really like you and all, and you have been more than helpful. But I can't spend anymore time with you. Kiki and I are in the middle of a crisis. We're a couple now, and well, we've got a lot of serious stuff going on. "Dana."

"Sean, I need you to meet me. It's very important."

"Meet you? Dana, do you know what's going on?"

"Yes, of course, I do. I need you to meet me at the hotel I'm staying at. I didn't feel safe going home. I thought they might be there."

"What's up? They who?"

"The ones that took Kiki's sister and father," Dana answered breathlessly as if she'd run in circles prior to calling.

Porter sat the phone down on the dash and pushed the speaker button. He needed a free hand to set his GPS map. "Where are you?"

"I got smooth out of town, man, I'm in Alameda. I have my sister with me."

"Your sister?"

"You know my sister—Roxi—Damian's girl. Please, I'll explain it when you get here." Dana went on to give Porter the address, which he put in his GPS.

Dana hung up the phone and went back in the room where Roxi was laid out on the bed. "He's coming."

"What is Sean gonna do? He's in it with them. He knows what Damian is up to. Damian all but told him he was gonna kill somebody for him, and Sean just agreed to it. They are in some brotherhood. They are in it together."

"I don't believe that."

Roxi sat up and began looking around, as if about to gather her things. "Well, believe it. This isn't all about Jamon getting off. It's about settling some old debt. Now I don't know who owes who, but there is some buck-fuckin' going on. And you know how it is when money is involved. People kill for money!"

"No, Roxi." Dana was trying her best to hold her sister back from leaving the room. "Don't leave."

"I got to. He's gonna come in here and shoot me."

"No, he's not!"

Roxi shoved Dana hard and slapped her. "Look, just because he broke you off, don't start believing his shit. You always do that. You're weak-minded, Dana. A man is a two-faced . . . you know, like the old song says."

Dana grabbed her face at the site of the slap but didn't

cry. She was suddenly confused. This was her sister's life they were talking about here. What if Porter was playing her? Every time they were together, he asked about Kiki. She had given him Kiki's personal number and address, all her information, everything, and now this. "Oh my God, what if you are right?"

"I know I'm right. We can't call the police because Damian will kill that little girl before the cops even get close. Damian can smell cops a mile away. We have to get to the DA."

"Peter?"

"Why in the hell would I want you to call that white man? Kimani, the DA, that's who you shoulda been calling."

"Roxi, I can't believe what you're thinking. You've got me doubting everybody now."

"I'm outta here," Roxi proclaimed, slinging her matted weave wildly while gathering her things.

"Wait, Roxi. Sean Porter loves Kiki. He would never hurt her."

"You are crazy as that old dude that used to walk around talking to his self. He don't love her. Even I know that!" Roxi insisted. "I see his eyes. He don't love her."

Dana shook her head but didn't move from her spot on the floor. "I'm not going."

Roxi held out her hands. "Well, fine. Give me your keys."

Dana nodded toward the nightstand. She knew she couldn't keep Roxi there. She would simply tell Porter what Roxi told her and see how he reacted. If he was on Damian's side, who knew, maybe he would kill her. But Dana had to take that chance. Because Dana had looked in Porter's eyes when she said or he said, Kiki's name, and what she saw was love, or at least something. It wasn't murder. Dana knew that what she was doing here tonight was important. She would be blessed in her efforts, if Porter was truly trying to help Kiki. *And, Lord knows, I need a blessing*, Dana prayed quickly while watching her sister pull off in her car.

About twenty minutes later, Porter was knocking at the door. Dana opened it, moving out of the way as he burst in looking around for Roxi.

"Where is she?"

"You here to kill her?"

"Kill her? Why in the hell would I be here to kill her?"

Dana exhaled, falling into his chest.

Suddenly, from behind, Roxi entered the room with the large baseball bat that Dana kept in the trunk of her car. "Get away from my sister!" she screamed before waylaying Porter, knocking him out cold.

"Roxi! Ya damned fool! He wasn't here to kill you!" Dana screamed as both women stood over the unconscious Porter.

"He wasn't here to kill me, huh?" Roxi's tone was correctional, and she was huffing, wide-eyed and harried. She reached quickly under Porter's hoodie and pulled out his gun. She showed Dana, who nearly fainted again. "Let's tie his ass up."

"With what?" Dana whined, feeling panic coming on. She knew if she got outta control, Roxi would slap the crazy out of her, so she tried to maintain. But looking down at Porter, seeing that blood seeping onto the carpet from where Roxi had cracked his head, she was freaking out just a little.

"Hell, ain't you ever watched TV? Use your headband to gag him. Get that phone cord."

"Well, I'm sorry I don't live with mobsters like you do." Dana quickly ripped the modular cord from the wall.

Roxi began wrapping Porter's wrists, and Dana tied his ankles together.

"Get his wallet and take off his shoes."

"His shoes?"

"Yeah, get his wallet, and get them Gucci's off his feet. We're taking 'em."

"Oh, Roxi, this feels so wrong."

"No. A bullet in your ass feels wrong. Now let's get ghost!"

Chapter 63

Shayla mindlessly fiddled with her earPod.

"What you got there?" Frank asked.

"I miss my iPod." She pouted.

"Well, at least you got your earphones," he joked.

She smirked. "Papa, they are not earphones, they're earPods."

Frank laughed. "Back in my day we only had a few names for things—cola, burgers, you know."

"I bet there was only Fords in your day too, huh, old man," Garret said, entering with another bag of fast food. He tossed it at Frank, who, still without his glasses, barely caught it. "You're so outta touch!" Garret looked at the goon who sat by the door and told him, "It's my shift."

"Shift? Damian didn't say we were doing shifts."

"Well, we are. So you go do whatever it is you do when you aren't here."

"Fine by me," the goon said, before giving Frank an over-the-shoulder glance. It was as if the goon suddenly felt something un-cool about Garret's intentions where the old man and the little girl were concerned.

The door closed, and Frank stood facing Garret. Frank was a little taller, but not by much. He'd always wished he was taller. Men like Sean Porter were always his envy. *But I was fast*, Frank remembered suddenly. He then thought about his childhood and shuddered slightly. *Oh my God, my life is flashing before my eyes. This little prick is about to kill me*, Frank thought in a moment of instant clarity.

Garret set his attention on Shayla. "I bet you take nice pictures," he said to her. Grabbing her, he stroked her hair as if she were a fully grown woman, a woman who wanted to make love to him.

Frank's stomach turned. "Get your hands off her!" he yelled, rushing at him.

Garret shoved him back and tightened his grip on Shayla's arm.

She began to whimper, "Garret. please! Please don't hurt me. You don't want to hurt me. I know you don't."

Turning back to her, his grin said it all. Frank knew what Garret was planning. "Come on," Garret told Shayla, heading toward the bathroom. "It's not gonna hurt, Shayla. You're gonna like it."

"No, Garret! No! I won't. Please!" Shayla begged, pulling against him.

Shayla appeared weak, and Frank could see she wasn't feeling well.

Garret pushed Shayla into the bathroom and she fell to the floor, screaming. Garret laughed wickedly.

Suddenly Frank wrapped the iPod accessory around his neck, catching him by surprise. Garret grabbed at the wire cutting into his skin.

"I'm outta touch, huh. Well, check this out, punk—these aren't earphones, these are earPods," Frank growled, pulling tighter and tighter with every ounce of strength he could muster. Yes, he was young again.

Garret turned to him, his eyes bulging slightly as he strangled. But youth was on his side. Pulling the gun from his belt, he aimed it at Frank's middle.

Frank felt it, and with lightning fast reflexes, grabbed at the gun, wrestling with the young man, who just a second ago was struggling to breathe.

Chapter 64

The sound was one Shayla had never heard before. She hesitated before looking out of the bathroom door. She just knew tonight was the last night she would live. But it was okay if she died. Tomorrow had its own grief. She wasn't stupid. She'd heard some crazy things, sure, but she wasn't dumb and figured out what they all meant.

Could Kiki really be my mother and this Sean Porter cat, my father? How could she do this to me? How could they all do this to me? I want to die. I don't want to face Kiki and deal with all of this.

"Just go ahead and kill me, Garret. I want you to!" she screamed.

The sounds of the struggle ended, and now the survivor headed toward the bathroom. As the door opened, Shayla released a terrified scream.

Chapter 65

Porter's eyes opened but it was still dark. He then realized he was in a closet. He heard voices. They weren't speaking English. *Where the hell am I?* he asked himself, trying to remember. He began struggling against his restraints, hoping to make enough noise to alert the owners of the voices. Suddenly the closet door opened, and two small Mexican women began to beat him with toilet brushes, screaming at the top of their lungs.

Chapter 66

"Why would Damian want to kidnap me?"

"I'm not sure he did. I went to the jail to beat up on, I mean, talk to Jamon," Tommy told her. "And he was squirming and twitching but told me that Damian was innocent as an angel."

Kiki chuckled. "You have to stop trying to make me laugh."

"I know. But I just can't deal with all this drama anymore. I'm just not into it."

"You're a cop. Ummm, sorry, but it comes with your badge."

"Maybe I should give it up."

"Please . . . you are made to be a cop."

"But your dad didn't think so. He wanted me to be a doctor."

"My dad was wrong. He's been wrong about a lot of things."

"Kiki, this wasn't his fault. Not for being a bad man, anyway."

"Excuse me?"

"Your father is hardheaded and stubborn and all that stuff, but he has a kind heart. He really does."

Kiki pretended to be choking. "Is this coming from you? You two fight like cats and dogs."

"Yeah, but he's the only father I've ever known. I know he's yours. No jealousy from me though. Because, whether you know it or not, over the years you sort of lent him to me, and I'll always love you for that. But, truth be told, I've come to really love him too."

"Tommy," Kiki began before hugging her tight. Tommy wasn't crying, heaven forbid she let a tear fall, but Kiki could see this was wearing on her.

Tommy pulled away and stood up. "I'm going to go see if those results are back from the lab on that blood sample from that building Sean's stinky buddy, Harry, took us to."

"Sean is on it. You can take a break. Put the badge down for a minute. You're too close to this one, Tommy. Just wait it out with me. Come on, sit down."

"Like Sean isn't close to it? Shayla is his daughter!!"

Kiki noticed something about her tone. "What's wrong, Tommy?"

"Nothing."

"Yes, there is. Why do you hate Sean Porter so much?"

"I don't know. Maybe it's just that 'father thing' with me. I have a father too, but I wish he would just waltz into my life right now and try to claim me. I'd kick his ass. I'm just not feeling this change of command that you've got in store for Shayla. Okay, so she's been kidnapped, and probably somebody knows she's Porter's daughter, at least by now. And then she's gonna have to come home and be his daughter. Ugh, I can't imagine suddenly being somebody's daughter after never having to deal with that crap."

"But, like you said, Tommy, you are somebody's daughter."

"Yeah, I guess." Tommy looked at her watch. "Where is Daddykins anyway?"

Kiki moved over to the window and looked out over the street. "Don't know. He's been gone a long time. Everybody has been gone a long time," she said, allowing a sigh to leave her mouth.

Chapter 67

"Tommy, you can go home if you want. I'm going to be fine. Everyone is here," Kiki told Tommy after shaking her awake. She'd fallen into a light sleep in the large white recliner and covered herself with a furry white throw. Kiki couldn't help but notice how pretty she was . . . like a sleeping angel.

Jolting awake, Tommy regained her composure quickly. "Oh, no, no, I'm gonna stay. I'm off duty, so I'm here for the night. Has anybody called? Did I miss anything? Who caught the bouquet?"

"Nobody caught anything, and nobody has called, and I think the police are getting concerned. They say normally kidnappers make contact before now."

"Well, we both know we're not dealing with normal kidnappers," Tommy made quotation marks with her hands around the word *kidnappers* before rubbing her eyes and stretching. "We're dealing with a sick person who is up to something so much more than a ransom. This is so personal. Don't they know that?"

"It's making me sick."

"I don't even know why they're treating this like a regular kidnapping. We know it's Damian Watson." Tommy looked around. The living room was crowded with detectives, surveillance officers, all talking, eating, waiting. "Where's Mr. Porter? He hasn't made it back from his wild goose chase—I mean, investigation."

"Stop it." Kiki chuckled slightly. "Seriously though, I don't know where he is, and I'm getting a little worried about him. He's been gone for three hours. I tried calling him, but his phone just went straight to voice mail, as if he turned it off."

"That's not like him. He'd been so attentive." Tommy grinned. "I sure hope he didn't get himself in trouble trying to do police work. We have a hard enough time with you guys in our way in the courtroom." Tommy pulled her cell phone out of the pocket of her leather jacket.

"Don't say that."

"I'm just playin'."

"Tommy, I hate every minute of this. I don't want to be an attorney anymore." Kiki sighed.

"Kiki, I remember when I was on vice. I was a fairly new cop. I had a female partner then. I remember she wanted nothing more than to be a cop and go undercover, you know, like they do on TV. Well, we got this case once. Bad case, hookers getting killed, all that. Anyway, we went undercover. Well, she got so into it, too into it, and well, the killer really thought she was a hooker and he killed her. We didn't even find her right away. She came in a box delivered FedEx."

"That's terrible."

"But, see, there's a difference between doing your job and letting your job do you. I'm a cop. I do my shift and then I go home. My job doesn't define me, and you can't let yours define you."

"Did you ever find out who killed her?"

"Damian Watson was behind it. I know it in my heart. He got the guy off just a month before he killed her. I think the guy was working for him," Tommy said, sounding cold and flat. "Hey, guys, any more sandwiches!" she then blurted out, changing gears instantly.

"Well, I guess I should start calling around, like, jails or hospitals," Kiki said, thinking maybe Porter had become a victim of Damian Watson too. *This was all getting to be just too much.*

Tommy called the station and inquired about Sean Porter possibly coming in on an interfering charge. She shook her head in Kiki's direction, after hearing that he'd not been in. Kiki then decided to call a few hospitals and took Tommy's phone and starting calling around.

Chapter 68

The police handcuffed Porter before removing the gag and phone cord. Once they removed the gag, the obscenities that flowed had the officers feeling justified in their actions.

"I'm an attorney!" Porter screamed. "You need to be finding the people who did this to me!"

"Consenting adults shouldn't get pissed when the game goes south," one of the officers said, snickering naughtily. "Where are your shoes?"

"Do I look like I was fooling around? I don't know where my shoes are! Look at my head!" Porter barked, feeling the heat coming from the back of it.

One of the officers glanced back there and seethed. "Yeah, that doesn't look like a love tap."

"What's your name, sir?" the officer asked, removing the cuffs and then starting on the phone cord.

"My name is . . . my name is, um . . ." Porter hesitated, trying to remember.

Chapter 69

"Daddy!" Shayla screamed.

Frank dropped the gun that seemed stuck to his hand. He could see Garret's feet out of the corner of his eye but refused to turn and look. He reached out to her, and she attempted to stand up on her feet. He could see her eyes widen at the sight of Garret's blood on his hands and shirt. Then she blinked, closing her eyes tightly.

Moving past her to the sink, Frank quickly attempted to get some of the blood off his hands, at least. Glancing into the mirror, he realized his eyes were wide too. He was feeling nothing inside and knew he was running on instinct. He just prayed they kept working for him until he got Shayla to safety.

Leaning against the door, he held his hand out for Shayla to stay back, just in case the goon would came back in after having heard the commotion, but nothing happened.

Shayla had been nothing but silent since stepping over Garret's still body. It was as if it hadn't sunk in what he had done, or maybe she had convinced herself that Garret was asleep, or acting, like they did on TV.

Frank couldn't bear the thought that she might be, right now, condoning or condemning him. Sure, Garret had scared her, but vengeance was wrong, no matter what. He'd taught her that himself. And now he'd gone against that very rule, taking a life on her behalf. Frank was sick to his stomach. This whole thing was beyond serious now.

"Come on," he whispered, gathering Shayla close to him. He eased the door and led Shayla up the steps into the night air. Frank quickly attempted to gather his wits. If only he knew where he was, he would know which way to dart once they hit the streets, but he had no clue.

"Papa, where are we going?" Shayla whispered.

Frank shushed her quickly. He had no money, but Garret had plenty in his wallet. Yes, he'd lifted his wallet. He had to. He had to do what he had to do, right? The opportunity to call a cab or catch a bus, or maybe even pay someone passing by to give them a lift was what was on his mind.

He'd scrounged though Garret's pockets, looking for a cell phone but found none. *Thought every young person carried a phone.* Maybe it was too small, or he was in too big of a hurry. *No car keys either, dammit! Desperate and full of fear—yes, the true makeup of a criminal*, Frank thought to himself.

The side of the building read *East Side Industrial Park*. Frank sighed. This place was nowhere near the city limits. Had they still been on the West Side, Frank could have stepped outside the building and immediately found help—a bus, a cab, someone who cared. But not here. Once he climbed out of this concrete maze of office buildings on the East Side streets, with its crackheads and all that, no one may even notice he was covered in blood.

Pulling Shayla along, who was fading fast, they walked,

ran, and dodged the invisible for what felt like an hour before reaching anything that looked like a street. The time had been hard to measure, but it had been a long while that she'd had a shot or anything to eat.

"It's cold, Papa," Shayla told him. "And I'm not feeling good."

"Damn!" he exclaimed.

This time Shayla didn't correct his language.

Lights coming ahead signaled to Frank that the goon probably was returning. After this long a time, seeing no people, why would he assume this was just a happenstance visitor to the industrial park? It had to be the goon coming back for his shift. Maybe it was even Damian. He would surely be upset at a new change to the plan that clearly wasn't his to begin with. Pragmatic control freak like him surely wouldn't be happy about this change.

Lifting Shayla onto his back, Frank backtracked into the buildings and hid her in the corner of a closed office until the lights passed. Within moments Damian's man would be looking for them. "We've got to get outta here," he mumbled, trying not to panic.

Shayla wasn't up to it. He could tell. He was going to have to think. He was going to have to make a sacrifice. He was a judge, for crying out loud. Well, he used to be. Before that, he was a defense attorney. *Don't tell me I can't plead a case.*

Looking around in the darkness, Frank felt nearly hopeless. He turned back to the window of the empty office and debated using his fist to break the window. *A broken hand? Would that be helpful?* he asked himself.

"What you doing here?" the man asked, startling Frank instantly.

Frank turned and saw the scraggly bum.

"Gimme your money!" the bum demanded.

A ram in the burning bush . . . thank you, God. Frank

instantly attacked the man. Wrestling the man to the ground, Frank's plan was to send the man through the window. They rolled and tumbled through the fine trim grass until Frank got the upper hand. Dragging the man to his feet, backing the bum up like a battering ram, he ran the bum's head into the glass, shattering it. "Sorry, man, but you picked a bad night to jack me."

Frank pulled the robe off Shayla and covered his hands then quickly smashed out enough of the window to climb through. Surely there was a silent alarm, so he knew he had to move quickly.

Picking up the phone to dial 9-1-1, Frank heard a click behind his head.

"Hold it, Frank!" It was the goon he'd befriended. "Frank, seems you been up to some regretful things."

"Yeah, but why do the same? Let me go."

"Can't do that."

"I thought we had an understanding."

"I understand you perfectly. It's me you don't understand. I have a job to do, and I do it well."

Yes, Frank understood. He understood that their new friendship was apparently no match for Damian's long-lasting control. Frank knew he couldn't fight a bullet, and slowly he raised his hands in surrender.

"We've got to get my grandbaby to the hospital," Frank explained, speaking slowly, stating the truth for the first time since the day Shayla was born.

It was midnight at Alameda Hospital. Normally it was quiet on a Sunday night; however, tonight everyone in ER was in an uproar. Two people were triaged in: a young Jane Doe, teetering on the brink of a diabetic coma, and a John Doe with a concussion, who didn't know where or who he was, and neither could be identified.

It was tricky for the doctor on call, not knowing whether

either was allergic to one thing or another. He'd had the girl in intensive care for about an hour, but the man had just arrived.

"So nobody is looking for these people?" the doctor asked the police.

"We're checking that now," the nurse said.

"I sure hope you find somebody looking for that girl. I hate when I see kids coming in like that just dropped off like a sack of potatoes. What kind of parent allows something like this to happen?"

"We called Child Protective Services, for sure. But, as for the man, they found him in a closet and haven't a clue who he is. He says he's an attorney, so I'm sure nobody will be looking for him until eight o'clock."

"Very true," the doctor agreed, snickering wickedly.

Chapter 70

"She's so pretty, Aunt Jewel. I got to see her before that lady took her," Kiki had said.

Her aunt just frowned and opened the curtains.

"They say you're getting out today."

"I get to take her home with us?"

"No, Kimani. The baby is not going home with us, not with you, not with me."

"What's going to happen to her?"

"That's for your parents to work out."

"But she's my baby."

"You aren't old enough to have anything, let alone a baby."

"But, Aunt Jewel, she's mine!" Kiki screamed.

"No, Kimani. You be quiet. We know what's best here."

"No, no, you don't. I want my baby! I want my baby!" she screamed.

Each time her head fell back, she jerked it forward as if hearing a noise. Kiki's mind drifted as she dozed restlessly in the recliner. "Shattered dreams, worthless years, here am I encased in a hollow shell," she mumbled, waking up.

Just then Detective Schultz's cell phone rang. He had come back to her condo to relieve Tommy who went back to work. "Schultz here. Really? You're kidding me. Alameda? Was an older man with her?"

Kiki sat up straight in the chair. She was on full alert now. They had found Shayla. She just knew it. She ran over to the detective and screamed, "Tell me, is she alive?"

He moved back slightly so that she wouldn't snatch the phone from him or possibly give him a black eye while grabbing hungrily for his cell phone. "Yes, Officer Park, we are most definitely looking for a little girl that fits that description. I'll be there." Schultz hung up the phone.

By now Kiki was sliding into her shoes and calling Tommy with the news.

"Ms. Turner, we're not sure it's her."

"It's her. It's her!" Kiki yelled at both the detective and Tommy on the other end of the phone.

"They found Shayla?" Tommy asked.

"In Alameda. Can you meet us there?"

"Us?" the detective asked.

"You know I'm going with you. I'm going with you," Kiki said with more determination than the detective had the energy to fight.

"Okay, okay," Schultz said, knowing he couldn't win this battle.

Chapter 71

Porter woke up in a start. He knew he was late for something. It was nearly midnight. Everything seemed so clear, yet so foggy all at once. "My name is . . ." he kept repeating, hoping the rest would jump out. The doctor had told him the amnesia was mild and temporary, but it was very agitating. "And where are my shoes?" he asked himself.

"You can't keep up with anything. You've always needed me to have your back. Without me, you're nothing." Sean looked around to see who other than himself might be speaking. Spying a closet, he gathered a plan to escape. He clenched his teeth and pulled the IV from his arm. His head swooned, but he was determined to get out of there. He climbed slowly from the bed, managed to get into his sweats and hoodie, but found no shoes. "Okayyy. Whatever."

He peeked out the door of his room and found that the hall was clear. At least he could figure that he wasn't under arrest. Although foggy, his memory was forcing pictures of violence into his mind. Clear pictures. He was behind the wheel. He saw the gun. He screamed for his brother to duck, but it was too late. He tried to keep control. He hadn't been drinking, so he should have had more control.

"Wait. I was drunk. That's why I wasn't driving. I was driving?" Porter asked aloud without realizing it. He saw the gun pointed down on him.

The white face looking at him was angry. The face that stood over him was cold and full of hate. The hand that touched his jugular, looking for a heartbeat, was cool. Amazing that he could remember that.

"Garret, they're not here!" a familiar voice called.

Porter wanted to turn his head, but he knew Garret would shoot him in the face for sure. Besides, he wasn't sure he even could turn his head.

"We gotta find them," the voice called.

"Stop ya yellin', M & M. I got it covered," Garret said, sounding cold and heartless.

Suddenly the angry white face grew closer, and the hands riffled his body, pulling free the pictures. "Yeah," Garret sneered lecherously. "I got 'em, M & M."

"Kiki," he heard himself say, before he heard another shot, felt the burn scourge his body and closed his eyes. "Garret? M & M? I need to get the hell outta here!"

Tipping into the hall in only the hospital slippers on his feet, Porter started for the exit. About that time, a tall, familiar-looking blonde was starting for the door coming in. "Tommy? Tommy!" he called, swinging the door open.

Her face lit up as she approached him.

"Yes! You know me."

"Of course, I know you, Porter. You've only been gone for—"

"Yes! I'm Porter!" he agreed, ignoring her puzzled expression.

She glanced at his feet. "Sean! What are you doing with those on your feet? Have you seen—"

"Sean! Yes! I'm Sean Porter!"

"Yes, you are. What's wrong with you?" Tommy asked, her attitude over his hours of absence, turning into concern. She moved in closer, taking note of the large gauge attached to the back of his head.

"I don't remember," he answered. "But I do remember this . . . Garret and M & M," he said, hoping Tommy would say something that would help him remember more, but she just stared.

A large nurse stepped up behind him. "Mr. Doe, we don't even have M & M's on the menu. You have been more than difficult and must come back to bed. You really think you're going somewhere, don't you?" she barked.

"Yes, yes, I did—do! I thought I was going toooo . . ." Porter pondered for a moment and then looked to Tommy for help with the answer to where he thought he might be going. "Help me out here."

"What happened to him?" Tommy asked, taking Porter by one arm, assisting the nurse, who had him by the other arm.

"He was brought in last night, John Doe, concussion. Somebody tried to knock his block off. Keeps blurting out stuff, but nothing that makes sense, so he can't go anywhere until we run more tests."

The nurse, Tommy, and the very confused Mr. Porter started back to his room.

"His name is Sean Porter. He's an attorney working with the police and the DA's office on a case. We've been looking for him."

"Funny thing, huh. Because, coincidentally, we got him," she said, a chuckle following her words.

"Court!" Porter yelled out as soon as the thought entered his foggy mind. "I need to get to the courthouse. I know who's behind this."

"Riiiight," the nurse humored. "M&M candies, Mr. Porter."

"No! M & M is behind all of this. I know it. He's the one who sent the pictures. He's the one behind this."

"Who is M & M?" Tommy asked.

"Kiki! Shayla! Frank!" Porter yelled out, "Oh my God, Dana!"

The nurse then nearly threw him in the bed, closed the curtain, and then proceeded to manhandle him out of his clothes.

"Wait, stop!" he cried out.

"Shayla is here, Sean. She's in intensive care. Kiki is here too," Tommy assured him from the other side of the curtain, hearing him struggle for his dignity.

As soon as it got quiet, she called to him, "Sean, think—Who is M & M?" she asked, but no answer came. "Sean?"

Just then the nurse opened the curtain, shaking her head, removing the needle, dumping it into the sharps disposal on the wall.

"I'm sorry, miss, but you have to"—Tommy flashed her badge, showing great irritation. "You should have asked me before you did that! God, I can't . . ." Tommy slapped her forehead and stormed out.

Chapter 72

Dawn: Monday morning February 19th, 2007

"I turned on his phone, and there are like fifty million calls from that DA you work for."

"That doesn't surprise me," Dana said, still feeling bitter about what occurred the night before. Never had she ever wanted to be a criminal. Life was a party up till now, and maybe this was the trouble her mother always promised her if she didn't get her life straight. But, dang it, I got my life straight, and still I'm out here running. And with my big sister, of all people. *Loyalty—bullshit! That's what it is—straight-up bullshit*! She pondered watching her sister act as if she didn't have a care in the world, going through Porter's phone as if she was his wife.

"You should go to work. Nobody knows you are in this with me." Roxi calmly took a large bite from her omelet. Porter's credit cards had taken them through the night and had covered the tab of this early morning feast.

"Are you crazy? I'm not going one inch toward that office. As soon as you finish eating, I'm calling Kimani and setting up a meeting."

"Okay." Roxi shrugged. "I'm down with that. That's who I've wanted to hook up with since jump—the DA. You're the one playing on the other side of the fence. I already told you what was over there. You trying to call that white boy you work for, to come help, and that nigga that I had to fix up in the room—All them is crooked folks. And I know crooked. Damian killed somebody right in front of me, Dana. He will kill that girl and that old man, if he feels threatened. He almost killed that Garret fool for changing up shit without permission, kinda like Pepper did, and right now, we're a threat. We done changed up all kinds of shit."

"But Sean didn't kill—"

"Forget Sean!"

Just then Porter's phone rang. Roxi answered it, "Heylo," sounding rough and ghetto.

Kiki stared at the phone a moment and then through the window of the ICU unit back at her girl who had lived her life thinking two of them were siblings, instead of mother and daughter. "Who is this?" she asked.

"Who is this?" Roxi asked.

Dana reached over and snatched the phone. "This is Dana Tomlinson. Who is this?"

"Dana? This is Kiki. Why are you on Sean's phone, and who was that?"

"Oh my God, Kiki. Oh my God," Dana panted, covering her mouth.

Roxi rolled her eyes and sucked her teeth. She felt safe here in Concord, safe enough to show a little confidence and control over her situation. They'd driven during the night to get here, but in Porter's car it was an easy ride. Maybe they'd found him by now. Maybe not. But even so, if he could tell anybody anything about what happened to him, it would be a miracle, Roxi figured.

"Tell her I need to talk to her," Roxi yelled out.

"Where is Sean?" Kiki asked.

"Sean?" Dana's voice peaked.

"In a damn coma . . . where he needs to be!" Roxi yelled again.

"What?" Kiki was trying to keep her voice low, but the conversation was getting crazy. She didn't understand what was being said. "Shayla is in the hospital. She's in intensive care," Kiki said, knowing Dana knew Shayla. She felt the need to bring Dana to a familiar ground.

"Shayla is in intensive care?"

"That poor baby. They musta not gave her that medicine. Tell Kiki I tried to get it to her." Roxi said, dropping her fork into her plate and holding her head in her hands.

"Is it a coma? Didn't she get her meds?" Dana asked.

"How do you know about that? Look, Dana, you need to talk to me. I need to understand what's happening. I need to know where Sean is and—"

"Kiki, was Sean Porter your man?" Dana asked

"Why? Dana, this is not the time."

Dana ran her fingers through her hair and nodded her head toward Roxi. "You loved him, huh?" she asked, sounding hesitant and pensive. "Well, he loved you."

"What's happened?" Kiki was about to panic. She felt it growing.

"God, Kiki! I'm so sorry. We have to meet you. We have to talk to you. My sister and I . . . I think we killed Sean."

"What?"

"We thought he was helping Damian. I think we killed

him last night, Kiki," Dana whispered, looking around the restaurant.

Kiki's head swooned, and she dropped the phone. Luckily for her, the nurse caught her just as she started to go down.

Chapter 73

The phone went dead.

When Dana called it back, it rang to the Alameda Hospital's reception. "She's at the Alameda Hospital." Dana began to gather herself together.

"We can't go there. The cops will be everywhere. Let's just stick with the plan and go to the DA's office at eight o'clock."

Dana hesitated, but her fear had a stronger hold on her. "Okay, Roxi, whatever you say. But even if they are looking for us, they wouldn't know us if they saw us."

"True. Amazing what taking off your weave will do, huh?" Roxi smiled, running her fingers through her short hair before sliding on her dark glasses and then looking at Dana over the top of them.

Chapter 74

It was almost time to leave Shayla. As much as Kiki didn't want to, she wouldn't miss this meeting with the judge for all the tea in China. Her father was still missing, and somebody at that meeting knew where he was. Somebody at the meeting knew who dropped Shayla off at the ER door and skirted off in the night like a big fat rat. Kiki had promised Porter she would get off the case, but now with Porter dead, and maybe even her father, there was no reason to. She would fight to the end to put Jamon and Damian and every other corrupt person behind bars. She was on a mission to avenge. She no longer cared why this all had happened. Someone thought it was a game, but no one was laughing. At least no one she knew.

"Kiki," Tommy called softly.

Kiki jumped slightly at the sound of Tommy's voice.

"Sean is here in the hospital."

"What?" Kiki exploded, jumping to her feet and clutching Tommy tightly by both arms.

"Somebody tried to bust his head open last night, and they found him all beat up in a closet," Tommy informed her, having made a quick call to the Alameda precinct that would have more than likely brought Porter in. "He was brought by the police with a concussion and temporary memory loss. He seems to think Dana, your receptionist, had something to do with all the kidnapping."

"She did. I wish I had time to find her, but we don't." Kiki looked at her watch and then again at Shayla. "I need to see him."

"Did you try calling Dana back?"

"Of course, I did, but they stopped answering Sean's phone. I think they are on the way to the courthouse. She said she and her sister wanted to meet with me." Kiki glanced again at Shayla.

"She's fine, Kiki. She's safe. Focus now. There are guards watching," Tommy assured, sounding sister-like again, pointing at the brute force watching the door of the ICU unit. "The minute she wakes up, they will call you."

"Tommy, what if she saw Daddy being killed?" Kiki whispered.

Tommy hugged her tight. "Frank's not dead, Kiki, he's not. You stop staying that," Tommy glowered, and Kiki pulled away from the hug.

Porter fought the sedative with all his might, climbing again from the bed. His thoughts were jumbled, but he knew what he needed to do and where he needed to be.

Dana and Roxi parked Porter's car in the paid parking and took a ticket. Roxi had figured even if he got a parking ticket for non-payment, he could handle it—if he was still alive.

"I wish you would stop saying that," Dana groaned.

"You act like he's your man or something. I mean, yeah, I feel kinda bad that he might have not been the bad guy I thought he was, but damn, I've been traumatized. I deserve a little pity too."

"You have not been traumatized. You've just been hanging out with bad people and getting what you had coming to you."

"Oh, thaaanks for the support," Roxi huffed.

Kiki was determined to stop in on Porter, so Tommy told her which floor and room and then headed downstairs. They were running out of time. It was already six a.m. Monday morning. Surely they were going to have put the siren on to break through the traffic that was building up.

So much had occurred since Friday night. What had started out as a good time at Harvey's had devolved into kidnapping, murder, and an underhanded reuniting of dream lovers." Kiki stopped her negative thoughts as soon as they came into her head. Sean was back, and the two of them were destined to forget the past and find love. Kiki had thought all night about how she would tell Shayla the truth, and with prayers to God that her father was still alive, she thought about how she would address their issues as well.

Tommy thought about how constantly she would tell Kiki to get over this mysterious SP, but Kiki was determined to forgive, wish, and haunt that man back into her life. It took damn near a lifetime, but it worked. Tommy thought about her life. *Who would be worthy of her haunt? Keliegh Jack.*

Just then Tommy's cell phone rang. It was Keliegh.

"Speak of the devil. 's up?"

"Got some information for you."

"Okay."

"Porter. You wanted information on Sean Porter."

"We found him," Tommy told her.

"I don't think so. There's no way you found Sean Porter."

"I know who we found."

"No, let me tell you who you found."

"Excuse me?" Tommy chuckled sarcastically as she passed what looked like Porter's big fancy car in the parking lot. A chill came over her. It was that familiar chill that sat her on alert and raised the tiny hairs on the back of her neck and caused her mole to start tingling. Looking around, she noticed two women walking quickly into the lobby of the hospital. Spinning on her heels, she started back toward the doors. "Save it. I gotta go!" she hung up.

Kiki peeked into the room. "Sean," she called softly. There was no answer, so she moved closer to the bed, pulling back the curtain. It was obvious the bed had only pillows under the covers, but she ripped them back anyway to be sure.

Just then the nurse came in. "Where is Mr. Doe?"

"I was going to ask you the same question—but it's Mr. *Porter.*"

The nurse ripped open the bathroom door. "I've got to call security," she said, showing her irritation at yet another of Porter's escape attempts.

Stepping into the lobby of the hospital, Dana and Roxi looked around for an information booth, but before finding it, Kiki stepped off the elevator with several security guards by her side. "You've got to find him!" she was saying.

"Don't worry, ma'am. He can barely walk, let alone figure out how to get out of this maze called a hospital," the guard assured her.

"He barely knows who he is, let alone where he's going," Tommy added.

Tommy and Kiki were walking their way.

"I told you that white girl we walked past was a cop." Roxi looked around nervously, quickly gripping her bag that contained Porter's gun.

"Stop, Roxi. Calm down. Don't even think about it." Dana called out, Kiki!" getting her attention. Kiki's face showed uncertainty, and so Dana smiled, hoping to edge her into some trust.

As they neared one another, Roxi's grip on the bag tightened.

Tommy remembered this woman clearly now. She was Damian's girl. Tommy's right hand eased up to her hip as soon as she re-entered the lobby. What the hell is she doing here at this hospital, and what connection does she have with Dana. And why did they try to kill Sean? And what does she know about Frank? All those questions led her hand to her holster and onto her gun, which she drew. "Hold it!"

Dana screamed, knowing that Roxi had a gun. She just knew her sister would try to use it, and die this early Monday morning.

Instead, Roxi's hands flew up in surrender, and she dropped the bag, saying quickly, "There's a gun in the bag, but it's not mine. It's that dude, Sean's, that lawyer. He came to kill me last night, and I hit him with a baseball bat. I think he's dead, but it was self-defense. I know where that old man and the baby are. Well, I guess you found the baby, but the old man, I know where he is."

The lobby emptied of people, who scampered away from the scene. Many stood outside looking in from a safe distance, while Tommy stormed fearlessly up to the two women. Without hesitation, she tossed one of the braver security guards a pair of cuffs. "Cuff her," she ordered, pointing at Dana as she began to read them both their rights.

Tommy roughly slapped the cuffs on Roxi and forced her to the floor, to sit Indian-style.

"What's the charge?" Roxi asked.

"Attempted murder, conspiracy to commit murder, kidnapping, aiding and abetting," Tommy went on. "Get me some backup," Tommy told the guard. "But do not pull anybody from ICU."

Kiki watched in silence, trying to take in all that was happening and being said before she spoke. "Where is my father?" she finally asked. It was one of many questions she had, but surely the most important.

Roxi, who was sitting on the floor in cuffs, looked up at Kiki with a twisted face. "I'm not telling you shit. I knew this was a mistake!"

"She had to arrest you. It's not personal. She had to. Talk to me. Look at me." Kiki moved into Roxi's sight. "I'm going to help you. You're going to help me, and I'm going to help you. You didn't kill Sean. He's okay." Kiki looked for affirmation from Tommy, who shrugged and reluctantly nodded. "Yes, he's okay, and Shayla is okay. She's okay, and thank you. Roxi, did you get her medicine? Did you?"

"Yeah," Roxi mumbled.

"Thank you so much. Roxi, I know you're a good person. Then, yes, I will help you as much as I can."

"Yeah, you can start by taking me outta these cuffs," Roxi snarled, directing her animosity at Tommy.

Tommy ignored her and simply walked over to the police officers, who had rushed into the lobby from ER to back her up. "Take this bag." Tommy handed one of the officers the purse to put into an evidence bag. "She says there's a gun in it. It should be registered to a Sean Porter. He's an attorney with Simon and Associates."

"Yeah, and he tried to kill me with it!" Roxi called out.

Roxi huffed. "Sellout."

"Kiki, Sean loves you. He came to help and we . . ." Dana paused. "Look, Roxi is my sister, you understand that. She has been through so much."

"Just tell her what happened. I wasn't beguiled." Roxi jumped in. Her tone was that of Damian's overly intellectual monotone. "I had not yet experienced Sean Porter's mind-numbing sex that apparently the two of you have to where you guys believe everything the nigga says and does. Remember, I knew him from coming out to Damian's house over the last three or four months. All I saw was that he was in cahoots with that maniac, Damian. Hell, for all I know, he was behind the kidnapping of the little girl and that old man."

"I didn't have sex with Sean, Kiki," Dana awkwardly interjected.

Kiki was only barely caring as she tuned in on Roxi. "Do you know what Damian's plans are?"

"Yes, I do. He was planning to get off scot-free from a murder rap. Your boss, with the help from somebody named Garret, was going to make it happen." Roxi looked at Dana and then back at Kiki.

"My boss?" Dana asked.

"I knew about Garret, but Peter?"

"Yup, that Peter Marcum is in on all the shit. He's a big-time frat rat, just like the rest of them good ol' boys—Damian, Sean, M & M, Garret, all dem—Drugs, sex, all that. They're all in on it."

"Roxi, no," Dana defended.

"I thought you said *Peter*?"

"Who the hell do you think M & M is?"

"How do you know all this?"

"You act like I ever sleep. I ain't slept a night since moving in with Damian."

"But what did I have to do with this? Why Sean? Why my family?"

"I think there was murder. Somebody got killed."

"Lionel or Pepper?" Kiki asked.

"No, not like recently, but like long enough for it to be like a secret," Roxi explained.

"A cover-up?"

"Yeah . . . has to be because, from what I heard, everybody knows about it. Even ya boy, Mr. Porter, I think."

"This doesn't make sense, Roxi. If they all know and have kept it secret, then why not just keep it secret?"

"Because, for some reason, this case made somebody decide to 'jump off the loyalty boat,' as Damian always said. Somebody was getting ready to snitch. And I got a big feeling it was Mr. M & M, because he was all up in bed with Garret. Not literally, of course, but you know what I'm saying. Marcum thinks Damian doesn't know what he was up to. But, see, Damian has plans for his ass, and trust me, they do not include a 401K."

"Who killed Pepper Johnson?"

"Damian did, but Pepper wasn't supposed to float up. And that was like really bad timing. Made everything very complicated." Roxy was very animated now. "I saw it with my own eyes. He sent Pepper and Pee Wee to get that money from Lionel, and when things went bad and Jamon was arrested and Pepper got away, he shot Pepper in the chest and in the head. Called him disloyal. It was"—Roxi paused while her eyes welled with tears for the first time since escaping Damian's capture, and Dana wriggled closer to her to offer support—"Horrible."

Tommy tapped her watch, and Kiki got the hint.

"Roxi, we have to go, but you keep talking in the car. Will you testify to all you tell me in court?"

"If you can protect me, I can testify."

"We can protect you." Tommy eased her out of the cuffs. "Why is Peter M & M? Do you know?"

"Malik Marcum. He's Jewish but goes by Peter so people won't know. He's got some racial issues," Kiki said under her breath, feeling so many things at one time. She looked at her watch. "Let's get these ladies to Montgomery's chambers."

Chapter 75

"So, M & M, I may be jumping the gun, but I'm about to call this a success. It's just about eight o'clock and there is no Kimani Turner, no Sean Porter."

"And no Garret Lansing either. What's that all about, DW? I wasn't counting on him being a no-show. Truthfully now, how is this supposed to play out?"

"You tell me."

"I told you I would get the charges dropped, but Kiki didn't relinquish the case officially. It's going to get ugly in there. I told you I'd use the pictures if I had to. So I'll do what I have to do to get this case turned back over to me."

"Doing what you have to do is always your way, *M*."

"You shoulda did your part."

"I'm doing my part. I'm keeping my brother out of jail."

"That's not funny. You know what we agreed on—You would talk to Kiki, or get Porter to do it . . . in that special way of his."

"Why you still hating on my brotha?" Damian blurted. "You have hated on him since day one. How you know he didn't do his part? You kill him or something?"

"You're insane. He's not dead."

"He was once."

"Trust me, if I had killed him, he'd still be dead."

"That's what I thought you'd say."

"What the hell does that mean?"

"You tell me."

"You remember if Bond was right-handed or left-?"

"It's not time for games, Dame. I don't give a care about Bond's hands. He's dead."

Peter was watching his words, Damian could tell. "Well, he was southpaw, and Sean was right-handed, just so you know." Damian was cool and calm, sounding as if he had all day to converse on the subject.

"So?"

Just then there was a commotion (even Damian could hear) on Peter's side of the phone.

Chapter 76

Kiki, Dana, Roxi, and Tommy sped through the streets in the squad car. Tommy used the siren to cut down on the interruptions, such as stoplights. It was eight on the nose when they pulled up to the courthouse. Tommy had informed the authorities of Roxi's high profile, so when the car doors opened and the women began to pour out, police officers raced to the side of them to escort them inside.

Just then Kiki saw and heard the screeching of tires as a big car sped past them. She could see that it was Sean Porter, and he was weaving his way through the traffic. His car had already suffered a few dings, and even now he appeared to not be awake behind the wheel. "Tommy, it's Sean!" she screamed, breaking from the guards and dashing toward the car that was headed into the grassy area, just missing the parking lot. The car came to a halt as if even in his nearly unconscious state Porter knew he had finally landed. That he'd made it to the courthouse. The door swung open, but only his leg dropped out, and he fell over in the seat toward the passenger side.

"Sean! Oh my God, Sean!" Kiki called, running toward him.

"Kiki, stop!" Tommy drew her service revolver just as shots rang out.

Kiki was hit, immediately going down right before reaching the door of the car. Porter sprung up in the seat and, as if feeling her need for protection, managed to flop from the car, falling on top of her, covering her with his own body.

Tommy screamed like a mad woman, firing rounds into the gathering crowd, hoping to hit the sniper, yet miss the innocent bystanders. She was a crack shot even under duress and knew if she saw him, she would hit him, but seeing him was a wild shot.

Suddenly, amidst the screaming and scattering, somebody returned fire on Tommy Turner, turning the courthouse into a scene of pandemonium. Tommy was fearless as she headed toward the only sister she knew, Kiki, and the man she loved.

Just then from the brush came a bloody and ragged Garret Lansing. Somewhere in the gunplay, Tommy had no doubt hit him. He looked crazed and war-torn.

Aiming carefully at Kiki and Porter, he readied his gun to take their lives at point-blank, but the revolver clicked. Empty.

Tommy was not so unlucky. She got in a clear shot, nailing Garret in the chest, just missing his heart, but surely making a fatal hit.

Garret dropped to his knees. "Kikiiiii," he called out before falling dead on the ground.

The officers grabbed Roxi and Dana and rushed them inside into protective custody, and Tommy ran over to where Kiki lay under Porter's protective covering.

Chapter 77

"Hey, Garret's dead," Damian said calmly, strolling into the courthouse as if it was the red carpet.

"Arrest that man!" Peter called out. His thoughts were scattered, but he was bent on self-preservation. Among all the craziness outside, Peter was still trying to maintain some semblance of order. But Damian's ultra-cool appearance was enough to just about take him over the edge.

"For what?" Montgomery asked, stepping from his chambers alongside Frank. They had apparently been visiting for a while.

Frank was unaware of all that had occurred but quickly noticed the uproar.

"Your daughter's been shot, Frank," Damian said, showing the slightest of emotion.

Frank tore out the door but was stymied upon seeing Garret Lansing laying dead in the street.

"You didn't kill him. You're not a murderer," Damian

said, having joined him at the door. "Now go to your daughter."

Frank needed no instructions. He ran out into the street, where Kiki lay unconscious under the weight of Porter, who was also knocked out, with Tommy struggling to move him from on top her.

Chapter 78

"Look at you, you're not hurt," Porter said, entering Kiki's room without assistance. He'd been up and out of the hospital a couple of days now.

Kiki pulled her reading glasses down and looked up from her new cookbook. Tommy always knew what she liked when it came to gifts and had bought her a really nice book filled with pasta recipes and lots of pictures.

Seeing Porter up and about made Kiki smile. "Shayla is getting out tomorrow," she told him.

"I know. You've told me a bagillion times."

"I'm just nervous, I guess." Kiki smiled, grimacing while scooting over enough for him to sit on her bed.

"Why? She knows the truth now, and all that's left is the healing."

Kiki burst into sarcastic laughter. "Like you're okay with the truth. Please . . ."

"Yes, I am. I'm totally fine with it. I've already had three visits with my shrink and everything. Remember, I just wanted to know who killed my brother, and now I know. All that's left is the healing."

"My! Aren't we the mature one?" Kiki noticed admiringly.

Porter's smile was crooked and boyish. The truth was, he was very unsure of how it would all come out. Kiki could tell. She laughed again, this time with more warmth, knowing all this had to be hard on him, all that happened the night when his identical twin brother, lay dying at the hands of Peter, aka Malik Marcum, and Garret Lansing.

Killed for being loyal to a brother. Wasn't what the whole fraternity thing was about . . . The irony was too great for Kiki to comprehend at that moment.

"And how about you? How are you holding up?" Porter asked her.

"Got my therapist on speed dial," she said, laughing aloud, and he joined her in the healthy laughter.

The silence between them was thick now as Kiki carefully touched his face, trying not to move her painful side. "I still love you," she said, not having said it for days.

"How can you love me?" Porter's eyes squinted. "You don't know me."

"I have always known and loved you. Maybe it was just a schoolgirl crush back then. Maybe it was the alcohol." She giggled, shaking her head playfully. "Or the way you sang to me and filled me with enough desire to give myself to you of my own free will. Give you all I had."

"What happened that night was rape," he admitted.

Kiki looked down shamefully. "Yes, it was, but what's come of it is love. Right or wrong, that's what's come of it."

"So you forgive me?"

"I do," she blurted out, sounding full of confidence.

"Marry me, Kimani Turner."

There was silence between them for a moment, until Kiki with her good arm pulled Porter into a big kiss. She smiled then. "Yes."

Again they stared into each other's eyes, something they were doing a lot lately.

"I got the results," she finally said.

"Oh yeah?" Porter said, before enjoying the taste of her lips again, seemingly trying to distract her from the conversation. "I got some results too," he teased.

The test results came back proving that Shayla was indeed Sean Porter's child.

"You know, we haven't really talked about like"—Kiki squirmed nervously—"like . . . that shower . . . ummm, day."

"Like . . . like . . . ummm that . . . ummm," Porter imitated. "You are such a kid."

"Stop. I'm a grown-butt woman. I'm the mother of a teenage daughter."

"Exactly! Ugh, teenagers."

"What do I tell her? How do I explain?" Kiki asked seriously. She wanted to play around, but Shayla's feelings were not game.

"Tell her I'm her father," Porter told her. "Tell her I love you and that I want you in my life and if she wants to come she's welcome."

"But what if—?"

"What if what?" Porter asked, knowing the questions were complicated. *What if Shayla rejected their feelings? What if she couldn't recover from the lie*? To those questions, he had no answers.

Kiki stared into his warm eyes until her stomach fluttered. "I love you, Mr. SP."

"Then I say, let's do the damn thing, Ms. Cute Little DA."

"Don't say *damn*."

"Sometimes you just have to," Porter purred, leaning into a sloppy kiss.

Tommy walked in about that time. "I'm sure I'm interrupting something lovey-dovey and all that ca-ca, but whatever."

"Nah, we're just talking about getting married, and so ya know once that happens, that's gonna end all that lovey-dovey ca-ca," Porter assured.

"Marrrriedddd, hmmmm. What does big daddy Frank think about that?"

"Are you kidding? We haven't told him. We're gonna elope," Kiki explained.

They all laughed.

"Yeah, we're gonna have our daughter Shayla drive," Porter joked.

They all burst out laughing again.

"Well, just hurry please and get well. I have been seeing Frank every day, and he's as grouchy as hell, complaining about his new glasses and new recliner and just about everything. Everyone is a mess except for me."

"Your time will come," Porter informed her.

"Don't jinx me, boy."

"That's right, Tommy," Kiki added. "Soon you'll be wearing pink taffeta."

Tommy pretended to gag and then hit Porter playfully. "I told you not to jinx me."

The three of them sat quietly for a moment before Kiki spoke. "I'm very happy right now," she said.

As if on cue, Porter's favorite burly nurse entered the room and said, "Me too. I get to give the four-hundred-pound man in the next room an enema," and the three of them burst into laughter again.

Chapter 79

Kiki wasn't the one to indict the District Attorney Malik P. Marcum for the murder of Bond Porter, as well as various other charges, including the murder of Pepper Johnson, drug trafficking, and contributing to the diligence of a minor. Jamon's testimony, along with Damian's, and all the evidence conveniently found in Peter's home, including the fancy Luger registered in his name, was enough to nail Peter to the wall.

Kiki was giving up law to become a chef, but she was at the trial every day, making sure that bastard got what he deserved for his part in putting Shayla's life in danger, and being a part of Garret's sick jealousy, traumatizing the man she loved.

Surprisingly enough, however, Jamon was convicted of the murder of Lionel Harrison. Harry, the homeless guy, got cleaned up real nice for court, and the DA's office, with new acting District Attorney Nigel Godwin, won that case hands down. It would be a long time before Jamon saw freedom again, no matter how much help he was to the state. Sometimes loyalty comes at a cost.

Damian got out of the country not too long after his testimony and was reportedly last heard to be in Trinidad. But since no one was accusing him of anything, maybe he just needed a change of scenery.

Kiki had heard rumor that Roxi and Dana were living the high life, along with their children, with new names and new identities under the witness protection program, as well as the goon that got Shayla to the hospital that night. The goon turned state's evidence, reporting on the drug deals he personally had been part of that Marcum had funded.

It was amazing how everything had pointed to Marcum in the end. But Kiki didn't care about all that. Shayla was safe, and that was all that mattered.

Chapter 80

Kiki could have lost sleep wondering about all the corruption she'd seen and heard in that courtroom, but she was only glad that she was out of the madness and that her family was safe. Shayla had been through so much over the last few months. Their testimony was crucial in connecting the dots between Garret and Peter. It had gotten very ugly at points, and Kiki wasn't sure Shayla would make it through.

Kiki felt her eyes burning with tears when she would reach for Shayla during the days in court, only to be met with distance. Even now that all the convictions had been made, Kiki was worried that she and Shayla weren't going to get over this as smoothly as she'd prayed they would. During the last year, during the trial, it seemed as if there had been one setback after another, and she was beginning to feel as though they'd never be close again. Through this entire ordeal, however, Kiki never left Shayla's side.

The testimony process was frightening, and Shayla was having a hard time accepting all she'd seen and heard, and felt during the days, weeks, and months she had to be in that courtroom. Thinking that Frank had killed the depraved Garret Lansing, the young man she once thought she had a crush on, was beyond traumatizing to her.

Just hearing what Shayla had told the courts that Garret Lansing had said and done to her caused Kiki to close her eyes tight.

Today, however, after the last verdict was handed down and after a moment of hesitation, Shayla took Kiki's hand and squeezed it tight. Kiki opened her eyes to meet hers and then pulled her into a tight embrace.

"This has been so stressful. I hope I never see a courtroom again. You can forget me ever being a lawyer. I'd rather be a rap star."

"I love you, Shayla."

Pulling back from the hug, Shayla stared at her, almost as if looking through her, and then, out of the corner of her eye, gave Porter a half-glance. "So, now it's all about the wedding, huh?"

During a more confident moment, Kiki had announced that she and Sean Porter planned to be married as soon as Peter was convicted. And now that it had happened, she was feeling a bit more timid about things. "Not if you don't want it," Kiki quickly reneged. "Not if you're not ready."

"Me? Kiki, don't do that. Don't start the guilt thing again." Shayla shook her head adamantly from side to side.

"I'm not. I just don't want to set us back again."

"Set us back? Kiki, it's not going to get harder to accept that you're my . . ." Shayla swallowed hard, showing that, true, it wouldn't get any more difficult to accept that Kiki was her mother, but it had yet to be any easier.

"I'm your mother." Kiki squinted from the instant burn of her own eyes. She'd been confronting the truth with more confidence the last few months and saying the words more often.

"Yeah, that," Shayla mumbled. "And that's not going to change. We're never going to go back to being sisters, as much as I'd like to." She chuckled nervously. "And you're about to move forward with him."

As Porter stepped forward, Shayla stepped aside, keeping distance between them. "She may love you, but I do not, Mr. Porter," she said, sounding sharp and clear.

Suddenly, as if regretting her words immediately, Shayla lowered her voice and her eyes. "I'm sorry, but it's just how I feel. I'll never get over those pictures. Ever." Looking again at Kiki, who hadn't moved or spoken, Shayla said in a near whisper, "Kiki, this is hard."

"I know, but I love him. I always have."

"I know." Shayla nodded. "But I'm not sure I can. I mean, I already loved you, so that was half the battle, but you and him being together, it's gonna be hard."

"I'll cancel it, Shayla, if you think we need more time."

"No, don't. You need to marry him, and I need to get over it." She looked again at Porter. "Besides, he needs you. He might forget who he is again."

They all chuckled.

Suddenly Frank grabbed Shayla's shoulders and squeezed. "I'm so sorry, Shayla. I never thought about anybody but myself. I was ashamed."

"Ashamed?" Shayla yelped. She was angry at Frank's thought, and it showed now. Up till this moment, she'd shown nothing but support for Frank, but now that the trial was over, it was clear Shayla had some unfinished business with him regarding her life.

Porter glanced at the presiding judge, whose attention was drawn to the heat permeating from their conversation, his concerned brow furrowed with the intense concentration he was placing on the family drama playing out in front of him.

Immediately Porter took Kiki by the arm and lightly began to lead Frank and Shayla out of the courtroom. “Let’s take this outside before we all end up on trial.”

Epilogue

Christmas Eve 2008

Circling the room, Porter held her head against his chest while they danced to Stevie Wonder's greatest hits.

Stevie's soulful words and deep-seated meanings stirred Porter's heart while he moved around the room with the beautiful woman in his arms. He knew he didn't deserve her, but he thanked God he was given the opportunity to love her. It was a thin line he treaded between permissible and punishable, passion and perversion.

Love for some is dark at the start, he thought to himself, poetry coming into his mind and heart, but now it is more than right, more than light.

"*I believe when I fall in love with you it will be forever*," Porter sang softly.

Kiki looked up at him and smiled warmly, pulling back from him in admiration.

"You're my angel from heaven. You know that, right?"

"And, you, you're always gonna be my dream man. What's your name again?" she teased.

"Just call me Porter."

"Ahh, nice to meet you." She giggled.

"And you?"

"I'm your wife."

"Then make love to me, wife," he said, sounding mature, controlled, and sexy.

Just then the phone rang. He answered it as Kiki scooped up the two champagne glasses off the table and headed to their bedroom.

"Congratulations, my brotha," the caller said.

"Damian, what a surprise," Porter said, sincerely surprised at his call, despite the foreboding he'd had, with the day going so perfectly and all. *Nothing's perfect.*

"Shouldn't be. My best friend got married. You didn't expect a call?"

"No, I didn't."

"But you're not disputing that we're friends . . . brothers."

"No, I'm not disputing the past, but things change."

"Not everything."

"Like?"

"Like the facts. And one fact that I know didn't change was that Sean was right-handed. His twin brother Bond, my best friend, was left-handed, and you, my man, are as southpaw as they come."

Porter said nothing. What could he say? It had all come back to him in the hospital while recovering from Roxy's home run hit using his head as the ball. As he recovered from the concussion, he slowly began to remember that night in all the details. It was Peter Marcum who had paid him to take the pictures. He and Garret were going to blackmail the judge. They hated Frank Turner for what they felt was discrimination, because of the fact that he had chosen and favored Sean over all of the others, that the judge pushed for Sean's membership in the fraternity, and even allowed his wayward brother, Bond, to come along just because Sean said he wouldn't pledge without him. Marcum and Garret felt Frank Turner favored only blacks, but they ignored the fact that Judge Turner despised Damian.

Peter Marcum was insane with jealousy, and so when Bond didn't deliver the goods, he lost his mind and convinced the naive Garret, with the agreement that he would get into the fraternity, to help him kill him. Together they murdered Bond Porter, or so they thought.

Sean was too drunk to drive, so Bond took the wheel, giving Garret a clean shot at the passenger side. He killed Sean immediately. Bond felt that he was responsible for Sean's death because he was driving Sean's car.

Can't change what happened. Sean was shot from passenger side. The second shot took out the tires and caused the car to roll, throwing the both of them out, and down the ravine. Garret collected the pictures off his body and shot him point-blank in the chest, just missing his heart, and apparently finished off Sean in the same manner. Only, his point-blank shot didn't miss.

It was Damian who had followed and got him to the hospital, only for him to be pronounced dead on arrival. But that was all the past now, and to hell with both Garret and Peter. Of course, Garret was probably closer to getting there than Peter.

Rushing back out to him, Kiki rolled her eyes at the sight of him still on the phone. She turned around. "Unzip me."

Her dress was almost too pretty to remove. She looked like the frosting on a cake. He didn't know where to start. But he knew he had to taste it.

"And get off the phone," she whispered.

"Yes, let me let you get back to your nuptials," Damian snickered wickedly. "Ms. Turner is waiting to take you on a trip. Don't fly without a net though. Wouldn't want no little 'yous and hers' running around next Christmas. Oh yeah, that's right—You're sterile." It was as if Damian now dared him to deny it, as if he'd been waiting for just this moment to confirm his thoughts. Apparently, Porter's silence satisfied him. "Well, I'll let you go now, but you'll be hearing from me soon, brotha. I could use a good, loyal P.I.," Damian jabbed one more time before he hung up.

Porter kissed his wife's neck, and she twitched with delight, holding her head to the side, making sure he had plenty of room to linger there at one of her most sensitive spots, behind her ear. Her hair had grown past her shoulder blades, so she had to move it out of the way now.

Porter found the simple act to be very sexy and was quickly aroused. He fought the urge to ruin this moment by rushing. Having stayed apart for a month prior to the wedding, this was a moment they had waited a long time to share.

Despite her curves, the dress fell like the last curtain call for the Lion King—royal and deserving of a standing ovation, which Porter couldn't help but give her.

Turning back to him and pulling the tie from the fancy shirt of the tux, she slowly undressed him. It was clear she knew exactly how far she was going to take this and at what pace she wanted things to go. He could tell she was about to live out another fantasy. She'd been sharing her sexual dreams with him for months now, each one more remarkable than the one previous. Kiki was like a kid in a candy store, when it came to sex, and smiled while shimmying from her full slip, which slid off her body like lotion.

Porter followed it to the floor, kissing her body all the

way down until reaching her heat. Taking her lower lips between his, he parted them with his tongue, causing Kiki to raise high on her toes and squeal with delight, until her high pitches eased into a low moan. He knew then she was ready for him.

"Give me a baby, Sean," she begged. "I want another baby."

Standing, he gazed deep into her eyes. "I'll try, with all my heart," he promised, knowing the effort would be fruitless. Lifting her, he slid her down onto his hardness, walking with her to the bed of their honeymoon suite that overlooked the ocean. The waves crashed with each crescendo the passion-filled couple reached as they desperately grasped for pleasures undiscovered, and finding most, they gave way to praises of joy.

Easing from her tight body, Porter allowed Kiki to rest from the somniferous activity they'd engaged in for the last few hours. They had all night, and he planned to take full advantage of that. There were no trials on his calendar, no criminals to defend waiting in his office. There was only Kiki and the sound of her light, love-filled breathing in his ear. Catching a glimpse of his reflection in the mirror, he could only smile at how much he and his brother looked alike. It was as if they were one and the same. However, Bond knew that Damian was right, and unlike his brother Sean, he could not give this woman, his wife, the beautiful Kimani Turner, all the love she dreamed about, for he was not his brother.

Upcoming Novel: First Chapter

SWERVE

. . . an unexpected turn of events

Gold studs down the length of her black leather pants protected her long legs from the wind while she rode. She couldn't help but enjoy the cool air as it whipped up under the helmet. Three-inch-heeled leather boots made her clearly over six feet tall, and a custom-designed, leather jacket hid the holster that housed her service revolver in a pocket she'd had especially made for this purpose.

Romia pulled into The Spot and parked. Stepping from her black Ducati motorcycle, she pulled the bright red helmet from her head, releasing her long raven tresses that bounced lightly around her shoulder blades. Turning the helmet slightly, she ran her hand over the emblem of the golden phoenix that covered the back of the headpiece and matched the one she had painted onto the side of the bike's monocoque frame. She then attached the helmet to the handle bar with a custom-made, short-locking bungee cord.

The symbolic bird that she'd found intricately woven into a large tapestry in her mother's attic while watching the neighborhood women cleaning it out after she died meant everything to her. One of the women seemed instinctively to know that she wanted to keep that tapestry and handed it to her, instead of shoving it deep into the bag she and the rest of the ladies were filling with her mother's belongings. Romia was only six, but even then felt deep inside that the bird meant she'd reunite with mother again, someway, somehow, someday.

Romia entered the bar she and her other colleagues frequented. Tonight it was nearly empty. Only two other officers, Hank and Aston, were sitting at the front table.

"You're late, Romee!" Out of nowhere, her former partner, Keleigh Jack, then appeared. He'd attended a wedding earlier that day but had discarded his suit jacket and slacks for jeans and a T-shirt.

Moving quickly to where she was, his body language was possessive as he quickly blocked her from view of the other men who might want to take a look at her. Romia recognized his moves. He was always less than discreet with how he felt about her. It was she who held off the "could have happened" between them. It just wouldn't be right, not with a partner, she'd told him.

Since they'd been re-assigned for a year now, nothing was growing between them beyond what was already there, so maybe she'd been wrong all this time about how he felt.

She and Keleigh Jack had been partners before he became a detective. He was now working with another female partner, Tamika Turner. Tamika, aka Tommy, was of mixed racial descent. Romia had heard rumors that she'd only recently discovered that her father was a black man, a former judge who didn't claim her until just recently. Romia could relate to living without a father and was happy for Tommy's discovery.

For each day Romia looked in the mirror knowing the

features on her on face could only belong to someone who was not fully black, she too wondered who her father might be. It wasn't as if her mother, before she died, had time to answer any of those important questions Romia might need to know in life.

Romia was fair. One could say she had an olive complexion in the summertime, her hair was loosely curled and hung long and thick down her back, which she felt was typical of a person of mixed race, one mixed with black. However, it was her steel grey eyes, not far off from bluish-grey, that had her wondering about her father, considering her mother was blond with brown eyes. And there were no answers in the foster home she was raised in.

Life wasn't bad there in the foster home, just lacking in the information department. Actually, her foster family put her and all her foster brothers in martial arts to keep them busy. Romia became a black belt by the age of ten. For the others, it was just fun, but for Romia, it was more than just something to do. It was life-changing. She fought hard and with a desperation that gave the impression her life depended on it. She wouldn't stop practicing until she perfected every move she attempted.

As she walked into the tavern that night, she looked around for Keleigh, but instead she noticed his date was sitting at the bar in a hideous pink taffeta dress. Barefoot and tired-looking, the little girlie looked like she needed a drink. But with a body like hers, who cared, right? Keleigh always dated Malibu Barbie doll blondes. You'd think a brother would have more imagination. But he didn't. He liked fake women that didn't give him a lot of lip. Maybe that was why the two of them hadn't gotten anywhere. Fake, Romia was not, and as far as lip, he was always getting put in his place with a little neck-jerking and what he called his mama's attitude, no ifs, ands or buts.

A dress like that could drive one to drink, Romia inwardly dogged. She slid up on the stool next to the girl, who had her feet up on the empty stool next to her. Maybe Keleigh had been rubbing her feet.

"I see you're digging that dress," she remarked to Shashoni, grinning wickedly.

Shashoni rolled her eyes. "We just left the reception hall. I haven't had time to get home and all that. I needed a damn drink—quick," she answered, still waiting for her drink that was apparently long overdue since having ordered it.

"You had a drink at the reception . . . quite a few," Keleigh said, trying to speak in a lower-than-usual voice.

Shashoni was pretty close to drunk, Romia could tell, now that she'd actually looked closer. She also noticed Keleigh's overprotective tone.

Finally the waiter brought Shashoni's drink. It was stiff one. As she reached for it, Keleigh intercepted it, pushing her out of her reach.

"What do you think you're doing?" she asked, reaching for the drink again.

He blocked her hand. "Enough, Shoni. You've had enough."

Shashoni looked around to see if anyone was watching their exchange. Romia too felt uncomfortable. Perhaps it was because the spotlight was suddenly on them, or so it felt.

"Here's your drink, Romee," the bartender said.

As Romia stood and turned to the bar to gather her club soda, a man reaching for his drink bumped her. Her arms rose over her head, out of reflex, and to keep from spilling her water on everyone. "Hey, watch it," she yelled, when he copped a quick feel in the process. She pushed him away from her, spilling the drink anyway.

"Watch it, ya asshole." Keleigh gave him another shove for good measure.

"What is this?" Romia asked, sniffing her sleeve.

Romia had never tasted liquor, having vowed never to drink spirits after the drunk driver killed her mother. They were walking together when the car came barreling around the corner right at her, and her mother pushed her out of the way right before the car struck. Instead of killing her, the car hit her mother, who flew over the front of the hood and crashed through the windshield. Her beautiful dress shredded, and blood splattered everywhere.

"I said I was sorry for what I said," Shashoni said, rambling on, sounding less than sober, apparently not noticing Keleigh's distraction with Romia's spilled drink.

"Smells like booze," Keleigh answered after he too sniffed her leather.

"What is this, Mack?" Romia asked the bartender.

"Sorry. Musta gave you that loser's drink." The bartender shrugged absently. "I've never done that before."

"I'm over that, Shoni." Keleigh shrugged and turned his attention back to Shashoni, who had laid her head on her folded arms. "I'm worried about your drinking right now."

"Look at my jacket. You messed up my jacket with this stuff. I don't drink this mess, Mack!"

Romia was having a hard time controlling her temper lately. She was feeling hormonal or tired, or something off, but lately she'd been getting upset very easily.

"I said I was sorry," Mack pleaded, sounding unconvincing.

Keleigh said, "Calm down, Romee. It's just a little spill." He then turned his head back quickly to Shashoni. "I care about you." His head moved back and forth like he was watching tennis.

"Since when?" Shashoni grabbed the drink and tossed it back before he could stop her.

He shook his head. "I didn't know you felt . . .

Shashoni lowered the near-empty glass slowly from her

full lips and glared at him. "You knew I did." She turned the tumbler up and drained the very last drop.

Romia understood immediately what was going on here. Shoshoni had fallen for Keleigh and made the mistake of telling him. That was obvious. Romia could see love in Shashoni's eyes and maybe a little in Keleigh's too. But she's must have said the *M* word, and now it was all ruined. Keleigh wasn't husband material, Romia could have told her that.

Who cared? Right now, her jacket had booze on it. Her problem was a lot bigger in her mind than Keleigh hitting and quitting some chick in an ugly pink dress.

"Dang! I need a towel." Romia leaned over the counter. "You got a towel back there?"

"We're partners," Keleigh whispered now to Shashoni, clearly hoping to keep his words private, but Romia heard.

Why did he have to explain that to this bimbo? Romia instantly thought, but did not ask.

"She's like my sister. I can't see her any other way. Why are you buggin'?"

Shashoni smirked, pulled her foot free from Keleigh's hand where he had laid it, as if he was going to start rubbing or re-rubbing it, after lecturing her on the protocol of being with him and where she fit in—partner first, former partner second, and then maybe you.

The girl then stood, smoothed the frou-frou pink dress down, slid her feet into the painful-looking pumps and stomped from the bar, leaving Keleigh with the tab.

While Keleigh dug for the money to pay, Romia noticed the slightly staggering young woman heading out the door and rushed to follow her, not waiting for the towel. "Shashoni!" she called, heading out the door behind her, thinking how crazy she looked taking off in that pink dress. "Let me take you home. I mean, sure you have on that lovely dress but—"

Suddenly the night sounds were added to by the sounds of a scuffle, which had increased recognizably in the darkness near where her motorcycle was parked. It was indeed a struggle.

Romia immediately went on alert. As she reached the back of the bar, headed toward her bike, the big man swung on her as soon as she cleared the corner. Her reflexes were cat-like, and she pulled back, avoiding his blow.

Sensing his every move, and he hers, it was as if fighting her shadow, or a sensei. He mimicked her technique blow for blow, as if having studied her moves. Had they fought before, maybe in competition? Did she know him?

Attempting to look in his eyes, Romia kicked and punched quickly, hoping not to lose eye contact with the stranger for more than a millisecond, but he blocked each blow with precision.

Just then a woman screamed.

"Shashoni!" Romia called out, thinking it was Keleigh's date being attacked somewhere in the distance.

Two more shots were heard, and the woman screamed again, "She killed him!"

Distracted by the woman's scream, Romia caught a blow that drew blood from her lip. As she stumbled back from the hard blow, the attacker took advantage of the time to scurry away. Romia's first instincts were to go after him, but the woman's bellows drew her attention in that direction.

Romia saw the body of a man bleeding, and the woman stood there screaming, all the color drained from her face. "Can you shut up?" She looked around for Shashoni.

"She killed him!" the woman screeched, pointing at Romia in a tattling fashion.

The bar began to empty, and the patrons began to scramble, heading for their cars to avoid the questions from cops that were sure to come. Others ran back into the bar to get Hank and Aston, no doubt, because within seconds they came out.

"What are you talking about?" Romia asked, realizing that the woman was accusing her.

"Freeze, Romee!" Hank yelled, drawing his gun on her.

"Hank, you're kidding, right?" Romia slowly attempted to rise from the body.

"Stay where you are, and put your hands up!" Aston Mitchell, another officer from her precinct, demanded.

The blood from her face was on her hands now, and she could easily see how bad this all looked.

Aston yelled at the woman who quickly ran toward the bar, "Move away, lady!"

Romia wished she had gotten a better look at her because she had a strange feeling this was to be the last she would see of the woman.

Keleigh quickly pushed through the growing crowd. "Romee, what the hell happened?"

Glancing up at him, her grey eyes were aglow against the light of the full moon. Her mouth was now covered with blood from the wound that at first seemed minor. "He went that way." Reaching under her jacket, she realized then her gun was gone. Her eyes immediately focused on the one laying next to the body. It was hers. "What the . . ." She picked it up.

"Drop it, Romee!" Hank yelled.

"What the hell are you doing, Hank? It's Romee!" Keleigh jumped between the officers and Romia, who was staring at the gun, the weapon that had apparently killed the man laying face down in the dirt. The man from the bar who had touched her breasts. This didn't look good at all.

Keleigh was looking stunned and a bit confused but stood his ground. There was no way he was going to arrest her or allow Hank or Aston too either.

"I-I didn't," Romia stammered. She heard the siren in the distance. *Someone must have called*, she thought.

"Drop the gun," he whispered over his shoulder, while standing between the drawn weapons and Romia.

"Get out of the way, Kel!" Hank ordered.

"No. Now come on . . . this is crazy! Get that woman out here to tell what she saw," Keleigh insisted.

"I don't know what happened. I don't know what's going on. It happened too fast," Romia said to Aston, who looked determined to arrest her.

"Romia Smith, you're under arrest." Aston began pulling out his handcuff from the back of his trousers where he had them clipped. He stepped forward. "You have the right—"

Keleigh refused to allow him to get close enough to put the cuffs on.

"Get out of the way!" Aston stepped toward Keleigh as if to go through him. Aston was going to prove he had no hesitation arresting a colleague.

Suddenly Romia dropped the gun, pushed Keleigh aside, and stepped forward, snatching Aston's weapon from him and dismantling it with one hand, twisting his arm behind him. She had to get away before the squad car arrived.

Keleigh swung on Hank before he could fire.

Aston freed himself from Romia's loose grip. She'd not really tried to detain him so much as buy a moment to think. He swung on her, but Romia easily ducked back and flat-hand punched him across the face, stunning him.

Everyone knew of her fighting skills. She could kill him within seconds, and he knew it as well. But she wasn't allowed to street-fight. It was all but illegal for her, but there was no way she was going to jail tonight.

"Come on, Romee," Aston said, holding his cheek while moving light on his feet as if thinking about contemplating taking on the challenge of fighting her.

He charged at her, only to have her hit him twice, this time with a closed fist. She held back on the power of her punch but still drew blood from his nose. He cursed her and swung again, but she ducked the telegraphed punch easily. Hearing the sirens closing in, she knew time was running out.

Aston kicked at her; he'd been practicing but was no competition. She caught the kick and turned his foot just enough to hear the crack. He yelped and crumbled to the ground.

In a guarded stance, she began inching her way clear, to break for her bike, as Keleigh wrestled the gun from Hank and tossed it aside. They were both breathing heavy from their momentary tussle.

Hank pulled a smaller weapon from the back of his pants. "Don't try it, Romia. I'll shoot you."

Romia raised her hands. "Stop! This has to stop!"

Again Keleigh jumped in, tackling Hank to the ground. Hank's gun went off, but ricocheted in the darkness, missing Romia by a mile as she leapt onto the seat of her bike, which started up without delay, as if sensing her need for speed. And she took off without even putting on her helmet.

As the squad car pulled in, she swerved around it, spitting up dust as she avoided the head-on collision. The officer behind the wheel hung a tight U-turn and pursued her. She could see the car right on her tail from the rearview mirror.

Why are they not listening to me? Why is this happening? Who was that woman? Romia wasn't going to stop and ask questions. Pushing the bike to top speed, she opened the distance between them. She had to get outta there, but where would she go?

Still hearing the sirens close behind her, she turned the bike into the first alleyway she approached. She was in an area known as the Palemos, a ghetto that was basically abandoned by the city dollars. There were many dark and deserted hiding places, and she planned to take advantage of one of them. They would be calling for backup, if they hadn't already, and so she knew she needed to get off the streets so that she could get around easier, faster, and without detection. They would never find her in this neighborhood. Everyone on the beat knew that if a suspect ducked into the Palemos you could forget finding them, unless you had a good snitch.

Screeching the bike to a halt, she quickly dismounted and pulled the helmet from the bungee. The golden phoenix glowed against the moonlight. She freed herself of the custom jacket that everyone knew she wore and recognized and tossed it aside.

Looking back as she started to run off, the regret was too much. She slammed the helmet on her head before looking around and then upward for a fire escape. Finding one, and without pulling the ladder down, she jumped high, gripping the bar tightly and pulling herself up to the first rung, and flipping her legs over her head and through the bars. Acrobatically, she then pulled herself toward her feet, flipping over the railing and climbing five stories, until she found a broken window with an opening big enough to climb through and ducked inside the empty office building.